Sawdust and Satin

Lake Chelan Book 1

SHIRLEY PENICK

Cover Photography by Wander Aquiar Photography
Cover Design and Formatting by Cassy Roop of Pink Ink Designs
Cover Models: Amanda Renee and Andrew Leighty
Edited by Deelylah Mullin

Contact me:
www.shirleypenick.com
www.facebook.com/ShirleyPenickAuthor
To sign up for Shirley's New Release Newsletter, send email to
shirleypenick@outlook.com, subject newsletter.

Previous books by Shirley Penick

The Rancher's Lady: A Lake Chelan novella
Hank and Ellen's story

Dedication

To the industry. To the countless authors whose stories have filled many a day and have spoken to my heart, thank you for your words. To the writing groups in the Seattle area and across the country who welcomed me warmly into the fold and encouraged me to give writing a solid, determined, try. To the cover models, photographers, cover designers, formatters, editors web designers, and even the swag vendors, thank you for doing the things for me, that I could muddle through and do okay with, but you all do it so much better.

And last, but by no means least, to my family and friends who have been so excited to see this progression and have cheered me on.

Sawdust and Satin

Chapter One

BARBARA AND HER HUSBAND Chris left the school building where the emergency town meeting had been held. She shivered as the cold wind whipped off Lake Chelan and slammed into her, stealing her breath and stinging her cheeks, nose, and eyes. It was bitter cold in January at the foot of the Cascade Mountains. She felt Chris shiver and he grabbed her hand and hustled them across the parking lot to his truck. He opened the door and bundled her in, before scooting around the front and climbing in the driver's side.

As he started the truck to let it warm up, Barbara's mind drifted back to the wedding dress she was working on. It was giving her so much trouble. The bride had a very specific look she wanted and Barbara was having a difficult time trying to find a way to get it done, that would look great. She'd been working on the damn bodice for two days and still hadn't found a solution. She was getting behind schedule and needed to figure it out immediately.

Chris touched her arm and said, "Barbara, answer me."

"Oh, sorry, I was thinking about the dress I'm working on."

"What a surprise." He sighed dramatically. "Can you wait one hour to think about that? I want to talk to you about the town meeting. It's kind of important, what with it being an emergency meeting and everything. I think we should discuss it. If the town dies, we'll have to move and that wouldn't be good for your business."

"I know. I'm concerned too. My mind drifted, I've never had such trouble with a dress before." The idea of the town fading out of existence was scary, but getting the dress right was urgent.

"I know your business is important, but the town dying is a larger issue, don't you think?"

She shrugged. "Well, yes—I suppose. It's just that I don't see *me* saving the town."

"No one person is going to save it, but we all have to do our part."

"I know, I'm sorry. My one-track mind drives you up the wall sometimes, doesn't it?"

"Not always, but yes—sometimes it does."

"Okay, I can try harder not to be distracted. But you have to remember this is my business and it's important for me to get my dresses perfect, which takes intense thought sometimes."

"I do understand, but you need to come up for air once in a while. Thinking about your business twenty-four-seven isn't good either."

"You may have a point." She nodded. "Anyway, about the meeting. I think we came up with some good ideas tonight, don't you? I noticed three distinct areas of focus. One, showcasing the artisans who live in our town; two, working to make it a wedding destination; and three, your idea. I think between all those we have some good plans to draw in tourists—especially since the economy is starting to recover."

"Yeah. You don't think my idea to capitalize on the video game was stupid, do you?"

Aw, here is the real reason he's being so insistent.

"No, honey. I think it's a great idea. The only one snarky about it was Adam and I think that has more to do with his immature rivalry with you—than anything. Is he ever going to grow up and get over it? It's been almost twenty years."

He smirked. "I thought he and Terry were going to come to blows, when Adam tried to put me down and called Sandy's game lame."

Thinking back, she laughed at the confrontation—they'd thrown some pretty low shots at each other. "Not too smart of him. Terry's protective of his big sister and proud of her game. And he should be proud. Whoever thought the stories she told kids while babysitting had the potential to become an internationally successful video game."

"Yeah pretty amazing. I do think we could use the popularity of the game to draw in tourists. In fact, when we get home, I want to talk to you about something."

Her breath caught in her throat. He sounded serious. His words gave her a flashback to her father saying the same thing, right before he walked out on them and left their family for a younger woman. Every time she heard *I want to talk to you about something*, she felt panic and fear. Her father had decimated their family and left them destitute—and it had all started with those words. At least that's how she remembered it. She knew she shouldn't put Chris in the same mold as her father, but what if he was going to do the same thing? What if her distraction had already pushed him away? It would break her heart; she still loved him. Financially she wasn't ready to have him walk away—she didn't have enough money saved up. She knew some people said marriages reached a crises phase at ten years. She'd always believed that was an old wives' tale. *What if it's true?* Their ten-year anniversary was this year.

"Barbara, are you listening to me?"

"Oh, sorry. I just…"

"I know, your one-track mind again," he complained as he pulled into their driveway and pushed the remote for the garage. "Do you think you could stay with me for a few more minutes once we get inside?"

"Uh, sure."

They walked into their four-bedroom ranch from the garage. Hanging their winter gear on the hooks in the mudroom, they went into the sunny yellow kitchen—

which seemed too bright and garish tonight. She normally loved this room with the oak cabinets and sunflower accents, but tonight it seemed obnoxious. She wanted to cover it all in gray or brown. *How can it be cheerful when I'm panicked?*

Chris moved to the kitchen table. All serious discussions were held there and in no way did she want to sit down.

"Do you want some coffee or a beer?" she asked, stalling.

He shook his head. "No, I'm good."

"I'm going to put on some water for hot chocolate. I'm cold." *Inside.*

"Oh, hot chocolate sounds yummy. You put on the water, I'll get the cups and packets."

She put some cookies she'd picked up from Samantha's bakery on a plate. Once they had everything and she could avoid it no longer—she sat across from her husband. His strong arms rested on the table and his big hands surrounded the mug of hot chocolate. Her breath hitched in her throat. *God, I love that man.* They hadn't spent a lot of time together recently with his night classes and her wedding dress business. *Have we grown too far apart? Is it too late?* She put her cold hands on the cup in front of her hoping to absorb some of the warmth. The rich chocolate smell nearly made her gag, she was so upset. She looked into his bright green eyes, noticed his dark blond hair curled over his forehead. Strangely, he looked sheepish. *What is that about?*

He took a deep breath and said in a rush, "I didn't want to say anything in the meeting 'cause I wanted to talk to you first. I have an idea. It might sound silly. I'm thinking about taking the land my grandfather left me and building an amusement park."

She gaped at him. *What? He's not leaving me? He doesn't want a divorce?* As relief swept through her, she couldn't breathe, she couldn't swallow, and she definitely couldn't respond.

"You hate the idea don't you."

She shook herself. "What? No, no, not at all. I'm shocked. An amusement park? Do you know anything about building an amusement park?"

He rubbed his hand over the back of his neck. "Not specifically, but for a lot of my online courses I have used amusement park rides as my semester projects."

"Really?" She laughed. "Your civil engineering classes allowed you to think about amusement parks? I thought civil engineering was all about building roads."

"No, civil engineering covers lots of areas—roads, yes. Also bridges, canals, dams, structures. Anything that needs building. Amusement park attractions are as complicated as bridges, if not more so. Plus, before I'd decided on which engineering discipline I was gonna major in, I took a lot of other classes in electrical and mechanical engineering. One of the classes was on robotics so I designed a Tsilly automaton."

"You used the game ideas for your classes?" She was amazed, but also slightly concerned he had spent so much time thinking about developing rides about Sandy's game. Did he still have a thing for her after all these years? They had only dated one year, before Barbara and Chris had fallen in love during their senior chemistry class. They had tried to fight the attraction, but it just got stronger with each moment they spent as lab partners. When they had finally admitted their love, it had ruined her lifelong friendship with Sandy. *What if he still has a crush on Sandy? No, that's a silly idea. We haven't seen her for over ten years—since the day we graduated from high school.*

Chris interrupted her thoughts. "I've always loved amusement parks, and I thought a Tsilly-based one would be fun to design. Whenever I needed a project, I thought of a new ride with the same theme." He looked embarrassed by his revelation.

"Hmm. And I thought you were studying boring subjects like physics." She narrowed her eyes at him.

"I did study physics, but I used fun things as class projects."

She laughed at his look of distress. "I wouldn't be opposed to you looking into it. Do you think the town would approve?"

"I never thought so before, but after the meeting... When Adam sarcastically suggested building an ark, I thought it might be a great design to house the different bible stories. We could start with Noah, but then modify the interior for other stories—like have a lion's den for Daniel."

"A fiery furnace for his friends. Columns for Sampson

to push down."

"Exactly. You can see it too, can't you?" He took her hand and squeezed.

"Yeah, I think the post-apocalyptic adventure would be great as one of those sit-in-the-dark rides where the cars move around, but the main focus is on a screen—like it's half movie, half ride."

"They call those dark rides." He rubbed his chin, thinking. "You have a point. If. I could get the actual game footage—"

"That might be a problem if we can't get Sandy on board with the idea. I hope Mayor Carol will be able to talk to her, or maybe Terry. If the rest of her family is on board, maybe she'd be willing to let you." She nodded. "Anyway, I see you've put some thought into this. You do have the land and there are plenty of ideas in the 'Adventures with Tsilly' game to turn into rides. But wouldn't it be expensive?"

He grimaced. "Yeah, I'd have to find some investors. If we built some of the key stories first and then added the different adventure areas a little at a time, we could maybe pay for it as we go. We would need a few rides to start with, I think. I liked your ideas of costumes for the town—we could have the operators for each area dress in costume."

"Why don't you gather up your ideas and see if you can get in to talk to Mayor Carol tomorrow and get her take."

"I will. Thanks hon, for being open."

"Sure. I love you. I want you to be happy." Maybe this

idea would bring them closer together as they worked through it. *This time I dodged the bullet. He isn't leaving... yet.*

"I'm going to go put some ideas down on paper—maybe work on a plan of attack—so I can be coherent when I talk to her tomorrow. Do you want to come with me as moral support?'

"Oh honey, I'd love to, but I'm working on a wedding dress for a client in Florida with a tight deadline and part of it is giving me fits. Hence my distraction earlier."

"Okay," he said, his shoulders slumping.

She knew he was always apprehensive about talking to people about his ideas. He was a smart man, but his self-confidence was low. He was a few months from his engineering degree, however, he still thought of himself as a grease monkey. *Maybe, I should squeeze in the time to go with him.*

"How about you call me when you set the appointment and I'll join you if I'm far enough along on the dress."

He straightened his shoulders and got up. "I'll do that." He gave her a smacking kiss on the mouth and turned toward the bedroom that doubled as an office. "If you get tired, go on to bed. I shouldn't be too long, but I do want to get my thoughts in order and you never know how long that will take."

She laughed, as she was supposed to. "Okay, honey."

As she cleaned up the kitchen she decided not to redecorate it—she did love its sunny, yellow warmth. She didn't have time to change it anyway—she was nearing her nest egg goal and she needed to spend all her time working. They were only a few months from the dreaded ten-year anniversary.

Chapter Two

CHRIS WOKE UP THE NEXT morning snuggled up with his wife. *Now this is the best way to wake up.*

When he'd finished last night she'd been asleep with the light still on, and the book she was reading on the floor. She had looked adorable with her long, dark hair spread across the pillow. He had picked up her book, laid it on the table. and crawled into bed with her.

She'd been working hard to build her business and supplement the income he made at the garage, so he hadn't wanted to wake her last night or this morning—she needed her rest. Maybe if he got the amusement park up and running, they wouldn't be strapped for cash. He made decent money at the garage, but it was never going to be a lot and he was tired of working at the same job he'd started in high school.

Of course, that was why he was taking online classes toward a civil engineering degree. But even when he did get his degree, how much work would there be in their one-horse town— assuming they could keep it from fading out of existence. He hoped the ideas they'd come up with last night would keep that from happening. *Starting over in a new location would suck.*

He crawled out from under the quilt his grandmother had made for their wedding. She'd called it a wedding ring quilt—it was blue and turquoise with some yellow. She'd passed on a few years ago. It was his favorite keepsake. His family had lived in Chedwick for three generations. *I don't want to be the generation that leaves.*

He got ready for his day, started the coffee, and gathered up his work from last night—which ended up being a rather hefty amount of info. Then he put it into the computer laptop satchel, wishing he had a brief case. But he didn't—the computer bag would have to do.

He hoped Barbara would go with him to see Mayor Carol. He wasn't sure how well he'd be able to present his ideas and having backup was a good idea.

He also wanted to get Barbara away from working so hard. Chris knew she craved the security money could buy—not surprising, given her father's desertion. She spent every second of every day on her business, seven days a week, and that wasn't good for anyone—or their marriage. He felt they had drifted apart too much and he was determined to change that. They had been married more than nine years, and he wanted to bring back the love and closeness they'd had in high school. *I need to think about how to do that.*

At his first break in the morning, he called the mayor's office. "Hi, Jennifer. This is Chris Clarkson. I was wondering if I could get an appointment with Mayor Carol for late afternoon."

"She has a four-thirty slot open, would that work?"

"Thanks, Jennifer. That would be perfect."

"Can I put down what the meeting is in reference to?"

"Um, well, just put down another idea for helping the town grow."

"Good. See you at four-thirty."

He then called his wife. "I have a meeting with the mayor at four-thirty."

"Okay, good honey."

She sounded distracted so he asked, "Can you go with me?"

"What? Oh, right. Mayor Carol and the amusement park. Sorry, I've got my head in this dress. How about you call me at three-thirty and I can see where I'm at. At the moment, it's not cooperating."

"I will. Good luck. Love you—bye."

"Love you too."

He went back to work thinking about all he wanted to say to Mayor Carol. He was so churned up about it he was making himself sick. He thought maybe he should go to his sister's restaurant for lunch and see if he could chat with her about it—maybe release some anxiety.

Chris walked into Amber's restaurant and knew he'd

never get to talk to his sister. The place was packed. Everyone was talking about Mayor Carol's big announcement from last night. He'd been distracted with the amusement park idea and hadn't given it any thought.

Some guys he knew from high school were sitting at the counter so he joined them and got pulled into their conversation.

"Are you gonna run for mayor, Chris?" Ted asked.

Chris laughed. "No, not interested. Any of you thinking about it?"

"Not us—any idea who might?" Fred asked.

Shaking his head, he said, "Not a clue, what do you think?"

Ted shrugged. "We were contemplating maybe Steve running."

"Steve Jameson?" Chris asked, stunned.

"Of course, Steve Jameson. Is there any other Steve you know?" Ted said.

"No—just surprised at the idea. I could see him running, but I can't picture him as mayor."

"Yeah, that was kinda our take on it too." Fred snickered.

Chris continued, "In fact, I can't imagine *anyone* else as mayor. It's gonna be strange to have someone else take her place—she's been the mayor here since we were barely teens. And to turn their house into a B&B sounds a little crazy too. From mayor to B&B owner…"

Fred nodded. "Things are changing, that's for sure."

They continued chatting as they had their lunch.

When he finished eating Amber rang him up so he asked, "Hey sis, do you think you'll be this busy tonight?"

"No, Wednesday night a lot of people go to Bingo or watch—"

"Perfect, I want to run something by you. I'll be back later."

"Yay, I get to see you two times today."

He tugged on her hair. "Lucky you."

"Yeah, lucky me."

He was glad he went to lunch. Chatting with the guys about the next mayor had calmed him down.

He called Barbara at three-thirty. "Hi, honey. Can you come with me to talk to the mayor?"

"Sure, I might as well. This dress is going nowhere fast. I think I have ripped out this one area ten times today. It's at four-thirty didn't you say?"

"Yes, four-thirty. Thank you, honey. I know you will figure out the dress—you always do."

Relieved she was coming, he hung up the phone and started getting ready for his meeting with the mayor. They had a shower at the garage so he could clean up. The mayor's office was two blocks over, so once he was cleaned up he could walk over, much easier than having to go home to get ready.

At four-fifteen when he saw no sign of her, he called the house again. His heart sank when she answered in her distracted voice. "Hi, honey. It's four-fifteen. Are you coming to the courthouse?"

"Oh my god, I'm sorry. I finally figured out the

problem I was having with the dress and lost all track of time. I'm sorry babe—I'm not going to be able to make it. Sometimes I hate my one-track mind."

"It's okay, sweetheart. I'll be home after I talk to her. Wish me luck?"

"All the luck in the world."

Damn. Okay, I can do this alone. I'm an intelligent adult.

He went up the steps and into the building. It was a distinguished older building with a large wooden staircase in the middle leaving two courtrooms, one on each side of the stairs. The judge's chambers were behind the courtrooms, down a hall, at the rear of the building on the first floor. It was quiet with the only sound being his heels on the floor.

He headed up the stairs to the second floor where the mayor had her offices and walked into the reception area. "Hi, Jennifer."

Jennifer looked up. "Chris, the mayor said to send you in when you got here. Go on in."

"Thanks."

He knocked once, then opened the door.

Mayor Carol said, "Hi, Chris, come on in."

He walked into the room, which was cozy and welcoming. Mayor Carol obviously wanted people to feel comfortable in her office. It was the direct opposite of the downstairs. Of course, the purpose was different between the two floors.

"Hi, Mayor Carol."

She smiled. "Have a seat, would you like something to

drink?"

"No, I'm fine, thanks." He took a seat and set his laptop bag on the floor next to him.

Carol leaned back in her chair. "So, what do you want to talk to me about?"

"I've had this idea for a while, but never felt it was the right time to mention it. The meeting last night made me feel differently." Chris wiped his palms on his knees. "You know the land my grandfather left me?"

"Yes, quite a few acres isn't it?"

"Nearly a hundred." He nodded. "I was thinking. What if I built an amusement park on it with the theme of the rides being 'Adventures with Tsilly'?"

"Now that's an interesting idea. What are you thinking of?" Mayor Carol focused on him with an air of expectancy.

"I have some information." He gestured toward his bag.

She waved her hand. "You can leave it with me to look at later. Tell me what you have in mind."

He scooted forward in his chair. "I was thinking of starting with a few key rides then building on to it as time and money allowed. It wouldn't be ready for this summer—I don't have the money to do it—but I was thinking maybe I could get a small business loan. Then look for investors."

"Don't worry about financing right now or how to do it. Tell me the big dream and let's see if it sounds beneficial to the town, then we can talk about the practicalities." She lifted her coffee cup.

"Big picture, I want to build rides for each type of adventure in Sandy's game. One area for the outer space exploration and one for the post-apocalyptic adventure and one for the geography, continuing on through all ten of the adventure areas in 'Adventures with Tsilly'. For example, if we used a boat ride for the geography level where we could put up miniature replicas of the area's attractions, for Europe we could put the Tower Bridge and Palace from London, maybe the Eiffel Tower and Notre Dame for Paris, and something like the Coliseum and Trevi Fountain for Rome. With mannequins dressed in the historical native costumes for each location."

As he went on to explain his ideas, Mayor Carol did not look at the coffee cup in her hands, she did not drink from the coffee cup in her hands, she did not put the coffee cup in her hands down.

When he stopped explaining, she nodded and put down the coffee cup. "I can see you've thought this through, although you would have to get the game company to allow you to use the footage for some of the rides you mentioned."

"Yeah, that might be a problem. But I have a lot of ideas drawn up—and actually engineered out—in the information I brought. A lot of it was done as projects for my night classes."

"When do you graduate, Chris?"

"I'll graduate in the spring. I've been working on this degree for eight years. I'm excited."

She smiled. "You should be proud of yourself. It's not

easy staying motivated so long."

"Thanks, Mayor."

"Chris, I think your idea has a lot of merit and if you can leave me your information I will take a look at it."

"I made a few copies of it before I came here, you can keep one." He'd about killed their little printer to make the three copies he felt he needed to make. He had run out of black ink about halfway through the second copy. Fortunately, Barbara was a fanatic about having all the supplies she felt she needed to run her business and there had been a three-pack of black and two of each of the other colors—which was a darn good thing, because he'd run out of blue a few pages later.

"Excellent. Now, how are you thinking about financing this?"

"I thought, maybe, I could get a small business loan to do the minimum starting costs. They have loans up to 150,000 dollars which would help with licenses and clearing the land, etcetera. Then I'd need to see about getting people to invest. Each ride would cost about a million dollars to build. I'd need several people with that kind of money to be interested. My ideal would be to start with a few rides for next year, then put up more as we are able to. I would like to make it a year-round park— which would take some doing—to get most of the rides in buildings. I've also written up a business plan to run the place, once the rides are built. I did it in my finance class."

"You might ask Gus if he'd be interested."

"Gus Ferguson?" Chris was surprised.

"Yes, he's a silver spoon baby and has a boatload of money. He might enjoy investing in you and this town. The game company might also be interested, since a location park might boost sales."

"Wow, do you think so?" He hadn't thought about the game company wanting in.

"Yes, I do. You probably want to take one of your copies over to Gus and let him look at it. Just drop it off and ask him to give it a looksee, so he can give you his opinion. Don't say anything else about him investing. Ask him if he could give you his opinion."

"I will. Thanks, Mayor."

"I'll talk to Sandy about it and have her feel out the game company."

"Really? That would be amazing."

"I think it would be good for her to hear this idea from her mother first."

"Yeah, maybe you can pave the way—so to speak."

"You should get the paper work started. Greg could help you with what you need. That boy,"—she huffed—"letting all those law classes go to waste while he runs a bar." She shook her head. "Oh well, it's his life. And now I'm going to go home. It's been a long day and I have some planning to do of my own."

"We sure will miss you as the mayor."

"Thanks, but I do think it's time. Fifteen years ago I took over the job *temporarily*," she said putting air quotes around temporarily.

"Not very temporary and your call, of course. Have a

good night then."

"You too, Chris. Keep me up to date on how things are shaping up—maybe every two weeks we should plan a quick update meeting. Talk to Jennifer on the way out to set up appointments."

"I will, thanks again."

He was in a daze as he closed the door to the mayor's office. He walked over to Jennifer. "She wants me to come back every two weeks for an update meeting."

"How about this time slot, every other week."

"Thanks, Jennifer. That would be perfect."

Chris was dumbfounded; the Mayor was treating this like a real project.

He stopped by the newspaper office. The place was a mad house of activity. Phones ringing, people talking, others madly typing away on their computer. He finally caught someone's attention and asked if Gus was in—they told him no and scurried off.

He wrote Gus a note asking him to take a look at his packet and that he'd call on Monday to ask his opinion. He paper-clipped the note to the copy of his plans, and snagged someone's attention asking if they could put it on Gus' desk. The guy pointed to the right one and said go ahead.

Chris walked over to the desk indicated and put his packet in the center of the blotter. Gus' space was surprisingly neat. Looking around the room at the chaos on some of the other surfaces, Chris was glad he didn't have to leave it on one of those tables. He knew it would get buried and never be seen again. But with Gus' nice tidy desk, it wouldn't be a problem.

He hoped Gus wouldn't think he was an idiot for wanting to build an amusement park. He didn't think Gus would want to invest in such a thing—a twenty-eight-year-old with a wild idea and some engineering classes. *Mayor Carol must have been trying to make me feel better about financing.*

He'd need to be like the tortoise—slow and steady—a little jump start with a small business loan would be the best place to start.

Chapter Three

BARBARA HAD TO STOP. She needed to pee and she was starving. So, she got up and could barely move—she was stiff from sitting hunched over the sewing machine. Her knees creaked and her back popped as she straightened. *Ouch, ouch. When was the last time I got up?* She limped to the bathroom and just barely made it. *Whew.* One problem solved. She didn't hobble quite as bad on the way to the kitchen. *Starving, but no, I can't eat in there, near the dress. Hmm, grapes wouldn't make a mess. Oh and look, cheese—not too messy. A few crackers. I can eat that small snack and not get it on the dress.* She popped a couple of grapes in her mouth while she made a plate of snacks. Munching on a piece of cheese, she noticed she was actually walking normally when she went to set the plate next to her machine and looked around her sewing room.

It was supposed to be a den, however she'd needed a large space for her sewing, and it was a nice big room. Wedding gowns took up a lot of space. The fabric wrinkled easily so she had to have large tables to lay the pieces of the dress on during construction. She also had rods attached to the ceiling where she could hang dresses when they were nearing completion—and she didn't want the trains to be folded up or drag on the floor. She had piles of fabric—satin, silk, even taffeta. Beads, buttons, and appliqués were in a chest Terry had designed for her, which had shallow drawers with many cubbyholes. Her area was well organized and kept spotless so as not to stain the dresses. She normally didn't eat in there, but she wanted to keep at it.

Then she heard the garage door open and Chris yelled, "Barbara, where are you?"

She walked over to the door. "In here."

Chris pulled her out of the room, grabbed her around the waist, and swung her around in a circle. "She loved the idea."

Barbara laughed. "Mayor Carol?"

"Yes. She said to get the paperwork together and submit it to the city for approval."

He was dressed up and looked sexy. *Maybe I should stop sewing and jump him.* "That's amazing, honey."

"It is. She's talking like it's a done deal. I got the paperwork to start filling out. She thought maybe Greg could help me. And I want to talk to Amber right away, so she doesn't hear it through the grapevine. Want to go with me to dinner? In an hour, maybe? I want to change my clothes and look over the paper work."

"I have one small part I need to fix on the dress—should only take me about fifteen minutes—then I can get ready."

"Perfect."

She went back to work on the dress. She wanted to finish off the area that had given her so much trouble the last few days.

Chris walked into the sewing room a few minutes later. "You're still working."

"Yeah, almost done."

He frowned. "Babe, it's been an hour since I last talked to you."

"What? It can't be."

"Six o'clock, honey."

"Darn, can you wait to eat a little longer? I really have to complete this." She hated to put him off, but she needed to get it done. It was for a wealthy client, and referrals from this bride could take her business to the next level. If she could make the woman happy. She had finally found a way to fix the problem, however it was a painstakingly slow process.

He sighed. "Fine, I'll get a snack."

"There are grapes."

"Like those on your table withering?"

"Um, yeah, I was planning to eat them, but that's when you got home and told me your great news."

"Well, get that done so we can go eat."

"Will do."

He was back a few minutes later. "Barbara, you have to stop. I'm starving."

"Honey, it's only… Oh my god, it's seven already?"

"Yes. Your fifteen minutes has now been two hours."

"I need to finish. You'll have to go without me."

"Dammit Barb, I know your business is important, but this is kind of a big deal for me and I want you to be a part of it."

"I'm sorry, but I have to finish this. It's finally going well and I've lost so much time."

"Fine, I'll go find someone who gives a damn," he said as he turned and marched out of the room. She heard the door to the garage slam as he went and started his truck.

She sighed. He didn't understand how her business worked. *The bride is paying me a lot of money, after all, and the possible referrals could change everything. I'll make it up to him when the dress is done.*

She finally stopped for the night. She was stiff from sitting all day, her vision was blurring, she was starving, she needed a bathroom break, and a shower. It was nine-thirty, but the dress was finally looking good. The house was dark except her sewing room and a light Chris had left on in the kitchen. Wondering where her husband was, she texted him.

Where are you?
Greg's

Finally done with the dress for today

Yay.

See you soon?

Gonna stay a while, talking to Greg about paperwork

OK sorry I didn't come with

No worries, don't wait up

Love you

Love you too, night

He didn't sound pissed, but he didn't sound especially happy.

She made herself a PB&J with a glass of milk and took the withered grapes. The dried and curled up cheese went into the trash. She took her plate of food and went to their bedroom to relax. Sitting on the side of the bed she scarfed down her 'dinner'. When she finished, she set the plate down next to her on the bed. *I'll take that to the kitchen, after I stretch my back out.*

CHRIS CAME IN AT eleven-thirty and found his wife still dressed in her sweats, lying flat on her back in the middle of the bed. Her ponytail was skewed to one side, her mouth was open making small puffs of breath, and she still looked beautiful to him. There was a plate on the bed and a nearly empty glass of milk on the nightstand. He shook his head, took the dishes to the kitchen, and put them in the dishwasher. Then he went back to the room, undressed, and pushed and pulled and rolled and dragged to get Barbara into bed. She didn't even wake up—she was exhausted. She was working too hard. *I have to fix that. Soon.*

As he laid there in the dark, he thought about all he'd done that night. Amber had thought the idea for using their grandpa's land to help save the town was excellent. They'd talked about their grandfather, who had lived in Chedwick after he'd married their grandmother. He had originally bought the land to raise cattle. After two years of trying, he had given up—he hadn't been a rancher. So, he'd sold his cattle to Hank Jefferson's father and the land had sat there empty. Both Chris and Amber knew their grandfather would be pleased with the idea. He had been a fix-it man and tinkerer. Always building some little thing to make his adored wife's life easier.

The guys at the bar had been enthusiastic about the amusement park. Terry and Kyle suggested building things from their areas of expertise—Terry with wood and Kyle with metal. He'd left a set of his ideas with Greg who planned to make copies for Kyle and Terry. He was glad everyone thought it was a good plan and he was happy to listen to ideas and advice. He hoped he could pull it off.

What if I fail? Go splat right in front of the whole town? No, I'm not going to think like that. I can do this. Can't I? He lay awake for a long time with his thoughts spinning in every direction. Finally, exhaustion claimed him and he slept like a rock.

Chapter Four

CHRIS AND BARBARA BOTH worked hard over the next few days. Chris spent his days at the garage and his nights on paperwork. Barbara spent all her time on the dress for the Florida bride—the structure of it was complete, but she still had to do the beading and finishing.

Friday morning Gus Ferguson walked into the garage where Chris had been mopping the floor and asked Chris, "Do ya have plans for lunch?"

"No."

"Can ya get away?"

Chris looked around the empty garage, which was exceedingly clean due to the lack of customers. "Probably."

Gus called out to Frank Miller the garage owner, "Can I steal Chris from ya for the rest of the day?"

"Yep, kinda slow today."

"Ya want to close up for a bit and come to lunch?"

"Sure, what time? Amber's?"

"Twelve-thirty. Yep, Amber's."

"Sounds good to me. Let's get cleaned up, Chris. See you in a bit, Gus"

When Chris and Frank walked into Amber's at twelve-thirty, the hostess directed them to the meeting room. Amber's place was a bit of everything. She had a hostess area to the right of the front door. To the left was a diner-type restaurant with Formica tables and a lunch counter with bar stools. Along the back wall was a huge salad bar. To the right was a fine dining area with white tablecloths and sparkling crystal. Behind the diner part was the kitchen. At the rear of the fine dining area was a meeting room, which could hold about a hundred people.

Chris and Frank looked at each other, shrugged, and walked to the banquet room. When they opened the door they stopped in their tracks. The town council was there, the mayor was there, both their spouses were there, and most of the rest of the town was there. *What in the heck is going on?*

Gus caught his eye and called out, "Come on up here boys, I saved ya some seats."

Chris couldn't believe his eyes. Barbara and Amber were both seated up front, and he went to sit by them. Frank went over with his wife.

Gus was with the Mayor and town council at the front of the room.

Chris whispered to Barbara, "What's going on?"

"I have no idea. Gus called and told me to be here at twelve-thirty and he wouldn't take no for an answer."

Gus stood. "I took the liberty of ordering some sandwiches and soup for y'all, so we can get down to business right away. I asked y'all to come here today because I didn't want to say this over and over to everyone. I'm only gonna say this once. I've lived in this town since I reached my majority and I have no intention of letting it die. My folks left me a bit of inheritance when they passed."

Mayor Carol snorted.

"Maybe a lot of inheritance."

Mayor Carol sniffed.

"Okay, okay, they left me an obscene amount of money. But I don't plan to just hand it out to anyone not willing to work hard and use it right. I've helped some of ya out from time to time, when ya got in a bind or needed a new piece of equipment." Chris looked around. Several business owners were nodding their heads, including his boss Frank, and his sister. He had no idea Gus had helped his sister. Interesting. Chris picked up his sandwich and took a big bite.

"And now I believe young Chris here has an idea that'll be a good place for me to invest a chunk, but it's gonna take all of us working together to make it happen. Chris, come on up and tell the folks here what you've got in mind."

Chris felt all the blood drain out of his face and his stomach knot. The sandwich in his mouth turned to sawdust and he had to force himself to swallow. Barbara put her hand on his arm and gave it a squeeze. He saw, shining from her eyes, absolute confidence. *Okay I can do this.* He squared his shoulders and stood.

He walked to the front of the room and looked out at his friends and neighbors. Barbara, Terry, Kyle, Greg and Amber all smiled at him nodding their heads with confidence. Mayor Carol stood on his left and Gus stood on his right. He cleared his throat. "I want to build an amusement park with rides which go along with Sandy's game. Kind of like a mini Disneyland."

"Tsillyland." someone said.

"Yeah, well, today it is chilly so it would work in the winter," another heckler said doing a word play on the pronunciation of Tsilly.

"I haven't picked a name yet. I have some designs and plans I drew up in my online engineering classes. Rides, animatronics, traffic flow, a business plan, etcetera. Whenever I needed a class project, I used the idea of an amusement park, not planning to ever build it. Even though I do have the land my grandfather left me, I never thought our town would want something like that or there would be a market for it. But after our town meeting, I thought maybe it was time to talk to someone about it. I didn't think it would be half the town…"

Everyone laughed and Gus said, "Chris left a copy of his plans on my desk, and he gave a copy to our mayor here. We like the idea. It's gonna cost a bundle, but I'm thinking it might be a good draw for tourists. I'm willing to put fifty million dollars toward building it and a resort."

"Oh, I wasn't planning on a resort."

Gus looked him in the eye. "Ya are now."

Mayor Carol spoke up, "All those tourists need somewhere to stay."

"But…" Chris felt like his head was going to explode. Fifty million dollars and a luxury resort? He didn't have the ability to pull this off, did he?

Gus said, "No buts, we need a resort in our town and you've got the ground for it. I bought the town hotel this morning. It can be our low-budget accommodations." He looked across the room at Marc Winthrop. "Marc, can ya get a work team into my hotel tomorrow and get the place in shape?"

"Sure can, Gus. We're pretty slow right now, might have to see if I can pull the guys off the crews at the ski resorts."

"You do that. Clean it up, modernize it, and make any repairs it needs. I want it ready to house the workers we are gonna need to build the park and resort. A month or two at most."

"I'll go over this afternoon and take a look around."

"Good 'cause I want ya done with that so ya can help lead the teams we'll be bringing in for the resort and park. I think we can bring in some people and get a mini park and mini hotel up by summer. Then, once those are done, you'll need to be helping Mayor Carol on her B&B."

Marc swallowed. "Yes, Gus."

Chris cleared his throat. "Um, Gus, we can't get anything done by this summer. I was thinking next summer for the first phase."

"Well now if ya had to go out and get financing that would be true, but since I'm standing right here with the money, I think we can expedite it and get a small version of your idea done up in the next six months."

"We can try."

"Try shmy, let's get 'er done. Now, Terry and Kyle, you'll need to get into it, too. Anything we can use that's made in our town will be both an artisan draw and a savings, since there's no shipping. I'll work on the promotion stuff, maybe call in some big wigs from magazines and TV, but that'll have to wait 'til we have some of it going. Chris, you're going to have to do this full time. You'll need to draw a salary—we can talk more about that later. Frank, can ya find some other helpers?"

"Yep. Got a half dozen kids and new high school graduates looking for work. Figured I only had Chris a few more months until he graduates, so I've been talking to them already."

"Some of them could be gofers for the construction crews too. Barbara, ya need to start on the costumes for the town and park."

"I can't, Gus. I have wedding dresses commissioned out for six months."

"Tell me, Barbara, do ya truly love every step of creating a dress?"

Barbara was silent as she thought about it. "I love the design. I love creating the form of the dress. The beading, hemming and finish work, not so much."

"See now, what ya need to do is to do the part ya like

and let some of the townsfolk help with the parts ya don't like so much."

"Oh, I don't make enough on the dresses to pay others to help with them."

"But if ya draw a salary for the work on the costumes, then ya could, couldn't ya?"

"Um, well, maybe."

"Ya think about it. Now, I know the fifty million won't cover the cost of the whole park—the resort will take about half of it, but maybe Sandy's game company would be interested in investing. 'Specially if we have the game in the resort rooms for people to play while they visit—kind of a win-win for them. Amber ya have first dibs on opening a restaurant or two in the resort or maybe room service."

"I'll give restaurants some thought, but I think I'll pass on the room service. Not my cup of tea," Amber said.

"Greg, every resort has a bar. Ya can decide if ya wanna expand."

Greg nodded.

"Now, as far as what I want back. I want two percent of the profits put into the new *Gus Ferguson* fund I opened today, which'll go toward people who apply for assistance on their businesses. Anyone have questions?"

The room sat dumbfounded. No one was talking, no one was drinking, and no one was eating—he'd given nearly everyone something to do or think about.

"No questions? Good. All of ya get on out of here and get busy. We're gonna make this little town rock."

Chris went over and sat by his wife, his mind racing with ideas, his heart pounding in terror. He felt like laughing and throwing up at the same time. Could he do it? Could the town support it and come together to make it happen?

He looked over at his wife. She looked nearly as shaken as he felt. She gave him a weak smile. Yep, she was feeling it too.

Gus came over to them and sat. "I know it's a lot to take in, just wanna add one more thing so ya have all the facts. I think ya should both draw a salary of 50,000 dollars a year while we get this set up and then we can increase it based on the profits from the park."

They both looked at him with their mouths hanging open. They barely made over 50,000 dollars a year between them.

"It's going to take hard work and dedication to get this off the ground—you'll earn it. The salary will give ya the ability to work on it and not have to do other things to keep afloat. Barbara ya certainly can keep up your wedding gown business, but start farming out the hand sewing and parts ya don't like to some of the other ladies in town. That'll give them an income and you some freedom to work on costume design and creation. Maybe some ladies could help with sewing the costumes too. You can decide who to bring on and pay for their help, just write up what ya think it'll cost and I'll get a pool of money set aside for that. Now, ya two go on home and hash it out. Chris, I'll meet ya Monday morning eight AM at Ambers." Gus walked away after he said his piece.

Barbara looked at Chris. "I don't think I can manage to hash it out right now, I need to let it sit."

"Yeah, I know what you mean. I feel like I've been run over by a train. I suggested this idea less than a week ago and now I'm supposed to quit my job and go full force into it? I feel like throwing up."

Barbara got a strange look on her face. "What if we table it for the rest of the day and take our minds off of it for a while."

Chris was relieved. "What did you have in mind?"

Barbara leaned in and in a low sultry tone whispered, "I know what would take our minds off of it." She looked pointedly at him as she stroked his thigh under the table.

Sex? I can do sex. That will certainly take my mind off all this. Great idea, baby. "Yes, that would do it. Hard and fast or long and slow?"

"Hard and fast the first time, long and slow the second, sticky and sweet the third."

"I like how you think, woman. Let's see who's first to get home and naked."

Barbara jumped up and hurried to the door. When Frank called to him, Chris heard her laugh.

"Now, Chris, I want you to know today can be your last day at the garage. If you're ready to start this up, I've got a couple of kids looking for jobs and we're slow right now—it would be a good time to take them on and start teaching."

"Um, well, okay. If you're sure." Was he ready to walk

away from his job? He just didn't know—and most of his blood had drained to parts south from his wife's suggestions, so he wasn't thinking clearly.

"Yep, I'm sure. You'll need the time to get this ramped up."

Speaking of ramped up, he needed to get home to his sexy wife. "Frank, I'll come by this weekend to clear out my stuff."

"No hurry, next week would be fine."

Chris held out his hand. "It's been good working for you, Frank."

"It's been good having you." The two men shook hands and Chris walked away in a daze. He had quit his job. What was he thinking?

Then he thought about his wife waiting for him at home and made a beeline for his truck.

Chapter Five

BARBARA RACED HOME. If she knew her husband, he'd
be right behind her. The thought of him closing in on
her made her heart race. She was pretty sure it had been
a couple of weeks since they'd had a romp in the sheets.
She knew during most of that time she was responsible for
the lack of intimacy—she'd been caught up in work and
exhausted at night. Thinking of the look of desire that had
started to build in his eyes made her tingle all over. She
was going to rock his world today.

She decided a trail of clothing from the back door to
the bedroom would be a fun way to excite him. So, she
dropped a boot right inside the door, then every few feet
she dropped another article of clothing. Almost to the
bedroom she dropped her bra, then hung her panties on
the door knob and closed the door.

She ran into the bathroom to freshen her breath and spritzed on the perfume he liked. Now where should she be? Standing in the middle of the room? Lying on the bed? She decided on the bed and yanked down the quilt and sheets. She lay down on it, as she heard the garage door open.

When Chris walked in the bedroom he was naked too, with a huge grin on his face. "You brat. Leaving me a trail of clothes to follow? I nearly came in my jeans. Now you're going to get it."

She pretended to yawn. "Took you long enough. I nearly fell asleep waiting."

"Oh really. Let's see if I can wake you up then," he said as he pounced.

He grabbed her wrists and held them above her head with one hand and squeezed her breast with his other teasing the nipple to a hard bud. His mouth was wild on hers, devouring her. Urgent and insistent his tongue dancing with hers. Then letting go of her wrists, he kissed his way down her neck. His breath was hot on her other nipple as he sucked it into his mouth and bit down gently. She arched up, writhing, he moved on to the other breast and gave it the same attention.

"Chris, please."

He reached down, running a finger into her. "So wet for me."

"Yes, I want you inside me now. You promised me fast and hard."

"You got it, babe," he said as moved back up her body.

He thrust into her in one smooth motion, embedding himself all the way to the hilt.

"Yes," she moaned. "Do me, honey. Hard."

He moved one hand to her clit, teasing it while he pulled out and plunged back into her. His mouth ravished hers.

She wrapped her legs around his hips and met him thrust for thrust. It didn't take her long to come so hard she saw stars. Squeezing him with her inner muscles, he groaned as she milked him to completion.

He collapsed on top of her unable to move.

She ran her hands down his back to his ass and squeezed. "Perfect."

After a while, he rolled off, pulling her with him. She landed on top. He stayed inside her—which she loved.

"Don't want to squish you," he said as he squeezed her ass.

"I love the feel of you on top of me."

"I love the feel of you under me, but I want you to be able to breathe too. After all, I have more ideas for you as soon as I recover."

She wriggled on top of him; she loved the feel of her bare breasts on his chest, his hair lightly abrading her nipples.

He swatted her ass lightly. "Stop that. Give the poor man a moment to recuperate."

She could feel him starting to harden inside her. She wriggled some more.

"Feeling feisty, are you?"

"Me? Feisty? Not sweet, little, innocent me."

He laughed. "Sweet? Yes. Innocent? Not so much. It was you who left a trail of clothes from the door to the room. Doesn't sound innocent to me. Sounds feisty."

"Hmmm, you may have a point. Let's see if I can continue to be feisty." She put her mouth on his and bit his lower lip, then kissed him passionately.

He groaned. "Are you trying to kill me, woman?"

"Oh no, I have much better plans for you than death and you are just going to have to man up."

He flexed his hips. "Yes ma'am."

She sat up which caused him to go deeper. His breath whooshed out and she reveled in the passion she saw in his eyes. She eased up his long length and came down slowly, watching the pleasure on his face. She did it again, inch by inch—so slowly he groaned her name.

"Dear god, Barb."

"Yes, honey?"

"Killing me."

She leaned down and licked, then nipped his right nipple. Then the left. "Oh, we can't have that." She lifted off him and slammed down twice in quick succession. "Better?"

He growled and squeezed her breasts, which hardened her nipples. "Woman, you're asking for it."

"Yes, I am. Give it to me, big boy."

He laughed. "You got it, babe." Then he flipped them over without losing penetration and started a slow pace that drove her wild.

She panted, grabbed his ass, and squeezed hard. "Faster, Chris. Now."

"Sorry, I believe round two was long and slow."

He pumped into her, slowly, over and over, each escalating the pleasure little by little. The sensations so delicious and building so slowly, she wasn't sure she would survive it.

When she started to come apart she bit his lip. "Come with me, now."

He groaned his release, calling out her name as she screamed his.

When she woke a while later, she looked at her husband with his head nestled between her breasts. She played with his hair, which had gotten a tad long over the winter. She felt him wake up and he looked at her with sleepy green eyes and a slow grin.

"Hey, babe."

"I'm starving. You?"

"I could eat."

She smacked him. "Good, let's go see what we can find."

"We could," he said as he started kissing his way down her chest, "or I could have a little taste of something much better than food."

"Chris!"

"Yes, baby?" he said as he moved between her legs, opening them wide with his shoulders. He leaned down and licked her. "Mmmm, tasty."

She said breathlessly, "Oh god."

"Nope, just me, baby," he said as he settled in to feast.

He knew how to bring her to a quick hard climax using his lips and tongue and two long fingers up inside her. When she'd come for him twice, he got up. "Now, about food."

She opened one eye. "Can't move, you're on your own."

"Not a problem, you rest now and I'll go rustle us up some dinner. I've got more plans for you, babe, and you are going to need your strength." He pinched her nipple and got up.

She opened her eyes to watch him. He was magnificent, with a sculpted chest, ripped arms, long legs, a high tight ass and he was hard. "Isn't that painful?"

He grinned at her as he pulled on his boxers. "Some, but I will use it to full advantage after I've gotten you some sustenance."

"Now you're trying to kill me," she grumbled.

"Nope, manning up, as you required," he said as he walked out the door.

She flopped back on the pillows. *I've created a monster.* Then she smiled a secret smile. *A very excellent monster.*

Chapter Six

CHRIS WHISTLED ON THE WAY to the kitchen. What a fine way to spend the day. Then he remembered why he was spending the afternoon in bed with his wife and the whistle died.

Can I build a successful amusement park? And now a resort on top of it?

Having the money was awesome, but the responsibility of it all was overwhelming. He didn't know a thing about running either one. *What is Gus thinking handing over millions of dollars to a guy who is twenty-eight. I'm a grease monkey for god's sake.* Sure, he'd taken some engineering classes and would graduate in a couple months, but did that really make a difference? Not in his book it didn't. What in the hell had he gotten himself into?

Okay, calm down. All he needed to do right now was

make some dinner for his wife. He was not going to panic now. Tomorrow he could panic.

Dinner. I can handle dinner. He looked in the fridge and found two steaks. That would work. The steaks could start cooking while he did some preparation for later, he went into the living room and started a fire, and made a cozy nest of pillows and blankets. Back in the kitchen he found a couple of potatoes and a bag of salad. He scrubbed the spuds, poked holes in them, and put them on a couple layers of paper towel in the microwave. Then got out the butter, sour cream, and chives to top them with. He chopped up the chives, as well as a cucumber and some tomatoes for the salad, turned the steaks over and started the microwave.

He looked in the freezer and was delighted to see some whipped cream which would go nicely with the strawberries he'd seen in the fruit drawer. And there was some chocolate syrup too. She had said something about sticky and sweet earlier. He grinned as he put the strawberries on a plate with a bowl of topping and a bowl of chocolate syrup. Then he put their desert in the fridge for later. He found some candles and lit them, took the steaks out, fixed the potatoes, and topped the salad, grabbed a bottle of wine and opened it. Once the meal was on the table, he went to get his lovely bride and found her dozing.

"Come on, baby. For you, I have prepared a feast."

She sat up, slumped back down. "Too tired, you wore me out."

"Naw, you're just faint from hunger." He got her robe, sat her up in bed, and slipped it over her head. It was kind of a lounging robe that fell to her feet in a swirl of flannel. "Come on, sweetheart, your banquet awaits."

"I'm coming. I'll be there in a sec."

He went back to the kitchen and poured the wine. When she came in, he gestured to the table with a flourish. "Come, my darling, and sup with me."

She rolled her eyes at him and sat. "Mmm. Looks good. I'm starving."

As they ate, they chatted about everything under the sun except for the amusement park and Gus's outrageous suggestions. By silent pact, they avoided the elephant in the room. Time enough tomorrow to tackle it.

When they had finished, she said, "That was excellent, Chris, I'm stuffed. I can clean up."

"No, baby. You relax, I'll take care of it. My turn to take care of you. Have another glass of wine."

"It might put me to sleep."

He waggled his eyebrows at her. "Aw, but I know the way to wake you up. Take the wine into the living room. Earlier I started a fire."

"Okay," she said as she got up and walked toward the living room.

He heard her laugh and then she called out to him, "Chris, this looks like a scene for seduction."

He smiled. That's exactly what it was. He had lit some candles and had arranged a cozy nest on the floor next to the fire.

He hurried through the cleanup, then he grabbed the strawberries he'd taken out of the fridge so they wouldn't be too cold, and the rest of the wine before he went into the living room and found her naked in front of the fire. The soft flickering light bathed her skin in a warm glow and caught the highlights in her hair. *My god, she's beautiful.*

Her back was to him and she looked over her shoulder. "Coming, honey?"

"Not yet, but I will be."

She laughed a throaty laugh that sent goose bumps over his skin. He put the strawberries and wine on the coffee table he'd moved to the side and dropped his boxers on the floor, already hard as a rock. He snuggled up to her back, reached for her breast, and kissed her shoulder.

"Mmm. What kept you?"

"I had no idea what was waiting or I'd have dumped all the dishes into the sink and run water over them. Instead I dutifully cleaned the kitchen, loaded and started the dishwasher."

She turned toward him. "I think all that deserves a reward." Spotting the strawberries, she said, "And what is that?"

"A little desert." He smirked.

She reached over him and snagged a strawberry, dipping it in the cream and chocolate then pushing him down on his back. "I think that's a fine idea."

Then she proceeded to torment him as she swirled the chocolate and cream on his penis and ate the strawberry. Then she bent down to lick him clean. She sucked him into her mouth and drove him wild. When she'd sucked him to a massive orgasm, she smiled up at him. "Excellent desert."

He lay there panting. *Not exactly what I'd planned—but I'm not complaining. And turnabout is fair play.* As she'd find out as soon as his heart recovered and he could move again. Which might be next week.

They played with the strawberries and chocolate and whipped cream, which made them both sticky in interesting places.

"We need a shower," she said when her brain started functioning again.

"Hot, wet, and soapy. I can get behind that."

"No more sex for you, stud, I'm exhausted."

"Oh, no. I'd never consider having hot, wet sex with my wife in the shower. What were you thinking anyway? I just plan to wash your back...and front...and... Well, that's all I plan to do. However, if you get out of control and beg me for more? I wouldn't be a good husband if I said no, now, would I?"

She rolled her eyes and got up heading for the bedroom. He took the strawberry mess into the kitchen and dumped it in the sink to run water over. He would clean it up later, as well as their nest in the living room. Right now, his wife needed cleaning and he was happy to oblige.

It was steamy in the bathroom by the time he joined her and she was wet all over. He got in behind her and grabbed the shower gel. Squirting a liberal amount on his hands, he ran them over her body. She felt good all warm and slippery. He paid careful attention to her breasts, which made her slump against him.

"Chris."

"Yes, darling, it's me."

"I know it's you. No one fires me up like you do."

He grinned. "Good to know."

He moved his hands down her waist and around to her back and squeezed her cute little butt. Then he went up her spine to her shoulders soaping the soft skin, and then down again running the soap across the back of her legs and then up the front. There he paused at the apex of her thighs. Parting her legs a bit more with his feet, he went to work on *cleaning* her folds and hidden treasures surrounded by them.

By then, she was panting and holding on to the bar built into the shower.

He ran his fingers back and forth and in and out until she exploded, and she started sinking.

He held her up and grabbed the handheld to rinse her off and wash the shampoo out of her hair. "Ready to get out?"

"Oh no, it's your turn now."

She got the shower gel and gave him the same treatment until he was panting. Then he held her up against the shower wall and plunged into her. Their bath time fun had been enough to fire them both up; it didn't take them long to come, which was good because the water was starting to cool.

"Now it's time to get out before the water gets any colder."

He laughed. "Yeah we don't want to get cold and have to generate body heat."

She slapped him on the ass. "No more. Bed time."

"Yes ma'am. I think you wore it out anyway."

She looked down. "I don't trust it not to have other ideas—it seems to be easily encouraged."

"Yeah, well, it does seem to favor you. That's for sure."

"No more tonight, buster," she said wagging her finger at it. "We're going to dry off and go to bed. To sleep."

They fell into bed exhausted. Too tired to think about Gus and his suggestions.

Chapter Seven

BARBARA EASED OUT OF bed, not wanting to wake Chris. Putting on some sweats she headed to the kitchen. Coffee, she needed caffeine stat. While the coffee pot did its thing, she took care of the strawberry mess. Chris had been sweet making dinner last night and cleaning up. Both in the kitchen and in the shower. She smiled as she thought about how he'd made her feel special and well-loved. They needed to take an afternoon off more often. Maybe they should schedule it into their calendars.

Her contentment faded as she thought about the reason they had taken the afternoon off. How could Gus think she could pawn off her wedding dress business and work on an amusement park and town costumes? Didn't he realize how much work she'd put into building her reputation? It was her name and business that could be damaged. This wasn't some hobby for her. This was important, vital even. She had no intention of neglecting her clientele while she spent all her time on costumes. She didn't care how much he was willing to pay her—this was her future and she wasn't going to ignore it. She would be happy to design outfits and help with decorating the amusement park, in her spare time, but her wedding customers came first.

She made some toast and took it and her coffee to the kitchen table. She grabbed her sketchpad and did some drawing while she ate. It soon became apparent she didn't know enough about the game or what Chris had in mind to go much farther than an outfit or two for Kalar. Of course, dressing Kalar was the easy part. She was a tall, well-built warrior woman with long dark hair, and strong features. Kalar was the guide in each adventure—she had clothing appropriate to each time, or location, in which the adventure was set. Later, she'd think about outfitting the other characters, as she had no idea how to proceed.

Now she had a wedding dress to finish.

Chris came into her sewing room later. "So, back at it," he said.

"Yeah, this one has a lot of beading."

"Are you going to get some of the town ladies to help you?"

"No."

"But honey, how can you do both this and work on costumes?"

"Chris, I'm not going to let Gus railroad me out of

my business. I've worked hard for it and I don't want us putting all our eggs in one basket."

He frowned "What do you mean by that?"

"I hadn't thought about it until it came out of my mouth, but I guess I don't want to depend on only the amusement park or the town's ideas for all our income."

"You think it's going to fail? It's not even started and you think it will fail?"

"No. Maybe. No. It's not that I think it's going to fail. Oh, I don't know how to explain it. I just feel more secure with my own source of income."

Chris sighed. "Oh baby, I'm not going to walk out on you like your father did, leaving your family destitute. I'm in this until death do us part."

"I know that—I do. It's just… I need the security."

"I understand. I was hoping you would stand with me and we could make the park something special. I want us to work on this together," he pleaded.

"Oh, I will. I still plan to design the costumes for the town and help with the park decorations. But I need to keep working on the wedding dresses too."

"Gus never said to stop. He suggested you have some of the other women in town help you with the parts you don't really enjoy anyway."

She shook her head. "But what if they make a mess of it or get the gown dirty?"

"You could have them come here and work in your space—it doesn't have to be at their own homes."

"It would be too crowded to have other people in here,"

she said as she waved her hand around the room.

"We could work out another area for fabric storage. Or maybe you should open up a shop somewhere."

"No, I like being able to work from here. I don't know. I'll think about it some more."

Chris looked disappointed, but he didn't voice it. "I'm going to check on my classes and then go to the fire department; we're having practice today. I'll be back in a few hours."

He left her room and she could tell he was hurt, but she just couldn't give it up. She knew he loved her, but she didn't know if he'd *always* love her. What if he stopped? What if the love died? *I need my own income—one not tied to his dream.* She'd help him with it and she'd help the town with costumes to help build tourism. She would be a team player, but she'd also work on the wedding dresses.

Chapter Eight

CHRIS WAS DISHEARTENED BY Barbara's attitude even though he knew why she was the way she was. They had talked about her father walking out on her family when she was a little girl—but he wasn't her father. *Dammit I'm not going to leave her or take away her security and income. I love that crazy woman.*

The amusement park was a risk, but with Gus' backing it wasn't a huge risk. He could always look for another job if it failed. He was going to give everything he had to make it work. He wished Barbara would stand beside him, because sometimes he needed her to back him up with her encouragement. They were a unit and this was a time where he needed her. He sighed and decided to think about it later. He would work on a way to make her feel more secure.

Chris went online, he needed to see if there were any new homework assignments he needed to do. He'd been spending a lot of time on the amusement park and hoped he'd not gotten behind in his school assignments. He was glad he'd be graduating in June. He logged on and decided to check email first and saw one from Irene Smith—his lab partner from a few semesters ago. She had graduated last June, but they had kept in touch every month or two.

When she asked him how he was doing, he decided to tell her about all the plans for the park and see if she had any advice. Since she'd been born and raised in her family's amusement park in Colorado, she could have some good ideas. After he had sent the email he logged into the college network to do his classwork. He watched the video from the professor and noted the reading for next class. The assignment was pretty simple so he did it right away and turned it in.

Just as he was about to log off, his email pinged with a message from Irene. When he opened it he saw she was enthusiastic about his plans and had many suggestions and tips. Chris replied, thanking her for her input, and joked that he wished she were closer so he could pick her brain. He decided to print out her email to keep with his plans for a handy reference.

As he hit print Irene IM'd him.

Hey Chris.
Hi Irene.
Love your amusement park idea.

Thanks, excited to work on it. As well as terrified.

You know, if you're serious about wanting my input, I could come to Washington for a couple months while you're in the planning stage. Winter is a slow time for me so...

Wouldn't want to put you out. Don't know what I could pay for your time.

Wouldn't need to, don't need to be paid. Other than maybe somewhere to stay. Think of it as one friend helping another. I've got experience you don't and I'd be happy to share.

Seriously?

Yes, I'd love to see this Lake Chelan you're always bragging about.

Seems like a lot of trouble for you to come all the way here.

Not really, it would be fun to be in on building a park from the ground up or at least planning a park from the ground up. I'd need to be back in Denver by mid-May to get started on jobs we have set for the spring and summer.

Well, okay, if you're sure.

I'm sure, can you look around for a place for me to stay?

Um, sure.

I'll let you know what my plans are when I get them. I think this'll be fun, don't you?

Yeah sure, well, I gotta get going now. Got fire dept practice in a few. I'll email you later.

I will too. Ttyl

Chris logged off the computer and wondered what had just happened. Was she really going to come spend four months helping him design the amusement park? He had only been joking when he said he wished she were closer.

Right now, he needed to get a move on—it was time for practice at the fire station and Greg would ream him if he wasn't there on time. Volunteering on the department included attending trainings, so they were well prepared for calls. He had no idea what they were practicing today— it could firefighting techniques, paramedic updates, mountain rescue, water rescue, or something else entirely. *Dear god, I hope it's not water rescue. It might be sunny, but I bet it's fricken freezing out. Kyle will be there too, so I can ask him about a rental for Irene.*

As he hurried out the door, he wondered about Irene. *Do I really want her to come? I could use the backup and it certainly isn't going to be Barbara. Will Irene try to run the show and push me into her ideas? If I need to, I can be firm. She does have expertise. So, it could be valuable. Couldn't it? Besides, what would it hurt if she comes to give some advice?*

Chapter Nine

MONDAY MORNING AT EIGHT, Chris walked into Amber's restaurant. Gus was waiting for him at a table, and he went over to join him. "Morning, Gus."

"Morning, Chris."

The waitress poured them both coffee and took their orders.

"Ready to make some plans?" Gus asked once their breakfast was ordered and they both had started on their coffee.

Taking out some supplies and laying them on the table, Chris said, "Yes sir, I have my pad of paper and pen ready to take notes. Is this our first official business meeting?"

"Yep. I'm thinking we should meet on Monday and Thursday mornings to get this going. It'll be a business expense—keep track of it for your income taxes. Most tax folks say the best way to do that is to keep a daily planner, write your expenses right on the day, who ya meet with, etcetera. Then if ya ever get audited, ya have the info in black and white. Either buy a planner or put it on your smart phone. You'll need a credit card to use only for business expenses."

Chris nodded. "I'll put the info on my smart phone and I have a credit card Barb and I got for emergencies we've never used. I'll use that and we can get another one for emergencies."

"That works. Now here's what I'm thinking. We'll start talking this morning about the amusement park then move on to the resort. I think we should do both of them in stages. If we can get maybe three outdoor-friendly attractions done by summer, we could have a special pre-opening of the park for the summer and early fall months before the weather turns too cold. Then shut down for the first winter while we get the indoor rides ready."

"Sounds like a good idea, but that time table is fast for amusement parks. If we keep it small we might be able to do it. Since the indoor attractions will require buildings it'll take longer to get them completed. If the crew can get the buildings built during the summer then they can work on the inside during the winter months."

"Exactly. I was thinking one of the outdoor rides could be some spinning cars or something. You could use it as the talking to Tsilly and moving through time or space to start the adventure."

"Oh, that's a great idea. I hadn't thought of a starting

attraction, but it would make sense—and people love spinning rides."

"Seems like it'd be easy enough to engineer."

"Yeah, it's not terribly complex and many amusement parks have them. It should be straightforward to get it built. First ride planned. Another outdoor attraction could be a roller coaster or Ferris wheel—although I don't know how either would tie into the game." Chris took a drink of coffee.

"No, but people do love both kinds of rides—so even if we have to stretch the game idea it'd be good to include them," Gus said.

"Again, there are a lot of them that would be fairly easy to build. People love carousels too—that's another possibility."

"Yeah they do. Ya could also put out some of them treasure chests to get the kiddos excited. Maybe talk to Kyle and Terry to see if they could help with some parts or they might have some ideas for gettin' it going. Jeremy might have some input too, seeing as he's written Tsilly adventure books. Keep thinking about any other simple rides that could be done by summer. And you'll need some restaurants. Maybe one fast food joint with outdoor seating and one nicer one."

"I'll get Amber to give me some ideas. By the way, a college friend is coming for a couple months to help with the design for the park. She graduated last year with her engineering degree and has been working at a civil engineering firm since then. Her family owns an amusement park in Colorado. She said she doesn't need to be paid, just a place to stay."

"Hmm, I don't have any problem with her coming to help, but she needs to be paid. I don't want her coming back later, saying we ripped her off."

"Oh, I don't think she'd do anything underhanded. I did talk to Kyle and he has a nice rental she can use—it's fully furnished and the rent is reasonable."

"I'd rather be safe than sorry, we'll pay her a good rate and pay her housing. Now the resort."

Chris groaned inwardly. He was freaked out enough about the amusement park let alone a resort. "Gus, I don't know much about building a resort."

"That's okay 'cause I have a friend who owns the Marquee chain of hotels. I talked to him this weekend and his company might be interested in opening one here. In case they aren't, I asked him about building a resort in stages and he seemed to think we could build the main building, which would house the registration and infrastructure, and maybe a hundred rooms. He said if we had a good crew and could break ground soon we could get it done in six months. Then later, wings could be built on or some separate buildings to grow it."

"Wow."

The waitress brought their breakfast. While they got busy eating, Chris thought about what Gus had suggested. Gus must have realized Chris needed some time to think about it, because he changed the subject to Mayor Carol's announcement and they contemplated who might make a good mayor.

Once they were done eating, Gus handed Chris an envelope. "Here's the first quarter salary checks for you and Barbara. I've got some rooms on the second floor of the newspaper building ya can use as an office and meeting room if ya want."

"Sounds like a good idea," Chris said as he watched Gus take four of the small squares of jelly and put them in his jacket pocket. Then he took a handful of the sugar packets and put them in another pocket. Chris watched the most wealthy man he knew steal sugar and jelly from his sister's restaurant.

"I have to get back to the newspaper, you'll get the check," Gus said. It wasn't a question.

Chris nodded. "Sure, my first business expense."

After Gus left, Amber came over and sat across from him. "How did your meeting with Gus go?"

"Good. He's got good ideas. He gave me checks for twenty-five thousand dollars and told me to pay for breakfast, while he put sugar and jelly in his pocket—like some homeless person would do. Very strange."

Amber just laughed. "Yeah, he does it every time he comes in here. When he first did it, I thought he couldn't afford jelly and sugar. Once he paid for my new stove, I decided I'd think of it as interest. He nearly always eats here three meals a day—when he actually uses those sugar and jelly packets is a mystery. I wonder if he's got a room full of them and if you opened the door they would avalanche."

"No telling. Might be interesting to see what else he helps himself to in town. Anyway, he mentioned during our meeting that I should have a couple of restaurants in the park for a summer mini opening. Maybe a fast food one and also a regular sit-down-and-be-served one. Can you help me figure some of that out?"

Amber nodded. "Sure, be happy to. Can you come back? Maybe at two, when we have the lull and we can talk?"

"Sure can. Thanks, sis."

Chris spent the rest of his day talking to the various people who could give him some help with the ideas he'd talked to Gus about.

BARBARA FINALLY HAD the beading done on the wedding dress. She texted Chris to see where he was, and if he wanted her to make some spaghetti for dinner.

Hey honey, where are you?

Talking to Jeremy.

I was thinking about making spaghetti, interested?

Yes. I'll be done with Jeremy in half an hour.

Can you grab some French bread on your way home for garlic bread?

Absolutely.

Barbara happily went into her sunny yellow kitchen.

He didn't sound disappointed with her anymore. She turned on some music to cook by and hummed along as she made the spaghetti and meatballs he loved.

Chris came in, kissed her cheek, then sniffed the spaghetti sauce. "Here's the bread."

"You go get washed up, I'll put this under the broiler to heat up." With a knife she sliced the bread down the middle longwise, then slathered it with butter and garlic and put it into the oven under the broiler. She took the spaghetti, meatballs in sauce, and salad over to the kitchen table she'd already set. The wine was ready to be poured, since she'd opened it earlier and there was also glasses of ice water. She got the bread out from under the broiler, nice and toasty brown on the edges, soft and buttery in the middle. Chris came in and they sat down to eat.

"How was your talk with Gus this morning?"

"We worked on some paperwork and decided on how to work the finances. He's opened an account for building the park and hotel. He also gave us checks, for the first quarter salary."

"Seriously?"

"Yeah. I put mine in our joint account. And yours is in my bag"

"I hardly know what to say to that."

"Yeah, I am feeling a bit overwhelmed."

"I know you can do it," she said patting his arm.

"Thanks honey. I think I will be able to do it too. I emailed my lab partner and she said she'd be happy to come here to help me get the amusement park designed."

"Your lab partner?"

"Yeah. The one I designed the roller coaster with. She graduated last year and is working as an engineer-in-training. Her family owns a large amusement park in Colorado—she knows all about them. Her engineering company is slow during the winter, so she can come help me with the planning and design for about four months. I called Kyle and he has a place she can rent that's fully furnished."

"Oh. Well, you've been busy."

"You don't sound very excited."

Why would she be excited he was going to be working closely with another woman for four months? That didn't give her confidence. *What if he is attracted to her?*

"I'm surprised your lab partner is coming to help you with it. Is she bringing her family?" Maybe she was married—one could hope.

He said, "I don't think she has one. She's never mentioned anyone."

Damn. She didn't want to be paranoid, but Chris fell in love with her after working closely together for six months, and that darn ten-year anniversary curse was fast approaching. "Does she know anything about the game the park will be based on?"

"I don't know. We didn't talk about it. She'll be here in a few days. We'll know more then. I'll tidy up the kitchen, since you cooked."

"Thanks. I'd like a hot bath before bed. I was bent over those beads all day."

"Okay, sweetheart."

As she walked to the bedroom, she wondered if she'd been too hasty in not taking a more active part in the amusement park. Maybe she should get the game out and play it to see what kind of adventures and costumes would be needed. She could spend an hour a day on it—to get something ready to impress her husband and his *lab partner*. Plus, it would help her not feel guilty about taking the money Gus had given them for her half of the work.

Over the next few days, Barbara worked on her wedding dresses—and while Chris was gone she played the game and took notes. She didn't know why she was hiding her work on the park, she just didn't want him asking questions. Before she let him know she was participating she wanted some good ideas. There were a number of costume sketches and some background ideas for some of the adventures she'd drawn. Of course, it would depend on the kind of rides he was planning—but having visuals was always a good idea.

Barbara was at the school teaching sewing, which she did one Wednesday and one Friday a month. Several other people from the community volunteered to teach classes that are considered *extra* in today's educational climate. Amber taught cooking, Terry taught woodworking, Kyle taught welding, and Gus helped with the school newspaper and yearbook. Both boys and girls from all grades took the classes since the town decided their kids should be equipped in all areas of life. The seventh through twelfth graders even went to Frank's garage one afternoon each month to learn car maintenance.

On Friday morning, Chris called her cell.

"Hi, Chris."

"Hi, hon. Hey, can you meet me for dinner tonight at Amber's about six?"

"Sure, be happy to."

"Good, thanks. Gotta run, see you tonight."

"Bye, love you," she said to dead air. Chris had already hung up. He was busy so it made sense, but another five seconds wouldn't have killed him. She was happy to be meeting him for dinner; she wanted to hear all about what he'd been doing the last few days, his progress on the amusement park. She also decided this might be a good night to show him what she'd been doing. She had some nice ideas and was pretty confident.

After school let out Barbara ran home to shower and change into something sexy. She paid special attention to her hair and makeup, using styles and techniques Christ liked. She got out her notebook of ideas she'd been working on for the amusement park. Her sketchpad had costume ideas for the various adventures in this recent sequel of the game.

Barbara walked onto the restaurant and Amber gave her a hug. "Hi, Barb. Chris is already here. Follow me."

Barbara followed Amber to a table where she could see Chris from the back, but there was a stunning woman sitting to the right of him and they had their heads together over something on the table. Her step faltered, seeing her husband in such an intimate position with another woman.

Oh, hell no.

Barbara straightened her spine and stepped up to the table. "Chris, there you are, darling."

He turned his head and she laid a big fat kiss on his lips and sat in the chair to the left of him, across from her new nemesis. She plastered a big fat smile on her face and beamed at the blond woman who looked a few years younger than her and Chris. She had on a low-cut red dress and had been leaning forward probably giving her husband the opportunity to get an eyeful of perky breasts.

"Hi, I'm Chris's wife, Barbara, and you are?"

"Barb, this is my friend Irene. She's helping me design the amusement park."

"Hello Irene. Welcome to our town. Did you bring your family?"

"Um, no. I'm not married. It's nice to meet you—Chris speaks highly of you."

"Thank you. Chris and I have been in love for ten years, haven't we honey," she cooed.

"Um, yeah." Chris looked stunned—they had never been outwardly affectionate in public so when she kissed him and then talked about them being in love, she figured he was wondering what was going on. She had no intention of letting up. He'd just have to continue wondering.

"We're happy you could leave your life and come to our little town, to give Chris some help. Speaking of which—Chris honey, I brought some of the costume designs and some set ideas I have for the different adventures. Did you want to see them now?" she asked, placing a hand on his arm and running it back and forth.

Irene narrowed her eyes and leaned forward again, her dress gaped in front. "Chris and I have been working on some of the choices for the first half dozen rides. Chris, do you want me to show your wife the ideas?"

Poor Chris sat there looking back and forth between her and Irene like he was watching a vicious tennis match—he was adorably confused. He had no idea he was in the middle of a civilized catfight and he was the mouse they were both after. He probably didn't even notice Irene had been coming on to him, he was always pretty clueless about women's antics.

The waitress, Cindy, came over and he looked so relieved to see her, Barbara nearly laughed out loud. "What can I get you folks to drink? The usual?"

Chris glanced at Barbara. "Yes, Cindy. Our usual is perfect. My wife would like a glass white wine and I'd like a Rainer. Irene, what would you like?"

"Oh, I'll have a Manhattan."

"Coming right up."

Chris said, "So, um, honey, let me tell you what adventures we were thinking about to start with and you can show us your ideas for those. Okay?"

"Yes."

"Okay, since we want this to be a year-round park, much of it is going to have to be indoors. Maybe even some covered walkways. We talked about an ark shaped building for the bible stories. Some animatronic animals would be good for inside. What do you think about an outdoor petting area in the dryer months? Maybe get some baby critters—Hank might let us borrow some calves and chicks, or he might even have a foal. We could gather any puppies or kittens that were available."

Barbara thought about it. "Baby animals might be more work than they're worth, but the kids would love it. Of course, if you hired some teenagers to watch over the area and teach the kids how to pet the critters it might work. The teens could feed and clean up after the animals, too."

Chris nodded. "It's worth thinking about. Seems like Alyssa Jefferson would be the best idea—she and Rachel and some of their other friends. At least this summer and next before they graduate from high school."

Barbara said, "And biblical costumes are easy enough—robes and sandals mostly."

"Yeah, and I think your idea from the other night is good. The post-apocalyptic adventure would be great for a dark ride if we can get the footage from the game for our use. Which is going to take winning Sandy over. She usually comes home in early February for her mom's birthday. I hope we can talk to her then."

Barbara felt nervous about talking to Sandy. "That might take some doing, but if her mom and brother are both on board with the idea, it might make her more willing to deal with you and me. It's time we all made up anyway—I hope we can get there. The costumes for that are pretty set in stone, if we get the footage, but I did make up some sketches."

Irene said, "Chris and I also thought a boat ride would be good for the geography adventures, especially US geography. We were thinking maybe a playground could be used for the foreign geography with the idea of climbing and sliding down the alps or pyramids, a raft type ride could be used for whatever river is in the part of the world the current release is focusing on. Maybe climb the Eiffel tower. Since a playground can't be changed out like an indoor ride, we would design it to be built onto with each new area of discovery in the game. The first issue was Canada so Niagara Falls, Lake Louise, and Quebec would be excellent. Then the current sequel is Central America— maybe cliff divers, Mayan ruins, and the natural arch in Baja with monarch butterflies, macaws, and gorillas as animatronics, maybe."

"I think kids would love that, and it might give the parents time to rest a bit while the kids play. Each part of the playground would need an attendant or two—they could dress in the traditional dress for the country they were monitoring," Barbara said.

"Exactly." Chris beamed at her, which Irene didn't seem to like at all, judging by the sour look on her face.

Barbara continued, "You talked about a boat ride for US geography, you were planning on that being indoors right?

"Yeah, if we want to be a year-round park most if it needs to be indoors."

"This release of the game is all about Alaska—you

could do a focus on the national parks. There are eight of them and you could show both summer, with lots of wildflowers and bears feeding, and also the winter with a colder temp and dimmer lighting to indicate the long nights they have."

"Great idea, honey."

"What are you thinking for the outer space adventure? It's Mercury this time."

Chris shrugged. "Haven't thought about it."

Barbara said, "I was wondering if there was a way to simulate what it might be like on the different planets as if you were walking on them."

"We could certainly manipulate the temperature and light, and for the gaseous planets we could have mist in the room. Mercury is hot in the day and cold at night, isn't it?"

"Yeah." Barbara said thoughtfully, "I was wondering if a bouncing castle or something like that could show the weightlessness. But it also has huge craters. This adventure might be the hardest."

Irene perked up. "You know, with that adventure you could do the whole solar system, rather than focus on one planet at a time. Some kind of space shuttle-looking car, maybe flying through the air attached to a rail on the ceiling that takes riders into different rooms, which would be the different planets. It could be a static ride rather than changing it for each sequel, but you could sell souvenirs to focus on the current planet."

"Hmm, that might work. We could have the different lighting and temperature in each room," Chris said. "And with putting it all into the ride the first time, it wouldn't need to be changed every couple of years. I like it."

Irene smirked at Barbara as Chris turned his attention to the waitress when she returned with their drinks.

Bitch, don't think you've won this round.

They ordered dinner and the conversation continued in the same vein with both the women trying to one-up the other, until Terry came into the restaurant. He walked right over. "You look out numbered, bro."

Chris grimaced. "Yep, want to join us? This is my friend Irene from Colorado. She's going to help with the amusement park planning. Her family owns a large park in Colorado and she's already a civil engineer, hence she has lots of input."

"That should help you. Nice to meet you Irene, I'm Terry and my sister designed the game this big lug is going to pattern the park after."

Barbara smiled at Terry. He was always proud of Sandy's accomplishments. "Bragging on your sister Terry?"

"You bet."

"I think it's special for a man to brag on his sister," Irene purred at Terry.

Barbara just barely kept from rolling her eyes. *The woman is on the make with any man handy. Better single Terry than married Chris.*

Terry took over the conversation, talking about things to do in Chedwick and the surrounding areas. He was being charming to Irene, which suited Barbara fine. *Go Terry!*

When they had finished dinner and coffee, Terry asked Irene if she'd like him to take her home. Since she'd ridden with Chris, she said yes and he took her arm to escort her to his truck.

Barbara breathed a sigh of relief and looked at Chris. "That was interesting."

"Yes, but I have no idea what was going on between you and Irene. Are you trying to jeopardize my work with her?"

"Not at all." How could she explain to him that she didn't trust the woman? Especially around her man. "We just didn't hit it off too well. When I came in and found you with her, I guess I was jealous."

"Oh, baby, you have nothing to be jealous about. We will have a nice working relationship, I think, but that's all. I'm not interested in anyone except you—you are the one I love."

Barbara smiled. "Thanks honey, love you too." But she didn't trust Irene as far as she could throw her. Maybe Irene and Terry would hit it off and he'd keep her occupied. *One could hope.*

"Ready to go?"

"Yeah, let's go home. Maybe we can snuggle on the couch or something."

"Oh, I was thinking about jotting down some of the ideas you and Irene had so I don't lose them. Can I look at your sketchpad and notes? You seem to have some good ideas and I didn't get a chance to look at them closely."

"Thanks honey. I'm trying to be helpful," she said,

disappointed not to have her husband's attention.

"It shouldn't take me too long if you want to snuggle—or something—a little later," he said wagging his eyebrows.

She laughed. "We'll see about that when you are done. I think I'll read for a while."

They waved goodbye to Amber and walked to their cars. It was a cold clear night and the stars were beautiful. Many of them were visible even with the town lights dulling them slightly. It wasn't a big town, thus it didn't create much light pollution.

When they got home, Chris went to his study and she went up and changed into a long flannel nightgown and got into bed to read her story. It wasn't long before she started dropping the book. She laid it down and thought she'd doze until Chris came up for some *snuggling*.

CHRIS CAME UP A couple of hours later and found his wife passed out. It had taken him longer than he thought to look over the information Barbara had created. She had done a good job. There was a lot of detail and thought put into her ideas. He was happy she was showing interest. He got ready for bed and slid in next to his warm, sleeping wife, content to snuggle around her. She didn't wake up, but she did melt against him, her back to his front—and that felt fine to him as he drifted off to sleep. Life was good.

Chapter Ten

"I GOT EMAIL FROM SANDY," Chris told Barbara when he got home from the office he and Irene had set up in a spare room at the newspaper. Gus had a large area above the newsroom they could use to spread out. One part of the room was partitioned off, which would make a great meeting room. They outfitted it with a conference table and chairs, put in a projector with the ability to project from their computers and the ever-present white boards for meetings. It was a great setup.

They had gotten some desks and computers, along with the CAD and project management software to put on their new machines. The empty walls were now covered with white boards and corkboards. What had been a large empty room was now starting to look like an office.

Chris liked to see the ideas on paper rather than in the

software, plus it gave them a quick glance at where they were in the process and what they needed to focus on. The project management flow spanned a couple of the bulletin boards and they had all kinds of notes and brainstorming on the white boards. Some of Barbara's costume designs were tacked up, as well as some of Chris's ride designs

Barbara looked up from her sewing. "Sandy sent you email?"

"Yeah, I guess Mayor Carol called and told her about our plans. Which is probably good to have the first contact come from her mother rather than one of us." Chris shrugged. "She wants more information on what we're thinking. So she can prepare a presentation for her game company, to see if they want on board or if they will release the footage or if they have any restrictions. I told her we would be happy to partner with her company, if they were interested. I gave her the list of attractions and rides we were thinking about along with some of your ideas for costumes."

"Did she seem friendly?"

He thought about it for a minute. "No, not really friendly, but she was professional about the idea."

"Hmmm, it's a start anyway."

"I gave her your email address in case she wants to talk about the costume and decoration side of things."

"Okay."

"Are you upset about me giving her your email?"

She grimaced. "No, it's fine. I am just kind of scared to hear from her. After all this time, I don't know how to react."

He squatted and took her hand. "I think we should take our cues from her. For now, respond in a professional manner and keep it business. When we see her face to face, that might be a whole different story. Over email, we can stay away from any drama and make it about the town."

She nodded and squeezed his hand. "I can do that. Did you attach any sketches or drawings about what you are planning?"

"No, I sent her text. I did BCC you so you can see what I sent, and what she said."

She smiled. "Thanks. I'll look it over, later."

"How much longer are you going to be working? Want me to whip up some dinner? I could make burritos or that hamburger and macaroni stuff."

"I have about an hour left on this and it will be a good stopping place. If you want to make dinner, I'm not going to complain. We also have chicken you could bake with some potatoes. Anything you want to make is fine with me."

"I'll make dinner. Surprise dinner."

She went back to sewing, however her mind was on Sandy and what might happen. This could go either good or bad. They had hurt Sandy by falling in love. She could remember the day they had told her like it was yesterday and it still hurt to think about it.

It was a bright, sunny day in mid-March before spring break. Of course, the Lake Chelan area has 300 days of sun a year so it wasn't unusual. But the rest of the day was burned into her memory.

Chris and Barbara had been lab partners since the start of the school year. When they first got assigned to work together they had laughed about it, since they were both close friends with Sandy. It had been a great joke for them to be working without her right in the middle. How would they cope without her?

The two of them worked well together since they had complimentary skills and knowledge. She was a hands-on kind of person and loved the experiments and trying new concepts. Chris learned by reading and taking lots of notes. She drew pictures during lecture time, which helped her to remember what the teacher was talking about. Now they call it kinetic learning, but ten years ago that learning style wasn't well recognized, so people thought she was flighty.

As the weeks wore on, she had started to appreciate Chris more and more. He was such a strong partner and— good lord—the boy was easy on the eyes. She seemed drawn to him like a moth to a flame. Hiding her attraction to him with jokes and teasing had been hard. But she had no intention of stealing her best friend's guy.

After a while, she started begging off when Chris was going to be with Sandy. Previously they had spent all their time together doing anything and everything. Once Barbara started having feelings for Chris she started hanging out with Sandy in the afternoons, but made sure she was on her way home when Chris got off work. So, she wouldn't have to be around him and Sandy. She even started skipping lunch with them and went to the library to do *homework*. There wasn't anything she could do about seeing him in her chemistry class, but she didn't have to add her off hours to the amount of time they were together.

Chris finally asked her about it after a couple of weeks of avoiding him in the evenings. Chris had said, "What's going on Barb? You haven't been around with me and Sandy for a few weeks."

She'd fidgeted. "Oh, I've been busy. Lots of homework and chores to do at home."

"Uh huh, and what about lunch?" Chris crossed his arms.

"Um, I'm ah… dieting, yeah dieting. I um, don't want to be around food."

"Is it food you're avoiding or me? Sandy says you hang out with her every day until six-thirty and then run off like a rabbit. That's the time I get off work."

"Oh, well, I have to get home."

Chris raised an eyebrow. "Why? So you can sit home alone? I know your mom doesn't get home until seven or seven thirty."

"Um, I have to make dinner?" she'd said biting her lip.

He shook his head. "Your mom works at the diner and brings home your dinner. Try again."

"I have to help Kristen with her homework?"

"Not buying it, Kristen is older than you. What exactly

are you helping her with?"

"I know stuff she doesn't," she'd said crossing her arms and scowling at him.

"Yes, I'm sure you do. What did I do to make you run away from me?"

"Oh, Chris, I don't want to be around you and Sandy. It's too hard."

"Hard? Oh, like trying to pretend you and I are just friends. Like trying to pretend there are no sparks flying? That kind of hard?"

She had been surprised. "How did you know?"

"Because, I'm feeling it too. I don't want to hurt Sandy, but I want to be with you every second of every day."

"Chris, we can't do this. I couldn't bear to hurt Sandy," she said, her voice breaking.

"I know, but I want to grab you throw you against a wall and kiss you for hours, or days. Weeks maybe."

She gasped. "You can't do that, we're supposed to be working on our chemistry lab."

"We will, but there is a whole other layer of *chemistry* going on which has nothing to do with molecules and experiments."

"We are going to ignore it," Barbara had said firmly.

And they tried—they really did—but once they both knew how the other felt it had become harder, the feelings intensified.

One night they bumped into each other, literally, behind the grocery store. She was looking for her keys in her purse and he was looking through his wallet when they crashed into each other.

He about knocked her down and grabbed her arms to keep her from falling. "Are you alright?" he asked.

"Yes, I wasn't paying attention."

"Neither was I," he said as he continued to hold her arms even though she was steady on her feet now.

He looked into her eyes and she couldn't look away to save herself. Then he made an inarticulate sound and dragged her into his arms and lowered his head to kiss her. The kiss started tentative, but when she opened her mouth he dove in like she was his last meal and he hadn't eaten in a month. Enchiladas and hot sauce is what he tasted like, which is probably what he had for dinner, but there was another taste which was all him and that was even hotter than his dinner. He pulled her closer to him running his hands down her back and pulling her in against his hips. Her soft body loved his hardness, she felt like she was going to explode. Was it possible to get closer, even a piece of paper wouldn't fit between them, but it still felt too far apart. She'd kissed boys before, but this was a completely different experience. How could he be making her hot and needy with just his kisses and his hands stroking her back?

She moaned into his mouth. "Oh god, this is crazy. We have to stop."

"No, this is heaven right here on earth."

"Oh, Chris," she said as her fingers traveled up into his hair to grip the blond locks. He kissed his way over to her ear and nipped her earlobe causing heat to pool between her legs. Then he started kissing down her neck to the soft spot between her neck and shoulder.

"Barbara, you are so sweet," he panted. "I could kiss you for a week."

"Oh, Chris."

Just then a car drove into the lot and someone yelled, "Get a room."

That doused the flames roaring between them like a bucket of cold water. They jerked apart and Chris said, "I don't think they could see who we are, it's too dark over here."

"I hope you're right, I don't want Sandy to hear about this."

Chris shook his head. "Not from gossips anyway. We are going to have to tell her how we feel. I can't keep leading her on when I'm wild about you."

"Chris, we've never even been on a date."

"No, but we've spent a couple hundred hours side by side. I know how I feel. Are you telling me you don't feel the same?"

She slowly shook her head. "No, I think, I'm very much in love with you."

"Good, because I'm very much in love with you, too. We need to tell Sandy. Tomorrow."

"No, I don't want to hurt her, Chris."

"And lying to her is better?"

"No, of course not."

"Then, we tell her. Tomorrow," Chris said.

"If you insist."

"I'll call her and then let you know when and where."

The next day was Sunday and Chris asked Sandy to join him at the park during church—when no one would be around. It was a beautiful spring day with a hint of cold still in the air. Chris and Barbara had gotten there early and were sitting on top of a picnic table when Sandy arrived.

"Hi, guys. We haven't all been together in one place for a few weeks," Sandy smiled.

Barbara muttered, "A few months, actually."

"Has it been that long? Hmm, I guess it was over Christmas break wasn't it. So, what's up?"

Chris looked at Barbara and they both turned to Sandy and said in unison, "We are so sorry."

Barbara started crying. as Chris went on, "We never wanted this to happen, we never wanted to hurt you, but…"

"What? Spit it out Chris," Sandy said.

"We've fallen in love with each other," he said as he motioned between himself and Barbara.

"What? Is this a joke? In love? With each other?"

"No, it's not a joke and yes, we fell in love with each other."

"When? How? Have you been sneaking around behind my back?" Sandy shrieked.

"No, nothing like that, we've been lab partners in chemistry and—"

Sandy reached out and slapped him, hard. Then she turned on Barbara. "You bitch, you couldn't keep your hands off my boyfriend. You couldn't find someone else to hit on?"

"Sandy, it wasn't like that. We've never gone out or anything. We had never even kissed until last night," Chris said.

"Yeah, well, I don't believe you. Some friends you turned out to be."

"Sandy." Barbara sobbed. "Please listen, we never intended for this to happen."

"You obviously didn't fight it either. Just… Just… Stay away from me. I want nothing to do, with you two Benedict Arnolds." With that, she turned and ran away from them.

They tried a few times to talk to her after that, but she always turned her back on them and walked away. That was almost ten years ago and they still had never discussed it or even spoken to each other. Of course, they hadn't seen much of each other, since Sandy lived in Seattle and rarely came back. But now life was different. Could they make peace with the past? Maybe for the town's sake they could, otherwise… How were they ever going to work together? And even more importantly would Chris and Sandy working together be a problem? They were coming up on their ten-year anniversary, what if Chris started to find Sandy more attractive. They had a lot in common with this idea, she was going to take a good look at that email.

Chapter Eleven

CHRIS AND IRENE WERE WORKING on designing the spinning ride. They knew they needed round cars, but couldn't decide what they should look like. They went through a dozen ideas—cups, bowls, balls—nothing seemed right. They wanted it to be the precursor ride to the rest of the attractions, so it needed to be designed well and stand out to draw people to it.

Chris answered his cell; it was Barb's number. "Hi, honey." All he heard was sobbing. "Barb, what's wrong? Are you hurt?"

"N-no, c-can you c-come h-home?" she finally managed to get out between sobs.

"Of course, do I need to call the police or fire department?"

"N-no, I just n-need you."

"I'll be right there." Chris hung up the phone, logged off his computer, and grabbed his jacket.

Looking at Irene he said, "Gotta go. Take the rest of the day off if you want. See you Monday."

Chris drove home in a panic, heart pounding, hands shaking. What could be wrong? What if she was hurt or something bad had happened to their family? He ran into the house yelling, "Barb, where are you?" He shucked off his jacket and shoes while still moving into the house.

Barbara ran out of her sewing room and straight into his arms, still sobbing.

He hugged her while she cried then he scooped her up, carried her into the living room, and sat with her on his lap. No external injuries—she looked fine—which eased the tension in his body.

"It's okay, baby. Now calm down and tell me what's wrong." Chris ran his hands down her hair and back to sooth her, muttering nonsense to calm her down.

Her sobs were starting to subside to hiccups when she finally said, "The dress I just started? The bride can-cancelled it."

Oh, thank god that's all it was. Chris wasn't sure why that was such a disaster, but he wasn't about to say that. "Oh, I'm sorry, baby. Why did she cancel?"

"She-she ran off with her maid of honor and got married. They were planning the wedding when they both realized they loved each other."

Chris didn't know whether to laugh or fume. "Oh, my god, can you imagine what the groom is going through?"

"Yeah, poor guy. But, Chris—I already bought the material and already have it all cut out. Now all that is ruined, plus all the time I spent designing it."

"You should make her pay for your time and the fabric."

She shook her head. "Oh, they always do, with the deposit. I always charge them for my design time and the fabric up front, before I start on the dress."

"Oh, that's good." He was still confused about why she was upset, but didn't know how to ask without setting her off again. "Can you maybe resell the dress? Or sew it up for some future bride? Maybe put it in a store to sell?"

"I hadn't thought about it. I had this whole next month dedicated to that dress."

Ah, here is the real problem. Barb didn't *do change* well. When she laid out her plans, they might as well be written in stone. "Um. Maybe you could make some other plans."

"Chris, you don't understand."

Chris stroked her back. "Okay honey, tell me what I'm missing."

"This was my goal dress!"

"Goal dress?"

"Yes. I was excited to have this dress commissioned, to make my goal."

"What goal baby?"

"My fifty-thousand-dollar goal." Chris was confused and was sure it showed in his face, but she went on, "When I started the business I made a goal to save $50,000 in ten years. I'm just this last dress away from that goal and it's only been eight and a half years."

"My goodness, Barb. I had no idea, honey. That's amazing."

"Now, it's all ruined," she said as her eyes filled with tears again.

"No, it's not. Your next dress can be your goal dress."

"But I promised myself I'd reach my goal before I did anything else. And now I can't—not for at least another couple of months and it will be too late."

"Too late for what?"

"To work on the costumes for the town. They'll need them before that."

"Oh, maybe you should look at this delay as a blessing. Maybe you should switch your priorities a bit. Use this time to work on some of the townspeople's costumes. Regardless of the amusement park, I know the town is planning to go forward with using the game to draw tourists. Maybe you need to do that first—now—since summer isn't too far off. If you get the costumes started and out of the way, then when you start your next dress you'll feel less stressed about the conflicting commitments."

"Oh Chris, you make a good point." He waited while she thought about it, he knew his wife well enough that she would need to process that idea. "I *was* feeling overwhelmed. Maybe I could focus on the costumes. I'd get a lot done in a month."

"I know Amber has talked to me about costumes and so has Samantha."

Nodding she said, "Yes. That's a great idea, Chris. I was going to have to try to cram it in, but if I take the next few weeks I'd get a lot accomplished for the town."

"Yeah and you could still put together the wedding dress in your spare time and maybe put it in a store somewhere. So, if some bride needed something unique and readymade it would be there."

"If she fit in it, of course. But that's not a bad idea. Thanks honey."

He kissed her neck. "It's my pleasure to rescue damsels in distress."

"I feel kinda silly for getting upset and making you come home from work."

Chris shrugged. "Oh, we were pretty much spinning our wheels. Ha ha spinning our wheels on the spinning ride."

"Oh? How come?"

"We need to have round cars which will spin nicely and a good theme for the ride since it's going to be the ride that is *transporting* people to their adventure. We've been tossing ideas around all day and can't come up with a good one. We thought of cups and balls and every other kind of round item, but nothing works."

"Oh, I think bubbles would be good. Riding on the surface of Lake Chelan, floating and spinning people onto their adventure."

"Barb, that's an amazing idea. Bubbles would be perfect and we can make the platform look like waves and put Tsilly in the middle. You're a genius!" Chris hugged her tight.

"It seems we both are—you for my job and me for

yours. Guess that's why we have such a super marriage."

"Yes it is. We work well together. Now that we've solved all the problems except who should run for mayor, what shall we do with our afternoon off?"

"Hmmm, I might have an idea how you could use your afternoon."

"Your wish is my command, my darling," Chris said.

"In that case, I think we need a nap."

"Oh yeah, as long as we don't have to sleep immediately."

"Maybe in an hour we'll sleep. In the meantime—"

The fire alarm cut her off; there was a weed fire near the school. "Sorry, babe, I better go. Can you hold that thought for a bit?"

"Yes. You go. Be careful."

"Will do." He gave her a quick peck on the mouth and went toward the mudroom. He put his feet in boots and pulled up the turn out pants. His coat and helmet were in his truck. He switched on the scanner in his truck and heard some of the other guys signing the trucks out—they must have been at the station. He headed straight to the fire.

When he got there, he noticed it wasn't too large but needed some water on it. The trucks arrived at about the same time, so he helped Marc hit the plug on the corner while Terry and Greg got the pumper going on the far side of the fire. He and Marc hooked up a Y-configuration so they could attack two sides. Ted and Kyle both drove up and got out to man one side while he and Marc did the other. He saw some of the other guys pull up and they all fanned out. The fire was put out quickly.

Officer Ben brought over a couple of boys who looked guilty. One of them had no eyebrows—just singed skin. Looked like another case of roll-your-own. They really needed to put a warning on packages of notebook paper. He wondered what they had rolled into the paper to try to smoke—weeds, grass, leaves? He saw Adam out of the corner of his eye and smirked at him. Adam flipped him off, but had a wry twist to his mouth. Chris reciprocated the gesture. A long time ago, those two boys had been Adam and himself—before the falling out.

They cleaned up and went back to the station to take care of the hoses they had used and put more on the truck in case there was a call before the used ones were dry. As they went about the tasks, his mind drifted back to his wife. *Did she really say she had nearly fifty thousand dollars saved? What the fuck?* He was scrimping and worried about her working too hard and she had fifty K in the bank? *I think we need to have a little chat as soon as I get home. No sex distractions until we have a sit-down about this.*

He walked into the house and put his boots and pants carefully in their spot. Then called out, "Barbara, where are you?"

"In our room. Come join me."

He walked in and there she was, all dolled up for him in a sexy negligee. *Shit.* "Put a robe on we need to talk."

"Seriously?"

"Yes."

"About what?" She put her robe on over all the sexiness.

Damn.

He put his hands on his hips. "The fifty K you have saved away. Why didn't I know about that? That's a hell of a lot of money to hide from your husband."

"I wasn't hiding it."

"Barb."

"No, really. When I first started my business we decided that I would contribute three hundred dollars from each dress to the family fund. I have done that. Back when I first started, I didn't make a whole lot more than that per dress—but now I do. Some dresses I make well over a thousand dollars on. So, anything over operating expenses and the three hundred for the family, I put in a savings account."

"You could have upped the family contribution. Or asked me if I had any need for it."

"Oh, well I just never thought about it. Your paycheck and my contribution seems to give us everything we need. So, I didn't see a need to bring it up."

"If we had needed it, would you have mentioned it?" he asked.

"Sure. Well, at least I think I would have."

"Great. Just great. A big fat maybe." He turned and walked out the door, heading for the kitchen.

She followed him. "Chris? Don't be mad, honey. I would have told you if I'd known this would upset you."

"Upset me? Really? What if I had fifty thousand dollars saved away in some account you knew nothing about? How would that make *you* feel?" He got the bread and some lunchmeat out of the fridge to make a sandwich.

"Oh, I guess that would scare the crap out of me. I would think you were saving it to leave me." She folded her arms around her body and seemed to shrink before his eyes.

"God dammit, Barbara. I am not going to walk out on you." He threw the knife in the sink and went over to her. He took her by the arms and looked into her eyes. "I am not leaving you. I love you."

She nodded but her eyes had tears in them and a very large dose of fear.

It broke him and he hauled her into his arms. "Oh, baby. Are you ever going to believe me?"

"I do, it's just… I get scared sometimes."

"Someday I hope you really believe and trust me. Keep the money if it helps you feel secure. We don't need it."

"Thanks. I'm sorry. I think I'm just broken."

He sat at the table to eat his sandwich, but it just didn't taste good. He knew he was hungry, but couldn't care less. He forced it down anyway. He really had no idea how to convince his wife of his devotion—he just didn't. Maybe just loving her was the only answer.

After he finished eating, she sighed. "I wanted to spend the afternoon with you. You know, playing damsel in distress and hot fireman to the rescue? But now I've ruined it."

"No, sweetheart. You haven't. I am still a male and fascinated by you. I would be more than happy to demonstrate."

"Really? And then we can nap."

"Yes."

"Yay! Race you to the bedroom?"

"Nope, I'm gonna sweep you off your feet and carry you to our pit of passion."

"Pit of passion?"

"Pit. Of. Passion." Chris picked her up and started carrying her to their room.

Barbara put one arm around his neck and put her head on his shoulder. "I love the way you think."

"You're gonna love a whole lot more than that before you get a nap, sweetheart."

"Go ahead. Make my day."

Chapter Twelve

Sandy was due in today. Chris felt queasy and his stomach was rolling. She was coming for a week. First order of business was to get her together with him and his wife—to talk. They were all meeting at Mayor Carol's for dinner. Both Barbara and Chris were slightly terrified. They had both communicated with Sandy via email, giving her more information about what they were thinking with the amusement park and the costumes for the townspeople.

He thought she was also talking to Kyle about the plans for the city park with the Tsilly climbing structure and the Kalar statue. Kyle had designed some hanging signs, showing Tsilly and Kalar, to suspend from the old-fashioned light posts they had down Main Street. The town usually had flowering baskets on them in the summer, but what Kyle was designing could be permanent decorations. He had also come up with signs for some of the businesses, incorporating the game theme. They would be having the meeting to talk about all that tomorrow. Terry and Greg were also going to talk about some ideas they wanted to run by the group.

Tomorrow's meeting would be fun, providing they could get through tonight. Tonight was critical. They had to get past what happened ten years ago.

CHRIS AND BARBARA PULLED up in front of Sandy's house and looked at each other. Barbara felt sick to her stomach, but whispered, "We can do this." Chris sighed and they got out of the car, walking slowly up the walk and onto the porch, he pushed the doorbell.

Sandy opened the door with a polite, professional smile on her face. "Hello, Barbara, hello, Chris, come in please."

"Hello, Sandy," Barbara said and held out a bottle of wine which shook in her hands.

"Hi, Sandy," Chris said and his voice cracked.

Barbara and Chris took off their coats and hung them on the coat tree in the entryway.

"Mom's got some wine and snacks in the living room, come on in."

Chris and Barbara followed Sandy into the living

room they hadn't seen for ten years. Growing up, they had all spent many hours in this room laughing and talking, playing music and doing homework, eating cookies and drinking milk—or soda when they got older. There were plenty of pillows and lap blankets to snuggle into, and a roaring fire with lots of family pictures on the mantle. Chris and Barbara sat stiffly on the couch next to each other.

Sandy grabbed the wine bottle like a lifeline and asked Barb if she wanted some.

"Yes please," she said in a whisper.

"I think mom is bringing you a beer—if you prefer—Chris."

"Um, thanks I would…prefer a beer. As long as it's no trouble"

Carol breezed into the room with a Rainer in her hand and gave it to Chris. "Here you go," she said cheerily, perhaps too cheerily.

"Thanks, Mayor Carol."

"Just Carol tonight—I'm not the mayor at home with guests."

"Um, sure. Thanks, Carol."

They all sat there awkwardly until Carol said, "Have some snacks, we'll eat dinner in a few minutes."

Chris reached for a cracker and bumped the tray sending food flying. "Crap."

Sandy rolled her eyes and looked at Barbara. "He hasn't outgrown that?"

Barbara said dryly, "Not in the least. I think I clean up

more food from him than I ever did babysitting for those monster kids of the pastor's."

Sandy laughed and rolled her eyes.

Barbara chuckled, the two of them had traded off babysitting for those kids because neither one could stand them for too long. Easily half of the Tsilly stories had been made up to entertain and also guilt those little hellions into submission.

Sandy shook her head. "That's saying a lot. Oh, what brats they were. Do you remember the time they threw spaghetti all over when I had to go answer the door?"

Barbara grimaced. "God, that was a mess."

"I called you and you came right over to help clean it all up."

"And the night he put peanut butter in her hair because she wanted to read a book and he wanted to play a game. You came over and we spent the rest of the night shampooing her hair over and over."

Sandy laughed. "Their mom asked you what kind of conditioner you used because her hair was so silky."

"Oh yeah, that was scary. I had no idea what to tell her, so I told her it was an old family recipe made with peanut oil."

Sandy laughed. "Close enough to the truth."

"After that, we always babysat together to keep the little tyrants out of trouble."

"Yeah, and it worked pretty well."

Chris looked embarrassed as he and Carol tried to clean up the snacks. Carol whispered to him, "Never thought I'd see your klutziness in nervous situations come in handy, but it did tonight."

Chris whispered back, "Yes, it did, thank god."

They continued to reminisce about the past during dinner—until Sandy put down her fork and looked at Chris and then at Barbara. "You know, the thing that hurt me the most is that you would sneak around behind my back instead of telling me straight out you were interested in each other."

Barbara gasped. "But we did tell you straight out. We didn't sneak around behind your back."

Sandy looked at Barb. "No, you stopped hanging out long before you told me."

"That's because I was trying to avoid Chris. I didn't want to fall for him—I avoided him as much as I could. I had to be his lab partner, but I didn't have to be with him the rest of the time. I still hung out with you any time I could—when I knew he wouldn't be there."

Sandy shook her head. "No, you didn't. You stopped having lunch with me."

"That's because I knew he'd be there."

"No, he wasn't—he got put on a different lunch the last quarter. I ended up all alone," Sandy said sadly.

"I didn't know." Barbara looked at her husband. "Is it true you stopped having lunch with Sandy?"

Chris nodded. "Yeah, the only time I saw her was early in the morning before class and after work."

Barbara reached across the table and took Sandy's hand. "Oh, Sandy…I'm sorry, I had no idea. I sat in the library missing you. But I did come over after school to hang out."

"But you only stayed for a couple of hours, then I was alone. Chris didn't come by until after dinner, so when you guys told me you were falling in love, I thought you'd been spending that time together—before he came over."

Chris shook his head. "No, after work I went home to shower before I came over. I didn't want to arrive all grungy from the garage."

"We told you the instant we truly knew we wanted to be together. We didn't want to hurt you, but we knew you deserved and needed to know the truth," Barbara said. "In fact, Chris insisted we tell you immediately."

"Oh, and all this time I thought you'd been sneaking around behind my back. I'm sorry I doubted your integrity."

"We're sorry too. We missed you so much after that, it was like there was a hole in our hearts," Barbara said.

Chris said, "So, can we be friends again?"

"I think we can," Sandy said and smiled at them.

Carol jumped up. "I have the perfect thing to celebrate with—hot chocolate cake."

They all moaned and Sandy said, "I hope it'll be a few minutes. I ate too much chicken."

"I ate too many of my favorite vegetable casserole, I've always loved it," Barbara said.

"I think I had a dozen helpings of your Ambrosia salad," Chris said, rubbing his stomach. "But I can't turn down that cake with the frosting melting down the sides."

"It'll be about an hour; I'm putting it in to bake now,

then it has to cool a few minutes before I frost it. We want it warm, but not piping hot from the oven. Go on into the living room and relax," Carol suggested.

Chris countered, "We will as soon as the dishes are put away and we've cleaned up after ourselves. You go on in and start relaxing."

"Yeah mom, I'll put the cake in the oven and we'll clean up."

Carol hugged each one of them. "I'm so glad you can all be friends again."

Sandy said, "Me too and I noticed, Mom, that you planned the dinner specifically making each one of us our favorite food."

"Whatever is takes Sandy."

Chapter Thirteen

THE NEXT MORNING THE meetings started in earnest. Chris was excited to be getting together with the core team—including Sandy—to start making some major decisions. The first group was with Gus, Sandy, Carol, Barbara, and Irene. They would establish scope, permissions, legality, and any interest from Sandy's game company. They also needed to determine who should be brought on board to get things moving like lawyers, accountants, engineers, architects, set designers, and anyone else who might be needed at the start. After that, they would need builders, plumbers, landscapers, and all the people who would actually build the park.

When Sandy and Carol came into the office above the newsroom, he went over to greet them. "Welcome to my humble office. Can I show you around?"

Carol shook her head and went into the meeting room.

"Sure, I'd like to look at your boards." Sandy tilted her head toward their corkboards.

"We have all kinds of stuff tacked to them. I like seeing them in paper rather than just on the computer so I print out more that I probably need to, but it's how I think."

Sandy perused the drawings and ideas tacked up. She walked down the length of the boards looking closely at each one. Chris waited while she examined it. She walked back to him.

"The timeline looks good. I see you have one for this summer and then others projected out for the next couple of years. So it appears as if you're planning an area for each of the ten adventures, each with some kids' rides and then moving into the more adult rides to simulate the challenge levels in the game—not that you can have a ride for each level since there are so many of them. But by using amusements, rides, games, exploration areas, and rest spots you can give a varied experience. Very clever, Chris. It looks like you've done a good job of marrying the game to the park."

"Thanks. And you can see the treasure boxes Kyle has drawn up, ideas for costumes Barbara has created, and some restaurant ideas." Chris pointed out each set of drawings as he talked.

Sandy gestured towards his work. "And there are the engineering specs you sent me from your classes. Nice."

"Let me introduce you to Irene." They went into the meeting room, said hi to Gus, and he introduced her to

Irene.

"So Irene, you have experience in building an amusement park?" Sandy asked.

"No, not building it, but living it yes. My family owns a large amusement park in Colorado—not Disneyland large, but Six Flags-type large."

"It's cool that you have some practical knowledge to contribute."

"Yes, and I'm already a civil engineer. I graduated last year."

Sandy looked at Chris and asked, "Did mom say you would be graduating in the spring?"

"Yes, I'm in my final semester." Chris grinned.

"Congratulations, you've been working on that degree a long time."

"Yeah, but it's worth it and I enjoyed doing the classes in the evening after working all day in a physical job. It's been fun using my brain more at night. Irene was my lab partner on a roller coaster project."

Gus cleared his throat. "Let's get started, shall we? If you haven't gotten coffee and a donut, now's the time."

When everyone was seated and had a copy of the agenda for the meeting, they got started with Mayor Carol saying, "Thanks for coming, everyone. I'm sure you're all acquainted with the plans we're making to help grow tourism in the town to keep it from dying. A big part of it is drawing on Sandy's game to attract some of the millions of people who play it. So let's start with the game company's take. Sandy, can you tell us what your company thinks and if we'll have any problems legally?"

"Sure, mom." She looked around the table "My company is all for the idea—in fact they would like to be a co-sponsor for some of it."

The room seemed to sigh with relief at that and Chris said, "Awesome. What do they want to do?"

"They would like to sponsor an arcade either in the amusement park, in town, or both—and fill it with all the popular games we produce. A good arcade needs both video games and pin ball-type games. We've called in some consultants to take a look at some games to see how they could be shifted to pin ball games. The video games are pretty straightforward—the only equipment needed is a booth and a chair. Some of the artists have drawn up some ideas you can see in the handout. They would also like to see a few of the games in the resort since I assume the resort will play along with the game theme. Last, but not least, they would like to sponsor any of the attractions which feature actual footage out of the 'Adventures with Tsilly' game."

"Sponsor how?" Chris asked.

Sandy waved her hands. "As in pay to have the game built and have a say in how it's done."

"How many attractions are they thinking?"

"That's negotiable, but maybe six to start. We've thought about the different adventures in the game and think there are several where you will need the footage, and some others which might benefit from the footage— or some of the props we've used in filming the game. Of course, the first one which comes to mind is the Post-Apocalyptic adventure. Unless you come up with your own scenarios, it would be almost impossible to do without footage."

"Yeah, I've thought that all along. This is amazing news, Sandy," Chris said with a smile so big he could feel it stretching his face.

Gus spoke up, "Yep it is. I do have a bit to add about the resort. The Marquee chain of resorts would like to make our resort one of theirs. If we let them do that, they will foot the bill and bring in their builders, architects, and the like."

Mayor Carol asked, "Will they work with us to make it a theme resort to go along with the amusement park?"

"We can write that into the contract, Carol, and we can insist on working on the design and decoration of it. We can also require a game system in every room with all the games preloaded. As far as the land goes, Chris, you can do either a lease for say 99 years or sell the ground to them out right. You'll need to think about that."

"Yeah, I will."

Sandy said, "We can go over the handouts now or you can all take them home and read them over. We can schedule another meeting to discuss it or you can ask me your questions. If I don't know the answer, I'll ask."

Barbara said, "I'd like to take them home—rather than draw this meeting out—to go over them."

Everyone else liked the idea so Sandy added a few more details of what her company wanted to do. Chris then talked about the rides they had already designed.

Irene gave them contact information for people who provided parts or could come up with the various supplies they would need to build, and some engineering firms who specialized in amusement parks.

Barbara showed them the costume designs she'd been working on for various townspeople. Then they talked through many of the ideas and came up with new ones.

About noon Gus said, "Chris, I'm thinking you should be writing all of this up for a presentation to the town maybe next Thursday. With one of them PowerPoint things with bells and whistles."

He hated doing presentations—not creating them, that was easy peasy, but giving them? Chris groaned inwardly. *But it's all part of the deal, so I'll just have to suck it up. If Barbara is there with me, I'll be fine—and I also have Irene as backup.* He said, "I can do that."

"Good, now let's break for lunch."

Barbara leaned over to Chris. "Would it be okay if I leave now? I've shown everyone what I have in mind and I'd like to get busy doing it."

"Sure, honey. Thanks for being here this morning. I know you're not much of a meeting person."

"I'll see you later. Let me know if you are ready for a quiet dinner at home or want to go out with some of these guys later."

"Will do. Love you," Chris said as he gave her a peck on the mouth.

They all went to Amber's for lunch and back to the

meeting room in the afternoon. Different townspeople came in to pitch Sandy and the rest of them their ideas for incorporating the game into their businesses. Terry and Greg talked about their idea for a carousel. Kyle talked about the climbing structure for City Park, decorations for the old-fashioned lampposts on Main Street and treasure boxes. Kristen showed her charm ideas for Kalar and told Sandy about the idea of using some of the townspeople for finishing the charms. Samantha talked about cookies shaped like different elements from the adventures, and also cake topper decorations for birthdays or other celebrations. Amber talked about special dishes she'd add to the breakfast and lunch menus.

Sandy assured them all they could have the rights to do the things they discussed She also gave some of them some direction and suggestions, as did the rest of the *governing* group.

At the end of the day Chris was excited, but also drained from so many meetings. He and everyone else decided to go home for quiet dinners.

Chris walked into the house and hollered, "Barb?"

"Hi, honey. I was wondering what you were doing."

"Coming home to my lovely wife. God, that was a long day, I just want to be a couch potato for an hour or two. Is that okay?"

"Sure. I had a busy day too."

"Tell me."

"Marilyn Carmichael came over shortly after I got home and I measured her for her costume and we looked over some of the ideas I'd sketched up. We also talked about costumes for her staff at the hotel. We should be able to use one male and one female costume design for her people—almost a uniform. With the town planning to change Adventure worlds each month—to draw tourists—it will take three different designs for the summer.

"Amber was next—she came during her afternoon lull—and we looked through the ones I'd thought about for her and I got her measurements. Then after she went back to the restaurant, Samantha came by and we did it all over again for her. I'm planning to make up three different costumes for each person so they will have enough to get us through summer, one per month, but so they can wash them they will need three of each design. I'll need to have some of the other women in town help me with them so they're finished in time. There are a lot of people who want costumes."

"Nine outfits per person? Wow I had no idea. You have been busy."

"Nine, yes, but we'll start with the first month so that's only three per person. And, not all the adults in town will need a costume, just the retail places, basically tourist facing people. I estimate maybe a hundred."

"A hundred is still a heck of a lot of costumes. Do they all have to be unique?"

"No, many of them can be similar, but we will want them to showcase whichever adventure world we are emulating for that month, so they can't all be the same or it would be boring.

"It makes me tired to think about. Do you want to be a couch potato with me?"

Barbara smiled. "You know what, that sounds like a great idea. What do you want to do about dinner?"

"I stopped at Amber's on the way and got us two of tonight's special—her chicken potpie."

"You're my hero. Dinner and an invitation to be a couch potato. You may just get lucky tonight."

"Really? I might have to bring you dinner more often if that's the reward," Chris said teasing her and waggling his eyebrows for emphasis.

They sat in front of the TV with a nice fire in the fireplace and ate chicken potpies and salad. Then they snuggled together watching random shows, with a comfy lap blanket over their legs. They didn't take the time very often to watch the television, with her business and his night school, so they didn't have any programs they were devoted to. But it was nice to take some time to relax.

Barbara took the remote and turned off the TV, then she turned on the sofa facing toward him, half laying on the couch leaning across his lap. "Make out time," she said putting her arms around his neck and pulling his head down to kiss him warmly.

He smiled, pulled her close, and kissed her lips and nose and eyes and her mouth again.

She licked his lower lip and he opened his mouth; their tongues danced together. His hands ran down her back to cup her bottom and he squeezed. She moaned, and as he ran his hands up he slipped them under her shirt. *I love the feel of her skin, always so soft and warm.*

She complained. "Too many clothes."

"And lap blanket. I don't need that anymore. You are keeping me plenty warm."

"Let's get a few of these layers off, shall we?"

"You won't have to twist my arm. Do you want to take this to our bed?"

Barbara shook her head. "No, too far. Let's make love on the couch, like we were kids."

Okay. I can play along with that idea. "But what if our parents come in and catch us making out?" he said as he pulled her sweater over her head.

"That would be bad, but I don't think it's going to happen since yours moved to Florida. I haven't seen my father in twenty years, and mom's been gone almost six years." Barbara pushed the lap blanket to the floor and started unbuttoning his shirt.

"Oh yeah, right, but I was playing along with the kids on the couch theme." Chris unsnapped her bra and cupped her breasts, rubbing his thumbs over her nipples.

"Sorry, can't think when I'm getting you naked." She pushed his shirt off his shoulders and ran her hands down his chest lightly scratching his skin with her fingernails.

He pulled her close until they were skin to skin and kissed her again, his tongue dueling with hers, as she squirmed against him.

"Still too many clothes," she said.

"Mmm, but I don't want to stop kissing to get undressed," he said as he reached for the waistband on her jeans. He unsnapped it and slowly pulled the zipper down. His hand slid into her pants—under her panties, seeking her hidden treasures—while his mouth continued to plunder hers. "Wet for me already. Nice." He stroked her folds concentrating on the small bundle of nerves, which gave her pleasure.

BARBARA LAY THERE letting his touch ignite her passions for this man she was married to. He continued to stroke her, driving her higher and higher while he kissed her neck starting at her shoulder and moving up to her ear. He took her earlobe in his mouth and sucked on it. At the same time, he slid two fingers into her and used the heel of his hand to continue the torture on her clit.

"Come for me," he whispered.

She exploded from his words and the amazing feelings his mouth and hands evoked. She shattered into tiny pieces and he gentled his hands, while pulling every last sensation from her.

When she came back to herself, she lay panting in his lap. There was something hard poking into her side. "Still too many clothes," she said sitting up and unsnapping his jeans.

He turned her around and stood up shucking his clothes while she pushed the rest of hers onto the floor. "Better?" he asked looking at her.

She looked at him magnificently aroused. "Yes. I want you inside me. Now."

"Yes ma'am," he said as he lowered her to the couch and crawled on top. She put her legs around his waist and he entered her in one long stroke.

"Mmm, perfect."

Long, wet kisses and long, smooth strokes had her body climbing again. This time when she reached the top, he came with her as they shattered together. She loved the weight of him as he collapsed on her. She held him tight as their bodies calmed and their heartbeats returned to normal.

"Am I squishing you?"

"A little, but it's the best kind of squishing."

He rose up and kissed her nose. "Let's go to bed. This couch is a bit narrow for the both of us."

"Good idea. Leave the clothes—we'll deal with them tomorrow."

He nodded and grabbed their cell phones. Handing them to her, he scooped her up and carried her to their room. They got under the covers and snuggled together. With little kisses and murmurs they drifted off to sleep, content with their lives.

Chapter Fourteen

Tuesday Barbara went to the hotel to measure the staff for their costumes and finalized the design with Marilyn. She also started a list of fabric and notions she'd need to make those items.

By the time Chris got home, they were both exhausted. Barbara whipped up a quick stir fry and they caught each other up on their day.

Chris told Barbara that he'd spent the day in meetings where they talked through in detail what Sandy's company said about the part they wanted to play and solidified their expectations. The company lawyers would be writing up the contract and Gus had reached out to one of his parent's lawyers willing to review and help with the legal side of the plans. When he had shared about all the game company wanted to do, Barbara was flabbergasted.

She said, "They want to sponsor five rides, two arcades, a history lesson area on how the game was built, souvenirs, and shops to sell them in? And on top of that they want a drawing, animation, and game design classroom which they'll staff to give the tourists a taste of what writing a game is all about? That's a huge amount."

"Yes, they're fully on board with promoting the game and the park." He leaned forward. "In fact, they plan to put a link to the amusement park website, which we don't have, on their fan page and in the next sequel of the game."

"Now you also need a website and someone to create it."

"Yeah, I have to admit this is going a whole lot faster and getting a whole lot bigger than I was thinking of. It seems to be snowballing into something much more complicated than I had envisioned. I was thinking a small amusement park with a few rides. Not amusements and rides and treasure hunts and souvenirs and arcades and resorts and classrooms." He yanked on his hair with both hands. "Oh, babe. It's getting wild. Tomorrow we're talking to the Marquee hotel people. My head is already spinning and we have at least another two days of meetings. The resort tomorrow and the *practical* discussions on Thursday—like restaurants and bathrooms and trash and god only knows what else."

Barbara grinned. "Well, those things are needed."

"I know and I'm grateful for the help and the reminder to look into all that, but…"

"You're just overwhelmed."

"Yeah, and kinda scared to death."

"I do understand. But you'll have help, so try to stay calm sweetheart." She patted his hand and then frowned. "I have to admit I'm feeling a bit overwhelmed myself. I've gone from creating one beautiful wedding dress a month—two weeks for simple ones—to designing and sewing costumes for the whole town that they can wear every day. We're talking at the bare minimum a hundred people dressed in costume five to seven days a week. With the town planning to change themes every month that's about a hundred new costumes a month with three changes. That's three hundred costumes a month for at least the summer months. Some people will have similar designs, so that helps on the uniqueness front, but still." She had to admit—even if it was only to herself—she'd no idea the scope of what she had innocently suggested in the town meeting. *Should have sat on my hands and bitten my tongue, that's for darn sure.*

His eyes widened. "Wow, that's a huge number. You're going to have to either buy some stuff readymade or hire a fleet of women to help with the sewing."

"Yeah, I'm going to start talking to people the rest of this week to see who can help and who has their own machines and stuff like that. While I also keep taking measurements of people who will need and want costumes. Including you."

"Me?"

"Yes, you and whoever you are going to hire to work your park? You'll all need costumes. I assume you're going to hire a couple of girls to play Kalar."

Chris groaned. "You are supposed to be helping me calm down not heaping more issues on my poor, confused head. I hadn't thought about it, but you're right on both accounts. I will need a costume and to hire some Kalars. Do you think a Tsilly character is needed also?"

"Maybe. But you'll need to have someone design that costume—don't even think about asking me for that one. Weird dinosaur, lake-monstery things are not my forte and I don't want them to be. Now I think it's bedtime. Let's go forget about all this for a while."

"Excellent idea." He pulled her close for a long wet kiss.

BARBARA SPENT WEDNESDAY working her way through the other townspeople who needed costumes. She decided another week of that and she'd be ready to make a list of fabric and notions she'd need to make nearly a thousand costumes total for the summer. It would take her a few days to take her list of people and their sizes and calculate the amounts of everything. This was the largest thing she had ever worked on. Sometimes a bride would want her to outfit all the women in her bridal party but even on the largest wedding she'd ever worked on it had been ten dresses total.

She planned to spend Friday talking to people who

could sew, to see who she could enlist to help put together everything and also continue on making three hundred new ones a month. Although the winter months probably wouldn't require as many—at least the first year. This was turning out to be a huge project and she wasn't sure that Gus's fifty thousand a year would even cover the work it would be. Fortunately, he was footing the bill for the extra seamstresses too.

WEDNESDAY CHRIS TALKED to the resort people and, thank god, they planned to do it all with some input from the town and Chris as to decoration, theme, and uniforms for their staff. Sandy could easily work with them on it and she was happy to head that area. She planned to send Chris, Gus, and her mom copies of what they were talking about—so if they had ideas or opinions they could voice them.

While Barbara was busy meeting with the townspeople, Chris met with the *practical* issues people. They would need bathrooms, trash pick-up, food, and drinks—but if they wanted to stay with the theme of 'Adventures with Tsilly' they would want those practical items to blend in.

Chris started putting together his digital presentation. He wanted to plan out the entire scope, with what he envisioned as the finished park. Then do an in-depth design for each individual attraction. Starting with the ones he wanted to get in by summer.

FRIDAY NIGHT THEY needed to get out of their heads for a while so they invited Sandy and Carol to join them for dinner at Amber's. They decided on the formal dining area of the restaurant. Amber seated them at a table, which—in the summer—had a beautiful view of the lake. In winter it was too dark to see by five-thirty. Living this far north, they had long days in the summer and short ones in the winter.

Chris and Barbara had been seated only a few moments before Carol and Sandy arrived. Chris stood as they came over to the table, always the gentleman even in this day and age. He kissed both of them on the cheek and made sure they were seated comfortably before returning to his chair.

"We've had quite the busy week haven't we? Sandy, when do you have to leave to get back to Seattle?" Barbara asked.

Sandy laughed. "You guys have worn me out with all these meetings and planning. Going back to Seattle will be a lot less work. But it has been fun and I think the amusement park will be a draw for tourists. I plan to leave on Sunday—I'm back in the office on Monday morning."

"I've enjoyed having you home for this week, Sandy." Carol smiled at her daughter while she unfolded her napkin. Amber had several designs she created with them; Barbara always hated taking them apart. "I hope you'll be able to make a few more trips soon."

Sandy nodded. "Oh I'm sure of it. I will probably come do a week every month or so—especially during the park opening."

Barbara clapped her hands. "That will be awesome. I hope we can spend more time together. Maybe Chris won't keep you chained to the conference room next time."

"We can hope. I think it would be fun to a have a girls' day out next time—maybe even go into Chelan and go to the theater. We used to love to watch the Chelan Valley Players."

Barbara grinned. "Oh, I haven't gone there in years. Let's plan on it next time you're in town."

"It's a date."

"Hey, what about me?" Chris said.

"Honey, you'll just have to find someone else to play with."

Sandy and Carol laughed at Chris's pouty face and then he couldn't hold it any longer and laughed with them. They had a nice dinner and chatted about everything.

When they finished eating, Chris suggested they all go to Greg's for an hour and hang out a bit longer.

Carol picked up her purse. "I think I'll let you young people do that. I'm going home to get comfy."

"I can come home with you, Mom."

"No, Sandy. You go with your friends. I'm sure they can drop you off at home later."

"Sure, we can do that," Chris said. "Come on, Sandy. You'll see all your old friends there. Friday night—it's a happening place."

They said their goodbyes to Carol and loaded up in Chris's truck.

"Just like old times, only Barbara's in the middle now," Sandy said.

Chris nodded. "Yeah, let's see if we can shake things up at Greg's."

When they walked into Greg's bar, it was indeed a happening place. Most of the tables were full and the bar was two-deep. Both pool tables had games going and there seemed to be a lot of action at the dartboard. Greg had some local kids playing music and a number of people were dancing on the tiny dance floor.

Greg came straight over to them. "Well, if it isn't the three musketeers—riding again."

Barbara laughed. "Yep, here we are."

"It's good to see you together again. Sandy, it's great to have you in town. Your first drink is on the house," Greg said, as he looked her over—from the top of her head, down to her toes and back up to her eyes.

"Thanks, Greg—but it's not necessary," she said with a slight flush.

"Oh, but it is. I've wanted to buy you a drink since junior high. You always have been my ideal woman."

"Oh, yeah. Sure. A workaholic game developer is your ideal woman." She rolled her eyes at him. "I've always thought you were into the flashy blond type—you know, someone to tone down all that intenseness you've got going on."

"Nope, no flashy blonds for me—at least not lately." He shrugged and tried to look sheepish. "There was one or two back in my youth."

They all laughed, knowing he'd been with several flashy blonds.

"Enough of picking on the poor bartender. What do you all want to drink?"

Sandy said, "Since, I'm not driving and my drink is on the house, I'll have a margarita please—a big one."

"Me too," Barbara said.

Chris shook his head at them. "I'll have a Rainer. Gotta get my ladies home safe and sound."

"There's a table open over there—not too close to the band. I'll take a break and join you guys for a few minutes. By the way, you just missed Irene, she was here earlier and had a couple of tourists hitting on her."

Chris shrugged, "It's a free country and she's an attractive single woman."

Barbara looked at her husband. Attractive? He thinks she's attractive? Damn. She was of course, but did he have to notice?

"Yeah I agree, I just thought it was odd when she left with both of them."

"To each his own," Chris said.

Greg nodded and headed toward the bar. Barbara wondered why she would leave with two guys, maybe they were dropping one off, of maybe they were just driving her home. Being nice guys. She didn't give it any more thought once they sat at their table.

Before Greg could get back with their drinks, Terry walked in, spotted his sister, and headed for their table. Greg must have noticed, as he brought Terry a Rainer too.

Terry smirked. "Greg, are you playing waitress tonight?"

"No, just taking a break to say hi to your sis. Now behave, or I won't give you the Rainier."

"Mean," Terry said grabbing his beer and holding it out. "To friends and family."

"To friends and family," they all said clicking their bottles and glasses together.

They spent a fun evening talking and drinking and even doing some dancing. Greg drifted back and forth between the bar and their table. It seemed to Barbara that he was taking more time off than he normally did on a Friday night, but no one seemed to mind. Sandy and Barbara both danced with Chris and Terry, trading off between the two.

Chris and Barbara were dancing and she looked up to see Greg whirling Sandy away from Terry. Barbara said, "So what's with Greg taking so much time to hang out with us tonight? He never leaves the bar so much, and look—he's dancing with Sandy. I don't think I've ever seen him dance in his own bar."

"It's Sandy, he's always had a crush on her. Even when we were in little league and she was the scorekeeper. He would come into the dugout and make anyone sitting next to her move so he could sit there. He's three years younger than we are, so I don't think she has ever noticed." He looked over towards Greg and Sandy. "Yeah she's just dancing, but he's totally into her."

"I never knew."

Chapter Fifteen

BARBARA WAS PACKING frantically and wondering where in the heck Chris was. She'd left a dozen messages on his phone. She didn't have much time and if he didn't call or get home soon she would have no choice but to leave without him knowing what was going on.

Barbara startled when he spoke from the door.

"Whatcha doin'?"

"Oh, Chris. I'm glad you're finally home. The bride in Florida is having a meltdown about her dress and insists I come and personally fix it."

"What? You're going to Florida?"

"Yes. I tried to give her the name of someone I know in Florida who can do alterations, but she insists it has to be me. I'm leaving tonight and will be gone up to a week," Barbara said as she stuffed more clothes into her suitcase.

"A week? Now? But what about the presentation to the townspeople on Thursday? You promised me you'd be there for it."

"Oh, I forgot all about it when the bride called hysterical. She tried on the dress today and says it needs work because she's lost weight. Her wedding is in two weeks, so there isn't any leeway time. I have to go."

"What about plane tickets?"

"Her father is sending the company jet and a helicopter to get me to the airport in Wenatchee—they are very rich and if all her friends love the dress and service I provide, it might mean a hefty increase in my business."

"You can barely keep up with the business you have now. And what about the costumes?"

"The costumes will just have to wait, I'm almost done taking measurements and then I can order the supplies I need. Chris, this kind of client would take my business to the next level."

"That's what I'm afraid of," he said sharply.

"That's mean. This is exactly what I've been working so hard at—to attract this kind of client."

"Yeah, but I want you to work with me on the amusement park and helping the town—not working all the time and flying off to Florida to cater to spoiled brides." He folded his arms over his chest.

Barbara fumed. "Chris, I don't have time to argue with you. I need to be at the heliport in an hour and I have to finish packing and get my supplies ready. Can we talk about this when I get back?"

"Sure. Of course. I will be *happy* to take the backseat in your life. No problem," he said as he stalked out of the room.

Barbara sighed. She knew he wasn't going to be happy about this, but she didn't expect him to get all pissy about it. This was her career—she didn't get all bent out of shape when he quit his job and started doing this amusement park. She had supported him in his plans for it and even had contributed. They had spent most of Saturday and Sunday working on his digital presentation. Why couldn't he give her the same support? He had in the beginning, but not lately. She wanted this—she wanted this kind of client. Even if she did have to jump on a plane at a moment's notice. It wasn't her favorite part, but if she wanted high-caliber brides, she had to offer high-caliber dresses and high-caliber service. She wanted this kind of client so she'd suck it up and go. Chris would have to get over it.

THE RIDE TO THE helipad was silent and angry. Chris was still pissed at his wife, and it looked like she felt the same toward him. Maybe a week apart would give them some perspective. He was going to feel like a dork in front of the whole town, and now she wouldn't even be there to make him feel better afterward. Some *For better or worse* this was turning out to be. They would have it out when she got back from Florida—that was for darn sure.

Chris pulled up to the helipad and there sat a gleaming black helicopter. She'd certainly be traveling in style. He turned off the car and got out to help with her luggage— he was still a gentleman, even if he was a ticked off one.

He gave her suitcases, portable sewing machine, and the bag of supplies to the man who stepped out of the helicopter.

They looked at each other and he leaned over and gave her a peck on the mouth. "I'll see you in a week."

"Call me and tell me how the presentation to the town goes. I know you'll do great."

"Yeah."

She got on the helicopter and he got back in the car. Neither of them were happy.

Still irritated he headed for Greg's bar. He needed to vent and he wanted a drink. He could eat some of Greg's bar food for dinner. Fried cheese sticks and onion rings— or maybe taquitos. Greg had a deep fryer and a freezer full of anything and everything that could be deep-fried.

Chris sat at the far end of the bar and when Greg came over he said, "Whisky and leave the bottle."

Greg lifted an eyebrow, but brought Chris the whisky he liked. "Want to talk about it?"

Chris slugged back the first shot. "After a couple of shots. Gotta calm down a bit first. Can you rustle me up some chicken fingers and fries?"

Greg nodded. "When they're done, I'll take a break and we can talk."

"Sure."

Chris slammed a couple more shots. When one of the waitresses brought his food out from the back and handed it to Greg, Chris knew it was time to talk. He got up, carrying his shot glass and bottle. The whisky was hitting him hard on an empty stomach, and he was ready for food. Greg grabbed a couple of water bottles and they went over to a table, which wasn't in ear shot of anyone else.

"What's up?" Greg asked.

"Dammit, Greg. Barbara is on her way to Florida. Some bride called hysterical and needs her. So without even talking to me about it, she packed her bag and was nearly ready to walk out the door when I got home. If I'd been a half hour later, I'm not sure she wouldn't have left without a word."

"She didn't call your cell?"

"No. Well, I didn't get a call," he said reaching into his pocket for his cell. "Oh. It's off. How did that happen?" He turned it back on and his voicemail icon showed a dozen voice messages. "Oh, there seems to be some messages on my phone—maybe she did try to call me. It doesn't change the fact that she left. I've got the presentation of the plans for the park on Thursday and she said she'd be there. But no—some damn bride is more important than her husband." Chris grabbed a chicken finger and stabbed it into the bar-b-q sauce before cramming it into his mouth.

"So, she's not gonna be there to hold your hand on Thursday, is that what this is about? Or did you need her help preparing the presentation? I can understand you being upset if that's the case."

"No, it's all prepared and I showed it to her on Sunday. She helped me smooth it out."

"So, it's just you needing someone to hold your hand?"

"Fuck you," he said cramming another chicken finger in his mouth.

"Thanks, but you're not my type, big boy. Somehow, I think there's something else going on here. Spill it, Chris."

"Dammit, Greg—she doesn't trust me. She's frantically building her wedding dress business because deep down she thinks I'm gonna walk out on her, like her father did. She works a minimum of ten hours a day, six to seven days a week. I never see her unless she's hunched over that goddamn sewing machine. Until Gus pulled us all into the meeting a few weeks ago, we hadn't had any decent sex in months. I've tried everything to reassure her I'm not going to walk out on her, but she still doesn't fucking believe it."

Chris stuffed some French fries in his mouth while Greg sat there silent. Greg had known him all his life and he probably knew this rant was far from over. "Then some bride calls her and she's off to Florida for a week. What? There isn't anyone else on the planet that can calm this bride down? Barbara has to leave on a moment's notice? What about other commitments? I don't care if the bride is as rich as Croesus, and that this is the kind of client Barbara has been building her business toward."

Chris gulped down half the bottle of water Greg had set in front of him and picked up another chicken finger and shook it at him. "She's married and we have a commitment to this town. She's supposed to be helping design costumes and stuff for the summer tourist season."

"I thought she did have some costume designs. I know she showed me a couple ideas she had in mind for me."

"Well, yes. She does. She's got costume designs for Samantha and Amber, and probably others I don't know about, too. Oh yeah, and Marilyn and her hotel staff. But it's not the point—she's just adding that on top of her wedding dresses and now is working even more hours. I wanted to help her cut back on work hours, not add to them. She's exhausted at the end of the day—she can barely stagger to bed and she's asleep before her head hits the pillow. It's not exactly the kind of marriage I was hoping for," Chris complained.

"What if you sat her down and talked to *her* about this? Maybe came up with a plan for her to take some time off each week."

"Yeah, I suppose we can try it, but when she gets going on one of her dresses she doesn't come up for air—it's like she's possessed or something. I can't seem to get through to her."

"Can't get through to who, Chris?" purred Irene as she slid into the booth next to him.

Chris jolted and moved over a bit. "My wife. What are you doing here, Irene?"

"Oh, just came in for a drink." She looked pointedly at Greg. "Can you make me a Manhattan, Greg? I'll keep Chris company."

"Yeah, sure. Got to get back to work anyway. Talk to you later, Chris."

"Um, sure. Thanks for the talk." Chris poured himself another shot. *Now I have to deal with Irene. Great, just great.* He spent all day with the woman, and he didn't want to spend the evening with her too—but going back to the empty house didn't appeal either. He ate the last chicken finger.

She said, "Now, no work discussion. This is after hours, and I declare this a no-work zone. Let's have a drink and some laughs—maybe I can drag you out on the dance floor."

"That's not gonna happen, but we can have a drink. What do you want to talk about?"

"How about the weather," she said giving him a nudge with her shoulder and a wink.

He laughed. "Okay."

They talked about everything under the sun as he finished his bottle and she had a few Manhattans. She did eventually drag him out on the dance floor for a couple of wild dances and one slow song. He didn't mind the fast dances, but it didn't feel right to be holding her on the slow song— when it ended he said he needed to get home.

"Okay, but I think we've both had too much to drink to drive home. Let's share a cab."

"A cab? In Chedwick?"

"Fine, not a cab—but doesn't Greg keep someone on standby to drive people home who drink too much?"

"Yeah, he lets the dishwasher play taxi. That's probably a good idea."

Chapter Sixteen

CHRIS TALKED TO BARBARA every night, but the conversation was stilted. She was doing alterations on the dress and trying to help keep the bride sane. Chris was working on the park and attraction designs. He had dinner with Irene a lot, and sometimes they went to Greg's bar for a drink.

Thursday afternoon Barbara called him. He supposed that was something—at least she called him on his big day. She wasn't there to support him, but she was calling. He decided to be pleasant.

"Hi, Barb, how's it going with the bride today?"

"Not good, the woman is a basket case. But I wanted to call to wish you luck on your presentation tonight."

"Thanks, I'm kind of nervous about it."

"Oh honey, you know the information backward and

forward, and the presentation you showed me is excellent. Don't be nervous—you're going to wow them."

"Thanks, babe."

"I'm sorry I can't be there with you tonight. This bride is a little on the crazy side."

"Aren't all brides a little on the crazy side?"

"Yeah, but this one seems to be worse than most. You've heard the term bridezilla?"

"Yeah," he sighed. "I'm sure it's helping that you're there. I hope she appreciates your dedication to her."

"Thanks, but I'll be glad to get home. You know I like my solitude."

"Yeah, you've never been much of a party animal. And I don't like you being gone."

"I know, but it was an emergency and this was a challenging dress—"

Chris cut her off. "I know. We can talk about it later. I need to get going. I want to get there early to set up, so I have plenty of time to be nervous."

"You've got this, honey. Call me in the morning and let me know how it went."

"I will. Come home soon."

"As soon as I can."

He hung up and decided he didn't want to think about Barbara clear across the country. He gathered up his things and left.

Chris got to the school auditorium and set up his digital presentation to project onto the screen on stage and the two TV's on either side of the stage. The remote that would allow him to click through his presentation worked perfectly. He didn't know how many people would actually show up to hear about the plans. How could he want both a crowd and a small handful at the same time? A lot would show there was interest in the amusement park idea. A few would make him less nervous.

The auditorium was packed by the time the presentation was scheduled to start. Chris felt like throwing up. He was going to look like an ass—he just knew it. He was surprised so many people came. There were people there who had already mentioned they probably wouldn't attend, and while they wished him luck they just weren't interested. He wondered why they had decided to come. Mayor Carol and Gus were with him on stage to offer moral support. They had also saved a chair for Irene, but she was nowhere to be seen. Typical woman. It didn't bother him she wasn't there, even though she was supposed to be his backup. He knew she planned to attend—he hoped she was all right. He put her out of his mind to focus on not looking like a dumbass.

Mayor Carol started the meeting by thanking everyone for coming and introducing Chris.

Chris got up. "Now that you all know who I am, other than the kid you went to high school with or the guy who worked on your car... Tonight I'm here to show you my idea for a 'Adventures with Tsilly' amusement park."

Just then, Irene rushed up on stage and patted his chest. "Sorry I'm late, honey."

Chris was confused and flustered by her greeting,

but introduced her to the crowd as his engineer friend from Colorado who was helping him design the park. There were many murmurs after that, but he continued on with his presentation, explaining the overall park idea and the plans for different attractions. He told of Sandy's game company coming on board and which attractions they wanted to sponsor. Chris also told them about the Marquee chain of hotels and the resort that would be built along the lakefront. At the end, he asked if there were questions.

One guy in the crowd asked, "What about Barbara?"

"Barbara is working with the various business owners in town to design costumes for them to wear over the summer. She's also helping me come up with uniforms for the people who will work in the park."

"Where is she tonight? Are you two separated?"

"Oh, she couldn't make it tonight because she's in Florida helping with a frantic bride. She should be home in a few days."

There was some snickering at that, but Chris didn't think anything of it. Assuming they were laughing about difficult brides, he asked if there were more questions.

No one said anything more, so Mayor Carol closed the meeting.

Mayor Carol and Gus both congratulated him on his presentation and several other people from town did also. He was glad they felt it had gone well. While he was unhooking his computer Irene sidled up to him.

"You did spectacular, Chris."

"Oh thanks. I thought you'd left already."

"No, I was waiting for you. To see if you wanted to go out and celebrate."

Chris shook his head. "Aw, no, I'm kinda exhausted. I was a basket case about this presentation and now that it's over, I just want to go home and sleep."

"Then, I'll see you tomorrow."

"Yeah."

Chris got his laptop in his bag and started for the door. The custodian George, was waiting to turn out the lights and lock up.

"You did good, son."

"Thanks, George."

"You need to watch out, for the little blond, though."

"Who, Irene?"

George nodded.

"No, she's a friend helping me design the park."

"I think she's got *designs* on you, too."

"No, she knows I'm married and not interested."

"That may be true, but it sure looked like more from where I'm standing."

"No, she doesn't know many people here. I think she gets kinda lonely. We've gone out to dinner a couple of times while Barbara's in Florida."

"Just be careful. She was here when the meeting started, but she waited until you had the mic before coming in and making a scene."

"She probably didn't want to interrupt the Mayor. But thanks for the advice, George, I'll keep it in mind."

Chris went home to relax. He decided George was seeing things and put it out of his mind.

Chris called Barbara as soon as he woke up the next morning. Now that the presentation was over, he felt a lot lighter and not as resentful of Barbara being gone. He decided he had done okay alone and had gotten all upset for no real reason.

"Hi, Chris, how'd it go?"

"Great, honey. I think everyone liked it. Several people mentioned the presentation was well done and informative and offered me well wishes and luck on it."

"Excellent."

"They asked about your part in it too, and I told them what you've been working on. They were surprised to hear you're in Florida."

"I'm more of a stay at home person. It would be a surprise to most of them. In fact, it surprises me." She sighed dramatically.

Chris chuckled. "Yeah, me too. I can't wait until you get home."

"Shouldn't be too much longer, we're doing another fitting tomorrow. If it's good, I'll be home the next day."

"Yay for that."

"I miss you too. Gotta go finish this up, see you soon."

"Love you, babe."

Chapter Seventeen

BARBARA DID GET TO COME home on Sunday. She'd told Chris she had finally gotten the bride satisfied with the dress. They brought her back on the jet and helicopter. Chris met her at the helipad and gave her a big hug and a long, hot kiss.

"You are a sight for sore eyes, my love," he said.

"Right back at you, Chris. God, I'm glad to be home. The weather in Florida was beautiful, but I'll take cold and home, over warm and away any day."

"Let's go home and hibernate."

"Perfect idea."

He opened the door for her to get in the truck and put her suitcase and sewing machine in the backseat. He climbed in and started the truck. It was cold inside because he'd arrived early to wait for her. Chris reached for her

Hand at the same time she reached for his, and they held hands all the way home. After he parked, he drew her close for a warm, wet kiss. She put her cold hands on his face.

"Hey, baby—you're freezing. Let's go inside where I can warm you up properly."

"Actually, the cold and you feel like home. But I'll let you warm me up any way you want to."

"I'm kind of thinking naked warming would be the best."

"Sounds good to me."

CHRIS WALKED AROUND the truck to her side as she grabbed her purse. He opened her door and helped her down, not that she needed help, but he'd always been a gentleman and liked to open doors and that kind of thing. She had learned early in their marriage to let him do those gestures for her. He made her feel cherished. Chris got her luggage from the back and followed her into the house. After he set the bags in the kitchen he swept her up to carry her to the bedroom.

"I'll bring your stuff in later. Right now, I need to kiss my wife silly."

"You are getting no argument from me on that plan. I missed you intensely."

"I missed you too, sweetheart. I'm sorry I was cranky about you going, but I do hope it doesn't happen too often."

"Me too, Chris—but I do have to admit it *was* an emergency. The bride had been so nervous she wouldn't fit in her wedding dress, she was practically starving herself and the dress ended up being way too large. And too large on a strapless dress is not good—in fact a little tight is better, so it doesn't fall down around her ankles."

Chris laughed. "Yes, it would have been awful if her dress fell off in the middle of the wedding. I'm glad you could fix it. Now, let's get some clothes falling down around ankles, shall we?"

It didn't take long for their clothes to end up on the floor. He drew her into his arms for a perfect fit. Warm skin on warm skin felt so wonderful, they both sighed with pleasure.

They made love slowly, lingering over every touch and reveling in it. He kissed every inch of her skin with little nips and licks to vary the sensations. He took her up slowly, so slowly she was surprised at the strength of her orgasm. When she broke, she flew up to the heavens, shattering into tiny shards of light, and drifting slowly back down to earth. Then he slid inside her and with long smooth strokes brought her up to the heavens again. When she came the second time, he went right along with her, groaning out her name and burying his face in her neck and hair.

They dozed for a while, wrapped up in each other and when they awoke they started up again, with Barbara kissing every inch of his skin, making his muscles quiver and jump. She reveled in the feminine power she had over him.

When he couldn't stand one more soft touch, he begged, "Babe, you're killing me. Need to be inside you. Ride me, sweetheart."

She moved on top of him and slowly sank down until he was buried deep inside her. It felt right to have him filling her, completing her.

He groaned. "Perfect."

Then she arched her back and he went deeper. She started to ride him slowly. Up and down. He pumped up into her and the pace became quicker as they came together with an explosive power. She screamed his name as he shouted hers. Then, she slumped down on top of him. He wrapped his arms around her and pulled the blankets up over them. They stayed wrapped in their cocoon while they came back to themselves.

Once they had recovered and could breathe and move again, Chris said, "I'm starving, are you?"

"Yes, you used up all my energy. Food would be a good idea."

"I have a hankering for Amber's clam chowder, what do you think?"

"I think it sounds awesome, but you'll have to go out in the cold to get us some."

"If I don't we'll starve, because I will continue to ravish you," he said.

"Oh, in that case, I could use a short rest from all your amorous attention."

"As long as we take up where we left off, after we refuel, then I can tear myself away from you for a few minutes," he said wagging his eyebrows.

"I'll think about it while you're gone."

He got up, got dressed, and gave her long, wet kiss before he drove off to get some food from Amber's.

She flopped back in bed, happy to be home with her husband. She'd missed him and hoped she wouldn't be called upon to fly off for a bride again any time soon. She decided to put some coffee on to have with their *refueling*. She put on her sweats and warm socks and went to her sunny yellow kitchen to get the coffee started.

The doorbell rang and she went to answer it. There on her porch stood Irene with her head down looking through a large bag.

Irene said, "Hi, honey. I wanted to bring your glove back. I found it under the bed and thought you would want it before your wife comes back tomorrow. We wouldn't want her to suspect anything." Just then she looked up and gasped. "Oh, you're back. Here." She thrust the glove into Barbara's hand and ran down the sidewalk.

Honey? Under the bed? What in the hell was that all about? Could Chris—*would* Chris—*did* Chris really do that? The evidence was in her hand and ringing in her ears. *Oh, Chris! How could you? Just like my father. Only I had to hear it from the other woman—so embarrassing.*

At least her father had the guts to tell her mother. Instead of hearing it through the grapevine, she'd heard it from the man she loved. Which would be a different kind of pain.

How could he be with Irene and then be passionate

with her? Was it all an act?

There was no way in hell she was going to put up with that. She took her suitcase to their room and dumped her clothes out on the bed. She stuffed his clothes into it, along with his toiletries. The tote bag in the closet would hold his shoes, she dragged it all to the back door. She put it out on the back porch, locked both the front and back doors with the deadbolt. Then she sat by the back door, waiting in a fury of grief and betrayal.

WHEN CHRIS GOT HOME with their dinner, he was surprised to see their suitcase by the back door—he was sure he'd brought it in when they came home. He looked in the tote bag and there were his shoes. What the hell? He tried to open the door, but it was locked, so he got out his keys, but it still wouldn't budge. What was going on? He rang the doorbell and yelled, "Barb, are you okay, honey?"

"Don't honey me, you cheating bastard."

"What? Barb, unlock this door. What are you talking about?"

"Your glove is in the bag with your shoes."

"My glove? Oh, I've been looking for it everywhere."

"You didn't look under *her* bed."

"What? Whose bed? Barbara, open this door so we can talk about it." Chris rattled the handle.

"No, I'm too mad. Take your stuff and go spend the night somewhere else."

"Barb, what in the hell is wrong with you? I just went to Amber's for some food. What happened?"

"As if you have no idea why I'm pissed. Go spend the night with your sister. In the morning we can file for divorce."

"Divorce? Are you crazy? What is wrong with you?"

"Nothing. I'm going back to bed. You leave me alone or I will call the police."

"Have you lost your mind?"

"Go away, I'm too angry to deal with you."

"Fine. I'll talk to you in the morning and you are going to explain yourself. Your clam chowder is on the porch." He dropped the meal at his feet and grabbed his belongings. Chris stormed back to his truck and threw the suitcase and tote bag into the truck. He tore out of the driveway and down the street.

Chapter Eighteen

CHRIS STORMED INTO GREG'S bar and went straight to a small table in the back. He told the waitress, Jessica, to bring him a bottle of whiskey, no glass needed.

Greg slid into the chair across from him, setting down the bottle a glass and a basket of popcorn. "Jessica tells me you're kind of cranky. What's going on buddy?"

"You tell me. I don't have a fucking clue."

"About what?"

"Barb threw me out. She put my stuff on the porch and said she'd call the police if I didn't leave."

"Oh."

Chris narrowed his eyes at Greg. "You don't sound surprised. Why not?"

"You've been spending a lot of time with Irene. Maybe Barb heard about it."

"Why would that matter? She's just a colleague. But no, she didn't talk to anyone. I picked her up at the airport; we went straight home and straight to bed. Where we had some amazing *missed you* sex. Then I went to Amber's to get us some food, you know, to refuel. When I got home all my stuff was on the porch and the doors were dead bolted."

"It does sound strange. Did she say anything?"

"She called me a cheating bastard."

"Anything else?"

"Something about my glove."

"Your glove?"

"Yeah, I lost it a few days ago. She said she'd put it in with the shoes. I told her thanks, I had misplaced it and asked her where she found it."

"She said I didn't look under *her* bed. I have no idea what she's talking about."

"Obviously, something happened after you left, which had to do with your glove and some woman. When did you last have your glove?"

"I wore it to work on Wednesday, but then couldn't find it Thursday morning. You know I just shove them in a coat pocket—I assumed it had fallen out. I checked the house, the truck, the office and asked Amber if she'd seen it."

"Yeah and I remember you asked me about it too, but it wasn't here. What are you going to do now?"

"I'm going to sit here and get drunk, for the second time in what a week, ten days? Then I'm going to sleep in my truck." Chris huffed. "If I have enough alcohol in my body I shouldn't freeze."

"Don't be ridiculous, you can't sleep in your truck."

"I sure as hell am not going to Amber's, which is what Barbara said I should do. Amber would mother and nag me to death."

"You don't want to go to Irene's?"

"Hell no, she's just a colleague. Why do you keep bringing her up?

Greg lifted a shoulder. "You guys looked pretty close on Thursday at the meeting."

"What? Oh, she knew I was nervous and was trying to be supportive."

"She called you honey and put her hand on your chest, man. That is more than *supportive*."

"I think she was flustered about being late."

Greg rolled his eyes at him. "Humph. I don't trust Irene, I don't know why—I just don't. But, you can spend the night in the room upstairs. It has a bed and a bathroom with a shower."

Chris relaxed, that wouldn't be so bad—bunking upstairs. "Thanks man. Can I take the bottle up with me?"

"Sure, but take some food too. You said you went to Amber's for food. I assume you didn't eat it."

"No, I didn't. Make me up something and I'll go get my stuff out of the truck."

Greg slapped his hand on Chris's back. "I'll bring the whiskey and food up when it's ready."

Chapter Nineteen

B Y MORNING, BARBARA wondered if she'd jumped to the wrong conclusion. Chris had left a dozen or more messages on her phone asking what she was talking about. Each message became more slurred. At first he sounded confused, then he sounded pissed, and finally just sad. The messages ended about midnight and she assumed Greg had sent him to Amber's for the night.

She called Chris's phone, but it went straight to voicemail. *Probably because the charger is plugged into the wall on his side of the bed.* She called the office number. After a few rings, it was answered by someone in the newsroom.

"Hi, this is Barbara. I was looking for Chris. He must have forgotten to charge his phone last night. It's going straight to voicemail."

"Neither Chris nor Irene have shown up today. Do you want her cell number?"

"No, I doubt they're together."

"Are you're sure? They *do* spend a lot of time together."

"I'm sure, thanks."

She realized he was probably sleeping off the booze. She called Amber's house.

"Hi, Amber. I thought you might already be at work."

"Hi, Barbara. No, this is my late day. I won't go in for another hour."

"Oh, okay, can I talk to Chris?"

"Chris isn't here, Barb. Should he be?"

"Oh, we had a disagreement last night. I thought he might have bunked with you."

"No. Was this disagreement about Irene?"

"Well, yes. It was."

"Oh, honey, I'm sorry—but I don't think it meant anything to him. He loves you."

Barbara's heart sank. So it was true. "He has a funny way of showing that."

"You were gone for a week, he got lonely. He had dinner with her a few nights here, and I heard they were at Greg's bar a couple of times."

"Thanks Amber, I gotta go now," Barbara said as she hung up and started crying again. He had not only cheated on her, but he'd done it in public. How could he? Now she knew how betrayed Sandy had felt. At least they had told Sandy before anything had happened—and at Chris's insistence too. Betraying someone must get easier the more times it was done. She was afraid he'd show up any minute and she didn't have it in her to talk to him. Maybe she'd go visit her sister for a few days, decide what to do next.

CHRIS WOKE UP ABOUT noon, disoriented. He looked around and remembered he'd crashed above the bar. He had spent most of the night drinking, calling Barbara, and wondering what the hell was going on. His cell phone had died about midnight, but he still couldn't sleep—his mind whirled from both the booze and confusion.

He had finally passed out about four in the morning and slept hard. The sleep of a drunk. Now his head was pounding and he felt like crap. He got out of bed and hunted around for any kind of pain relief. He got a big glass of water and drank it down at the sink with the painkillers he'd found. Thank god. Then he refilled the glass and took it back to the bed.

Greg didn't have a landline up here. He searched his bags and didn't find a phone charger. He'd have to get dressed and go find out what had happened to his life. There was also no food, and he figured if he didn't eat something soon the hangover wouldn't let go—and the painkiller wouldn't help his queasy stomach. He got in the shower, got dressed, and decided to leave his things in the room, for now. He didn't want to drag all his stuff with him while he tried to find out what was going on.

He went down the outdoor stairs and got to his truck, plugged his cell phone into the car charger, and drove over to Amber's. She wasn't in the café. He ordered a ham and cheese omelet, orange juice, and coffee—lots of coffee. When he was almost done eating, Amber slid into his booth with a cup of coffee for herself.

"Hi, Chris."

"Amber."

"Barbara called me this morning looking for you."

He raised his eyebrows. "Oh?"

"I told her not to worry about you and Irene."

"What?" he spat out.

"I told her you were just lonely with her out of town and you having a few meals together and hanging out at Greg's bar didn't mean anything. I told her you loved her."

Chris fumed. "Why in the hell does everyone think I'm interested in Irene? I'm a married man and I love my wife. Irene is a colleague—nothing else."

"She said you guys had a disagreement and confirmed it was about Irene."

"Why would she think that?"

"You two *have* been kinda chummy and I heard a rumor you went to her house the first night Barb was out of town."

"What? I did not. I went to Greg's. Had a few drinks and some chicken. Then Irene came in and we sat and chatted, maybe danced a little. I was kinda buzzed by then. Greg got the dishwasher to take us home so we wouldn't be driving drunk. I went to my house and she went to hers. In fact, Jeff took me home first and her second. She insisted I go first, since she's living farther out and she didn't want me to fall asleep on the drive."

"Oh. Well, I didn't believe the rumor anyway. I know you love Barb."

"How did the rumor get started in the first place? If it got to you, then everyone must have heard it. You're not exactly gossip central."

Amber shook her head. "No, I don't like gossip."

"Is that why people asked where Barb was on Thursday?"

"Yeah, I heard some snickers about you enjoying Irene while the cat was away."

"I had no idea. It's all bullshit. Oh my god, do you think Barb's heard it? She's always been afraid I would abandon her like her father did. It's why she works so hard on the wedding dresses—to make sure she has enough cushion to make it, if I leave her."

"Didn't she just get back?"

"Yeah, and she was fine when I picked her up. She didn't get senseless until I got back from getting dinner here last night."

"Something must have happened."

"I'm going over there right now and get this straightened out."

Chris got in his truck and drove home only to find an empty house. The back door wasn't dead bolted any longer, so he went in looking around for any clues. He didn't find anything. He got his phone charger and a few other items. He decided to leave Barb a note. He got some paper and a pen out of a drawer.

Barb, Please call me. I don't know what happened, or what you heard, but it's all lies, I am NOT cheating on you. I love you and I know we can work this out, please call me sweetheart. Please! Love, Chris

He put his stuff in his truck wondering where she was and what he could do to get to the bottom of this. He got in his truck and started it, when he had a thought. Mabel Erickson often knew what was happening on their street. She was an old retired lady and she loved to watch the goings on in their neighborhood—maybe she saw something. He turned off his truck, walked over to her house, and rang the bell.

"Come in, come in, young Christopher. I was waiting for you to come by."

"Oh? Why were you waiting for me?"

She looked at him like he was an idiot, which maybe he was. "So I could tell you all about it."

"All about what, ma'am?"

"Oh, that floozy stirring up your wife, Chris. What else?" She took his coat and hung it in her hall closet, then she pointed to a chair. "Sit there while I make us some tea. This is going to take a while and I need a nice sip of tea so my throat doesn't get dry."

She bustled away into the kitchen, leaving him standing in the living room. He knew from past experience he wouldn't get one more bit of information until she was ready to tell him. He sat in her late husband's chair and worried while he waited impatiently for Mrs. Erickson to make him tea he didn't want, but would drink every drop of.

She came back in with a tray, which held a teapot, two cups, sugar, spoons, two dessert plates, and some cookies that looked like they came from Samantha's bakery. Thank god. In the past Mrs. Erickson had made her own cookies, but she was getting on in years and the fire department had been to her house a couple times when the smoke detector had gone off from burned cookies. Chris, like nearly every other male and a few females in town, was on the volunteer fire department. He'd seen the results of her baking and everyone had encouraged her to try Samantha's cookies. He was pretty sure Samantha dropped off a dozen every week to ensure she didn't cause a fire.

Mrs. Erickson poured his tea and asked, "Sugar or milk?"

"No thanks, plain is fine for me."

She handed him his cup and a plate with two cookies on it. Then she poured herself a cup and stirred in milk and sugar while Chris tried not to pull his hair out, but managed to smile warmly at the woman. She put two cookies on her plate and settled back into her chair. "Now, where were we? Oh yes, the floozy."

Thank god she was finally going to tell him. He was sure if she waited any longer, he would spontaneously combust. Then the fire department would have to come to put out the fire.

"What floozy, Mrs. Erickson?"

"That floozy Irene, of course."

Chris frowned. "What did Irene do?"

"I have to say the woman has the patience of a saint, but she's not using it for good. I've always wondered why some people have positive traits but use them for evil, you know like—"

Chris interrupted, "Yes, ma'am, we all do wonder, but what did Irene do, ma'am?"

"Oh right. Here I am going off on a tangent when you are wanting to know what I saw. I was sitting upstairs in my sitting room, just keeping a friendly eye on the street. You know how it is, Chris. I was doing neighborhood watch duty."

Chris nodded. "Yes, ma'am, and we surely do appreciate your diligence. So, Irene?"

"Yesterday she pulled up in front of my house and parked about four or maybe four fifteen. She sat in her car and watched your house. You got home with Barbara about four thirty and went right on in. I didn't see any lights come on except in your bedroom—I figured you two were having some *missed you* sex. And for quite a while it seemed, but I remembered when my dear Charles would be gone for a few days and we would go at it like rabbits—"

Chris cleared his throat and interrupted her again. "Yes, ma'am, I'm sure you did. So Irene?"

"Oh right, Irene. She sat in her car and waited, watching your house like a hawk. After you left several hours later, looking relaxed and happy, she went in for the kill."

"What did she do, ma'am?"

She glowered. "She was right in front of my house. I had a front row seat. She took a man's glove she had on the seat of the car and put it into a large handbag. Then she crossed the street and rang your doorbell while looking down into her bag. When Barbara answered the door, she didn't look up. She kept rifling through the bag as if searching for something. She said something and I saw Barbara stiffen. Then Irene whipped out the glove and looked up pretending to be surprised to see Barbara at the door. She shoved the glove into Barbara's hands and ran down the sidewalk. Barbara shut the door and Irene looked back and then walked to her car with a big fat smile on her face. Then she sat there in the car waiting. You came home a while later and when you tore out of the driveway, she followed you."

Chris sat there in shock with his mouth hanging open, trying to process what she was telling him.

"You know, I noticed you came home late the first night Barbara was gone, so I didn't believe the rumors that young punk Jeff was telling. About taking both of you to Irene's house."

"What? What did you say?"

"Oh, you know. Jeff O'Conner, the dishwasher for Greg, who brought you home the first night Barbara was gone. I assume you had a bit too much to drink, because I know he drives people home occasionally when that happens."

"Yes, ma'am, he did bring me home. But what did you say about him telling people?"

She looked surprised. "Oh, you don't know?"

Chris slowly shook his head. "No, I guess I don't. What's he telling people?"

"You know he's just a punk and no one with any sense would believe it."

Chris was gritting his teeth in frustration. He unclenched his jaw. "Believe what?"

"Oh, that he drove both of you to her house and left you there."

"What? He did no such thing."

"I know. Didn't I just say I saw him drop you off? And I saw you walk out the next morning, alone, I assumed you were walking back to the bar to get your truck. So, no I didn't believe a word of it."

Oh dear god, this was worse than he thought. Someone was actually saying he was hooking up with Irene. Well fuck, what was he going to do to convince Barbara of his innocence? By god, he knew the first thing he was going to do was to put Irene on the first boat out of town, with a one-way ticket. Designing the amusement park wasn't nearly as important as his marriage. But first he needed to know anything else his helpful and observant neighbor knew.

"Mrs. Erickson, is there anything else I don't know?"

"Oh, undoubtedly, but I don't know what else you *need* to know."

"Let me tell you straight from the horse's mouth,

I'm running Irene out of town on a rail. I won't have her interfering with my marriage."

"I always knew you were a good boy, Christopher. We don't need that floozy in our town sleeping with all the married men."

"Has she slept with married men?"

"The only one I know for sure is Brett. She seems to steer clear of the unmarried ones."

"Brett?"

"Yes, but he's no prize, I feel sorry for Janet though."

"Yeah, for a lot of reasons. Thanks so much for your support. Would you like some help cleaning up?"

"No, no, I can do it fine. Gives me something to do."

"Will you tell Barbara what you told me, if I can get her to come over?"

"Yes, I'd be happy to. Good luck to you." She got up and retrieved his coat.

He gave her a kiss on the cheek.

Chris walked back to his house. Barbara was still gone. He went back to Greg's to drop off his belongings, then he was going to go have a chat with Irene. He didn't feel up to talking it through with Greg, so he sent him a text asking if he could use the room another day or two.

Greg texted back, Of course. FYI after I came back down last night from bringing you dinner Irene was here trolling and asked Jessica if you were around. I sent her packing.

Chris replied, Thanks buddy

Chapter Twenty

CHRIS WENT BY THE OFFICE and didn't see Irene's car. He was about to drive out to her rental when he decided to talk to one more person before he confronted her. He wanted all the facts, so he headed for the school. The kids would be out in a few minutes and he and Jeff were going to have a chat.

He drove through the high school parking area looking for Jeff's old beater car and parked near it, then he waited for school to get out. He heard the bells ring and lots of high school kids came swarming out of their wing of the building, to go home.

There was a couple that reminded him of Barbara and himself in high school. She was wearing his letterman jacket, and he was carrying both their backpacks in one hand and had his other hand wrapped around her. He walked her to the passenger door and opened it for her, but before she got in, she turned her face up to him and they shared a steamy kiss. Then she hopped up into his truck and he walked around to his own door and got in. One more kiss and they were off.

Chris sighed and thought how simple life was at that age. He scanned the area again and didn't see Jeff, but his car was still sitting where it had been, so he wasn't worried. Ten minutes later, the lot was mostly empty and he was starting to wonder if Jeff had left without his car. Then he saw him herding out two smaller kids—a girl about eight and a boy about ten or eleven. Chris waited until they got almost all the way to the car and then stepped out of his truck.

"Oh boy," Jeff said.

"Yeah, I need to ask you a couple questions, Jeff."

"Yes sir, Mr. Clarkson. I kinda figured I'd be seeing you one of these days." He looked at the kids. "Cindy, Tom, get in the car. I need to have a minute with Mr. Clarkson."

The kids looked at Chris wide-eyed and nodded before getting in the car.

"My brother and sister," Jeff said.

"Jeff, tell me why you've been telling lies to the folks in town."

Jeff shifted from foot to foot. "I'm sorry, Mr. Clarkson, I knew as soon as I took the money it was wrong. But the kids needed new coats and I just couldn't pass it up. Then I was trapped."

"Tell me what happened from start to finish."

"You know the night I drove you and Miss Smith home from Greg's bar?"

Chris nodded.

"You know how Miss Smith wanted to be dropped off last. As soon as we dropped you off at your house, all of a sudden she was sober as a judge—she wasn't acting drunk anymore. She seemed perfectly fine."

"Go on."

"Well, she sits up straight and says to me, '*What's your name?*' And I say '*Jeff*.' And she says, '*Jeff, today is your lucky day. I'm going to give you one hundred dollars to tell one itsy bitsy lie.*' I didn't say anything and she says, '*All I want you to do is tell one or two people you brought Chris to my house.*' And I said '*I can't do that, ma'am, it would look bad for Chris.*' And she says, '*Do you think so? How about if I pay you two hundred dollars for one little lie to two people.*' And I says, '*But, ma'am, I don't think anyone would believe it.*' Then she laughs and says, '*Oh, Jeff, I don't want everyone to believe it I just want some of them to wonder.*'"

"Wonder?"

"That's what she said. Then she says, '*I only want you to pick two people to tell. One person who is a gossip and is happy to repeat anything, whether it's true or not.*' And I thought of Miz Tisdale because she'd repeat the sky was green."

"Yes she would. Who was the second one?"

"The second one I was supposed to tell was someone who didn't like you much. She says, '*You know, like someone he was rivals with or someone who dated Barbara.*' I thought of Adam and the fact he is always kinda hostile to you."

"Yes he is, you chose well. So you agreed to do it."

Jeff pushed his hands into his pockets. "Kinda, I mean she dropped two hundred dollars in the front seat and of course I picked it up. I was trying to decide if I should give it back or keep it and tell those two people—who nobody would believe anyway. But as soon as I picked up the money she trapped me. She took out her cell phone and snapped a picture of me holding the money and she says, *'If you don't do what I'm paying you to do I will tell everyone I passed out and while I was sleeping you stole the two hundred dollars from my purse and I caught you doing it and took your picture.'"*

"You're kidding," Chris said, amazed at the length she went to.

"Nope it's exactly what she did and then she says, *'And I'm a respected engineer and you are just a kid and everyone would believe me and you would go to jail, then what would happen to your siblings?'"*

"She threatened you?"

Jeff straightened and looked Chris in the eye. "Yes, sir, and I got scared. I took her money and I told those two people. And when I told her I had done it, I told her I wasn't going to do it again and she says, *'We'll see.'* Which kinda made me mad. But she just laughed and says, *'You've done your part, now I'll do mine.'"*

"I see, well, it seems like her idea worked, since there are a lot of people in town who heard your lie."

"I'm sorry, Mr. Clarkson. But I did buy the kids new

coats with the money and I had enough to buy them winter boots too. And some food. I know it's wrong, but so is my brother and sister being cold and hungry."

"Where's your mom, Jeff?"

Jeff drooped. "She's real sick, she can't work. I'm supporting the family on my job at Greg's. Please don't tell him so he won't fire me. He gave me a shot at the job and I've worked real hard for him."

"I won't tell him, but if I bring my wife to see you, will you tell her the truth?"

Jeff squared his shoulders. "Yes sir, I'd be happy to. It's been weighing on my conscience."

"Good, now take the kids home and get to work. If I hear you spreading any other rumors, true or false, I will rat you out in a heartbeat."

"Yes, sir—I mean, no, sir—I mean, I won't be telling any more gossip or lies. This time was bad enough. It made me feel dirty and bad about myself."

"As it should."

Chris watched Jeff get in his old car and drive off. He thought about all he'd learned and decided he was going to talk to Mayor Carol to see if the town could help out their family in some way. And he was going to mention to Greg that Jeff could use a raise, since he was currently supporting the family. First, he was going to call Doc Sorenson.

"Hey, Doc, this is Chris."

"Howdy, Chris, howzit?"

"In a god awful mess, but I'll get it under control. Hey, have you seen Tammy O'Conner lately?"

"Nope."

"Can you swing by her place and take a look? Jeff said she's real sick."

"I'll go right now."

"Thanks. She probably can't pay you."

"No worries."

"Thanks," he said again. Chris knew Chedwick had an emergency fund for helping with medical expenses—if Doc needed it he could use it. The town had paid for Doc's schooling back when Chris was in grade school. The mayor had seen doc was gifted medically. As a child, he was always taking care of wounded animals and cleaning up cuts and scrapes of anyone who needed it. The town had sent him off to college so they would have a full time doctor. Because of that, he did a lot of his doctoring for free or at low cost.

Chris felt he'd done his best for Jeff. Then his thoughts turned to Irene and they were blacker toward her than they had been earlier—and that wasn't an easy thing to accomplish. Time to go see her. The ferry would be by in about an hour, and he planned to have her skanky butt on it.

Chapter Twenty-One

BARBARA SAT IN KRISTEN'S studio. Her sister worked away on a pendant for her favorite client, Vangie. She was resetting an old cameo into a new, contemporary design. Barbara had told her all about Chris's infidelity, sobbing as she choked out everything she knew and how hurt she was.

Kristen put down her tools and looked at Barbara. "I'm sorry you're hurt, but I'm not buying it."

"What?"

"I don't believe it."

"What don't you believe?"

Kristen put her hands on her hips. "That Chris cheated on you. The man is totally in love with you."

"Everyone saw him out with her."

"Yeah, I was in town one of those evenings after

putting a box of stuff on the ferry. I stopped in for dinner at Amber's and Chris and Irene were there. I went over and said hi. Chris didn't look guilty or embarrassed to be seen. He introduced me to her as an engineer from Colorado who was helping him design the amusement park. They even had some sketches on the table."

"But—"

Kristen shook her finger at Barbara. "But, nothing, you're looking at his actions through a filter, from our bastard father walking out on us. You're judging Chris by our father's actions."

"But, Irene said—"

Kristen looked like she'd tasted something nasty. "Irene is a slut. She slept with Brett, you know."

"Brett? Janet's Brett?"

"The one and only."

Barbara was shocked. "How do you know?"

"I'm not nearly as isolated up here as you might think. Irene is living next door to Mary Ann, and Mary Ann is starting to help me with some of the finishing on the Tsilly charms, like we talked about at the town meeting. She told me all about Brett one day when she came up to get some charms to work on."

"That proves my point, she has no trouble sleeping with married men."

"But it doesn't prove the point that *Chris* slept with her. Did you talk to him? Did you talk to that snoopy old lady across the street? If anyone would know about Chris's habits while you were gone, it would be Mabel. She could probably tell you what time he used the bathroom and she sure would have noticed Chris not coming home."

"No, I didn't talk to Chris or Mrs. Erickson. It's not a bad idea, asking her. I hate to go around trying to gather evidence."

"Yeah, much better to convict him on nothing but one slut's comments and what were probably working dinners. Mary Ann didn't tell me about Chris visiting Irene's house, just Brett. Do you want me to call and ask her?"

"Maybe. But they went to Greg's too."

"Yeah, if I know Chris, he was avoiding going home to an empty house."

"This is all my fault?" Barbara huffed.

"I didn't say that, Barbara. I just don't buy Chris was cheating on you."

"I need some time to think it through. Can I stay here a couple of days?"

"Yes. I'm your sister, you're always welcome—but I think you need to put a time limit on thinking about it and then confront it. Plus, you have commitments on wedding dresses and costumes for the town, don't you?"

"Yes, but I did grab my sketch book and client book, I can work on some of it here. I need to call Christa and get the last few measurements she did for me when I had to go to Florida and then I can get a fabric and notions list together for the costumes and call it in to the distributor."

"Fine. Shall we say two nights for you to think and wallow? Mary Ann's coming tomorrow, we can ask her some questions."

"But I might need time to wallow and think after we talk to her."

"Okay, two nights, with an option for one additional after we talk to Mary Ann. However, in my humble opinion, I think you are going to be hightailing it back to your husband after we talk to Mary Ann, to apologize for believing lies about him."

"Fine. And for what it's worth, I hope to god you're right and I am apologizing. I love that man."

"Now go work on your stuff so I can get back to this. I'm on a short deadline. Vangie wants to wear it at a wedding," Kristen said, taking back up her tools.

"I'll make dinner later, so you can catch up."

Kristen looked back at Barbara. "Oh, if you're going to cook you can stay five nights. Six if you cook all three meals and cleanup too."

Barbara laughed. "Brat."

CHRIS PULLED UP TO Irene's rental with tires screaming and slammed on his brakes. He stormed out of the truck, banged on the front door, and hollered, "Irene, it's Chris."

The door opened and Irene purred at him. "Chris, I was hoping to see you today." She stepped back to let him in and dropped her robe, standing before him naked as the day she was born.

Chris looked her over in a slow perusal from head

to toe and back up. Then he said, "Not interested," and headed up the stairs to her room. Fuck how had he missed the signs? She was a skank from head to toe. All along he'd thought they were friends, colleagues and she was just playing him.

He got to her room, hauled out her suitcases, dropped them on the bed, opened them, and started dumping the contents of the chest of drawers into the suitcases.

When he turned to the closet and grabbed two handfuls of hangers, she screeched, "What are you doing?"

"Putting you on the ferry. Get dressed or you are going to be riding the ferry naked."

"But, Chris, why?" she said in a tiny, sad voice, her eyes filling with tears.

"Save it for someone who cares. You bitch, you told lies about me. You fucking blackmailed Jeff into telling lies about me. You tried to destroy my marriage, goddamn it. You are the first woman, in my entire life, I have ever felt like hitting. Don't fucking tempt me. Now get dressed. You aren't welcome in this town."

"I didn't want to destroy your marriage, I just wanted to hurt it a little so we could have sex. I sure don't want you forever."

"You selfish bitch, I'm not interested in you. I have a wife I love very much and if I can't convince her it was all lies; I don't know what I'll do."

"But you need me for the amusement park," she whined.

"The amusement park is *nothing* to me, without my

wife. *Nothing*, do you understand? The amusement park is something to do, a dream to build and own. My wife is my heart—without her, nothing else matters. If you've destroyed that for me, then you've effectively destroyed my life. Now. Get. Dressed." He stomped into the bathroom and started shoving her toiletries into a bag. When he was finished, he hung his head and prayed for the first time in years, for God to help him get his wife back.

Irene was dressed when he walked out of the bathroom. "Do you have anything else in the house that's yours?"

"No, only my coat downstairs."

"Good, let's go." Chris picked up the luggage and walked out. He got in the truck and started it; he saw her stop and pick up her robe and stuff it in her pocket. He stared straight ahead.

Irene got in the truck and turned to him. "Chris…"

"Don't bother. You have nothing to say I want to hear."

They drove to the ferry landing in silence. He unloaded her luggage and went in with her to make sure she purchased a ticket. The ferry was pulling up. He waited until she was onboard and then got back into his truck.

On his way to Greg's bar, Chris called Kyle and told him the house was vacant and the keys to it and the rental car were inside. When Kyle asked why, he told him Irene had to return to Colorado suddenly. He figured the rumor mill would take care of it from there.

When he walked into Greg's, he sat hard at the bar.

Greg came over and lifted an eyebrow.

Chris said, "I need a beer. Dear god. I need a beer."

Greg slid a Rainier in front of Chris.

Chris took it and chugged about half of it. "It has been one hell of a day, my friend. One hell of a day."

"Want something to go with the beer?"

"Yeah, fry me up something and come on back to the corner table and I will tell you a story you are not going to believe."

"Will do."

An hour and a half later, Greg sat there with his mouth hanging open. "You have got to be shitting me."

"Nope, it's all true."

"Good lord, I knew she was trouble—but seriously, how could someone be that evil?"

"I have no idea. Can you afford to help Jeff out with a bit of a raise until his mom gets on her feet? I called Doc on my way back from the landing and he said she has walking pneumonia and it's a good thing it hadn't gone any further untreated. It is going to take her some time before she'll be able to go back to work."

"Yeah, I was thinking about giving him a raise anyway, he's a hard worker. But do you want to reward him for his behavior?" Greg said lifting an eyebrow.

"I don't think he had a lot of choice in the matter, and I think he learned an important lesson. Plus, if he's sole support of the kids right now, it's not about him, but about them."

Greg nodded. "Yeah. You know, if I recall correctly, Tammy was pretty good in the high school jewelry classes. Maybe she could help Kristen from home, even if only while she recovers."

"Really? That's a great idea. Of course, I have no idea how any suggestion coming from me will be received. I can't imagine Barbara has gone anywhere besides up the mountain to Kristen's."

"You might wait a day or two until you get a chance to talk to Barbara. Tammy will need a week to sleep and take her meds anyway."

"Yeah and if it comes down to it, you can call Kristen and suggest it, since Jeff's your employee."

Greg nodded. "If it comes to it, I will."

"And, well, um, if you can, I mean, if you do, or want to, um…"

"Spit it out."

Chris cleared his throat. "Could you say a prayer or something, for me and Barb?"

"Of course I will. I'm not a big prayin' man myself, but this does seem like a perfect time for a little divine intervention."

Chris cleared his throat. "Thanks, man."

"Sure. Let me get you another beer."

Chapter Twenty-Two

Barbara sat in Kristen's workroom fidgeting while they waited for Mary Ann to arrive.

"Stop, you're driving me crazy."

"Sorry, I'm just nervous. On the one hand, if I'm right, I'm going to be devastated. On the other hand, if you're right, I'm going to have to grovel."

"I'm right and you won't have to grovel. Just apologize and blame it all on PMS."

"Kristen!"

Kristen waved her hand vaguely. "I know, I know, setting women's rights back a hundred years and all that, but when it comes right down to it? Play the woman card. It's what makes us different from the boys and what they crave. Being the big strong man who takes care of his little woman."

"Oh my god, that is wrong on so many levels."

Just then, Mary Ann drove into the driveway and Kristen sighed. Barbara looked at her sister and smiled, she thought Kristen had probably been spouting all that crap to take her mind off fretting. She had a good sister.

Mary Ann walked into the shop.

"Oh good, you're here," Barbara said.

Mary Ann looked confused. "Yes I'm here, but why is that good?"

"I have some questions and I hope you know the answers."

"I hope I do too."

Barbara took a breath and sat up straight. "I'm just going to blurt it out. Has Chris been hanging out at Irene's?"

"If he has been, I haven't seen him." Mary Ann pulled a chair up next to the other two at Kristen's workbench. "At least, not until yesterday."

Barbara's heart soared, then sank. "What happened yesterday?"

"About three o'clock he comes roaring down the street and slams on his breaks in front of her house. I think he left some rubber on the pavement he was driving so wild. Then he storms out of his truck and marches up to the door and starts banging on it. I was unloading groceries, so I had a front row seat. He yells out, *Irene it's Chris. Open up.* She does and it looks to me like she's in a silky robe. He shuts the door. Then I hear him yelling. I can't hear what he's saying except a few words here and there like nothing and wife and bitch. Not fifteen minutes later, he slams out of the door and throws her suitcases in his truck and she comes out and gets in. He tears off down the street. About an hour and a half later I see Kyle go in the house and he hauls out bags of food, puts the trash by the street for pick up tomorrow, and puts the *for lease* sign back up in the yard."

"She's gone?" Kristen asked.

"Looked like it to me."

"That was the first and only time you saw Chris at her house?" Barbara felt her entire body relax with the hope, Chris had been faithful.

"Yeah other than the first day, when he helped her move in."

"See, I told you." Kristen smirked.

"What's this all about?" Mary Ann asked.

"Oh, Irene tried to convince Barbara that Chris had been at her house while Barbara was out of town. Last week."

"Not that I noticed. I don't sit and stare at the house, but the room I'm using to help you with the charms is next to her house, and I'm in there a fair amount. And I have the curtains open for all the light I can get. I like natural light better for working than lamplight."

"Of course," Barbara and Kristen said in unison.

Mary Ann laughed. "Yeah, you both already know that. There have been some other visitors to Irene's house. Just not Chris."

"Oh, more than Brett?" Kristen asked.

"Yeah, Brett and a few tourists. One night, I think she was entertaining two at the same time."

"Eww," Kristen and Barbara said in unison again.

"Yeah, I shut my curtains that weekend, for sure."

"Weekend?"

"Yeah, they were there a couple of nights. To each his own I guess, but I don't want to watch or know about it. Anyway, when someone told me the rumors about Chris and Irene, I told them they were full of it. Of course, one of the people spreading the rumors was Adam. Why would I believe him?"

"Oh, he's always hated Chris. Some rivalry going back to little league, I think." Barbara had bubbles of joy running through her to hear it was Adam spreading the rumors and Irene was gone.

"Yeah, he'd be just the type to happily spread mean rumors about Chris," Kristen said.

"Which is why I told him he was full of it. I'm probably on his list now too."

"I doubt it; he seems to be more forgiving of the ladies—always looking to score."

"He and Irene should have hooked up."

Mary Ann shook her head. "She seems to like married men. No strings that way."

"Oh my god, do you think that's it?" asked Barbara flabbergasted.

"Yeah I do. I think she likes to draw men away from their wives for a roll in the hay and then send them back home."

"It does shine a different light on the subject, doesn't it?" Kristen said.

Barbara got up. "Thanks for letting me stay last night, but I think I need to go home now. Thanks for the info, Mary Ann."

"My pleasure," Mary Ann and Kristen said in unison. Which made all three of them laugh.

Barbara made a beeline for home, relieved her husband wasn't cheating on her. She alternated between laughing and crying all the way to the house. When she got home, Chris wasn't there, and it felt cold and empty. She found his note asking her to call, which made her feel better. But when she did, his phone went to voicemail. She wondered if he'd charged it yet.

Who could she call to see if she could find him, Amber maybe? But she'd already made a fool of herself with Amber, and she didn't want to repeat it. Maybe he was at the newspaper or he could be at Greg's or pretty much anywhere. She could drive around, but she wasn't in any shape to see people. She hated to call around trying to track him down, she'd try his cell again in a while.

After several attempts to call and getting no response she was getting worried. She would try one more time and if he didn't answer, she would leave a message. It was so quiet in the house and she felt so alone, she finally realized the fire and police scanner were not on, like normal, maybe something was happening that she didn't know about. She turned it on and sure enough there was a lot of talk about some boating accident. Chris wasn't on the radio but she heard Greg on it. She could pretty much assume that if Greg had left his bar then Chris was out there too and it sounded like this was not going to be over soon. So she decided to leave him a message to invite him over to talk tomorrow evening, that way he could rest up from the trouble today. She could make him something he especially liked for dinner. *Good idea.*

She called his cell one more time. This time when the voicemail message came on, she waited for the beep. "Hi, Chris, this is Barbara, um, I was thinking maybe we should talk. Would you like to come to dinner tomorrow, about six? Let me know if you're coming or not." Barbara hung up the phone and felt like a fool. Who called their own husband and invited them to dinner at their own house? Someone who had jumped to conclusions and thrown their husband out of the house, that's who. It would probably serve her right if he decided not to come at all. What an idiot she was. Now she had to wait to hear back from him. What was that phrase, about sitting on pins and needles? Oh, yeah, she could relate to it—her whole body was tense and tingly.

Barbara knew she wasn't going to get much—if any, sleep that night—so maybe she'd work on costumes for a while. Hopefully it would take her mind off her fear as she waited for Chris to call back. She had ordered what she needed to get started on them from the fabric wholesaler, but the order wouldn't be arriving on the ferry for a few days. She still needed to create patterns for the costumes and she always had plenty of butcher paper. Might as well get started.

THE RESCUE TOOK Chris and the crew all day. They were fortunate to get the people off the boats in time, right after they had gotten them off one of the boats had erupted in flames, so then they had a fire to deal with. They had to get the second boat away from the one in flames so it didn't go up too. What a fricken disaster that was. Once they got the fire out they had to find temporary shelter for all the people. He'd finally gone to Ambers for a late dinner, she'd called dispatch to tell them to all come in for food. Chris didn't notice his phone was turned off until about eleven. He turned it on, saw a message, and prayed it was from Barbara. It was. Thank god—or maybe, it was thank you, God. He frowned as he listened to it. Dinner *tomorrow?* Like he was a guest? Shit, that's not exactly what he was hoping for. Better than nothing, but it still seemed a little off to him. He didn't want to call and wake her up tonight, he decided to call tomorrow.

Chris called Barbara's phone the next morning about ten o'clock, but it went to voice mail. He left a message— yes he would come to dinner. He wondered why she didn't answer. Was she playing some game with him?

WHEN BARBARA AWOKE it was ten thirty, she never slept this late. She'd spent most of the night awake, waiting for her phone to ring. The scanner had finally gone quiet sometime after nine, but he didn't call. Finally, she was tired of the whole mess and dragged herself up to bed about four in the morning.

She reached for her phone on the nightstand and it wasn't there. Damn, she must have left it in her sewing room. She got up and hurried to see if Chris called, only to find it dead. She groaned. She'd have to plug it in and let it charge a couple minutes before she could turn it back on. It seemed like the universe was plotting against her. She could make coffee while she waited for her phone to get enough juice. And something to eat—she hadn't been eating much the last two days, being too upset to eat. But now that she knew Chris wasn't cheating on her, she should eat something, like toast—maybe with blueberry jam from the Blueberry Hills Farm in Mason.

Barbara made coffee and toast and finally her phone was charged enough to turn on. Yay! There was a message indicator with one voicemail. Yes, it was a call from Chris and he was coming. She better get after it, if she was going to cook something special and get the house tidied and herself cleaned up. Not only was she not eating, but she wasn't taking care of herself either and she kind of stank from not showering since leaving Florida.

Okay, clean up the house, shower, start dinner. I wonder what we have to cook. She didn't have time to order groceries from the Safeway in Chelan. That took three days, but that's why they had a deep freeze—to have food on hand to cook. Or she could go to the tiny market in town if absolutely necessary. They kept some emergency supplies in the winter, but for the most part, they were stocked for tourists in the summer. Beef was never an issue, since Hank Jefferson kept the butcher in town well-supplied from his ranch. If she didn't have to get out to buy stuff, that was even better. She was pretty sure there were some steaks and frozen corn on the cob in the freezer. Chris always loved meat or pasta—those were his two weaknesses. She went to the freezer to get them out to thaw while she got everything else going.

Chapter Twenty-Three

CHRIS ARRIVED AT SIX o'clock. Was he supposed to park in front and knock, like a guest at his own house? To hell with that, it was lightly snowing and he didn't want to come out and have to clean off his truck if he didn't stay. He pushed the garage door opener and parked his truck inside. Then he came in the back door and hung his coat in the mudroom.

He walked into the kitchen where Barbara was standing. She looked as nervous as he felt. He opened his arms to her. "I didn't cheat on you. I love you."

At the same time she said, "I'm sorry I didn't trust you. I love you." Then she rushed into his arms and sobbed.

He held his wife as she cried and he soothed her with long strokes down her hair to her back and whispered nonsense. He finally felt like he could breathe again; it had been a long three days.

As her sobs started to ease, he said, "Calm down now, sweetheart. I don't blame you honey. Irene put a lot of time and effort into making it look like I was guilty. I had no idea what she was doing and I certainly wasn't interested in anything she was offering."

"You mean, she did more than come tell me you'd been to her house?"

"Oh yes. Blackmail, bribery, lies. You name it. She did it."

"But why?" she asked, rubbing her forehead.

"I didn't ask, but near as I can figure she likes married men—she just wants them for a night or two of sex. I'm guessing it makes her feel powerful to draw a man away from his wife, but at the same time ensures there are no strings."

"Did you encourage her?"

"Hell no, and I think it's why she went to such extremes—because she's never had anyone turn her down or be indifferent to her."

"That makes sense, in a twisted sort of way. People are weird."

"Yeah, it does make you wonder."

"Are you hungry? We could eat while we talk."

"Yes, I am hungry. I didn't eat much today. Usually stress makes me chow down, but today I felt a little queasy all day. You're far too important to eat and carry on like normal. Let's eat while we tell each other everything we know about what happened with Irene."

"Good, sit in the dining room and I'll bring you a plate."

"I can get my own."

"No, let me serve my husband some dinner, okay?"

"Sure." Chris went into the dining room and found an intimate setting with candles, flowers, and a bottle of wine. He poured them both a glass and waited for his wife. While they ate, Chris told Barbara all the shenanigans Irene had pulled. Barbara was shocked at the tales. Then she shared what Mary Ann had told her and Chris was surprised about her entertaining multiple men, although he did remember Greg mentioning something to that effect. Then Chris told her about *escorting* Irene to the ferry and Barbara laughed at his high handedness.

"I have to admit I'm glad she's gone, but what about the amusement park?"

Chris shrugged. "We can get some other engineers in here to work on it. I was starting to lean that way—there are a lot of details to be designed and worked out. I think a couple of paid engineers from different disciplines would be the best idea. Besides, even if the park fails, you and our marriage are the most important things in my life. The park will be a fun job and I'd have some satisfaction of taking a dream to reality. Nothing compared with my wife and marriage."

"Oh, Chris. How can you say that? I'm not sure I could walk away from my wedding dress business."

"I do have to say, this marriage bump did make me think about some issues. It threw me for a loop when it first happened and I didn't know the extent to which Irene had gone. It hurt my feelings you would trust someone like Irene, but not me. It felt like a kick in the chest to have you not trust me to that degree."

Barbara looked chagrined. "I know and I'm ashamed by my reaction. It felt so similar to my father's actions."

Chris felt his blood pressure hit the roof. "Goddamn it Barbara, how long are you going to measure me by his stick? I'm not your father. I'm not going to trade you in on a younger model. I'm not going to walk away and leave you destitute. Why can't you believe that?"

"I don't know, it seems like it's the first thought that comes into my head and I have a lot of trouble getting it out of there," she said sheepishly.

"You need to try harder. You're working yourself to death trying to take on more wedding dresses. Socking away nearly all your profits for the day I walk out on you. I'm not going to walk out on you."

"My mother didn't think my father would either."

Chris crossed his arms and could feel the scowl on his face. "Your father always had a roving eye and I think he had more than one affair with women from town. It wasn't too big of a stretch for him. It would be a huge stretch for me. I don't have a roving eye and I'm not interested in anyone except you. I need you to believe it."

"I do..."

"No you don't. You're always waiting for the other shoe to drop. I think that's why you don't want to talk about having kids."

Barbara gasped. "Do you believe that?"

"Yes I do. Is there another reason."

"I just don't feel ready for children."

"Why?"

"They can be expensive and time consuming and I don't have time with my business."

"And you need to work so hard on the business…?"

"To save up a nest egg for emergencies."

"Like me walking out on you."

Barbara gasped. "Oh my god. You may be right."

"Yeah. I was afraid of that." He had thought it might be the case, but for her to admit it gave him chills.

"I'm sorry."

"I know, baby," Chris said sadly. "I'm afraid I can't go back to that. You not trusting me opened my eyes to some fundamental problems in our marriage. I think we need to work some things out before we can continue. Maybe we should get some marriage counseling."

"Counseling might not be a bad idea. But what do you mean by *before we can continue?*"

"I think, maybe, we should take getting back together slowly."

"Slowly?"

"Yeah, maybe get some counseling and work some issues out before I move back in."

Barbara stiffened. "You don't want to move back in? Are you saying you want a divorce or separation?"

"No, neither one. I love you and I'm fully committed to you, but I think we need to make our marriage stronger."

"And we will strengthen our marriage by you not living here? How does that make sense?"

"Well, for one, we won't procrastinate getting counseling. And we won't just fall back into our normal patterns and ignore the problems."

"What if we can't work the issues out? What if we drift apart?"

"I'm not talking years. I'm talking a few weeks or a couple of months at the most. Just long enough for us to take a look at our marriage and decide what it is we really want."

"You're punishing me for kicking you out."

"No, Barb. I'm not. I want us to have the time to build a stronger marriage where we have trust and faith in each other. A marriage where we are one flesh, instead of two going in opposite directions. Don't you want that too? Don't you want to wake up each morning and know, beyond a shadow of a doubt, I'm fully committed to you and I'm not going to walk out and leave you high and dry?"

"Yes, it would be wonderful."

"Then, let's take a few weeks and work to get to that place. Can we try it for maybe six weeks?"

"That seems like a long time not to see you."

"Oh, you're going to see me, alright. I have every intention of wooing you back to me once and for all. We are going to be spending a lot of time together—without the temptation to fall back into old habits."

"I guess it would be okay. I don't like it, but I can try it—for a few weeks."

"Then I'll see if there is anyone in town who does marriage counseling. I would guess the pastor could do it."

"Chris, we don't go to his church."

"No, but I still think he might counsel us. I'll ask Mayor Carol. She knows everything. Maybe she'll have some ideas."

"Where are you staying?"

"I've been staying in the room above Greg's bar, but maybe I should ask Kyle for somewhere I can stay for a few weeks. Maybe a vacation rental that isn't being used."

"You're going to pay to live somewhere else rather than be with me?"

"That's not what this is about—it's about us building a stronger marriage. I have full confidence in our marriage and our love for each other—that we will come out of this stronger."

"But let's make sure our counselor agrees with that idea."

"Sounds like a good plan."

"Okay. I made a cobbler for dessert. Do you want some?"

"Of course. Let me load the dishwasher while you get it ready. With ice cream?"

"Yes, with ice cream. How many years have we been married? I know you like ice cream with cobbler."

"Thanks, honey."

Chris cleaned up the dishes while Barbara got the warm cobbler out of the oven and scooped plenty of ice cream on top of Chris's portion.

"Let's take it into the living room," Chris said, "I'll get a fire going."

"Sounds good."

They cuddled on the couch while they ate their cobbler.

"This whole living apart plan. Does it mean no sex too?" Barbara asked.

"Yes. Well, at least at first. That might be a good question for our counselor."

"Then let's get started right away."

Chris laughed. "Yes, ma'am. Of course, even when we were dating we could still make out."

"What if we get carried away?"

"Hmm, maybe we should wait until after our first session and see what the rules should be. I'll try to get the first session before the weekend."

"That's only two days."

"Yes, but I'm highly motivated. I think I'll go now—so we avoid temptation."

"Rats."

After he got his coat on and was about to walk out the door, Barbara took hold of his jacket front, went up on her toes, and kissed him. Not a small peck, but a long, wet one with lots of heat.

When they finally separated, she said, "Hurry on the first session."

"Oh, I will babe. I will."

Chapter Twenty-Four

AFTER SPENDING A restless night, Chris decided leaving his wife last night made him a fool. He was on the phone early trying to find a marriage counselor. Mayor Carol suggested Pastor John Davidson. He was mostly retired with his son Scott taking over the bulk of the ministry. Pastor John was still happy to help with counseling people, since he had more life experience.

Chris's hands shook slightly as he dialed the number and waited for Pastor Davidson to answer the phone.

"This is John Davidson. How can I help you?"

"Pastor Davidson, this is Chris Clarkson."

"Hello, Chris. I've been hearing some interesting rumors about you."

Chris sighed. "Most of what you've been hearing is lies."

"That's good to know. I prayed you hadn't gone off the deep end. It does happen more often than one would hope, but it didn't sound like something you would do."

"Thanks. Barbara is my one and only, and I'm not interested in cheating. But those lies have shown a harsh light on our marriage and Barbara and I'd like to have some counseling. Would you be able to do that?"

"Yes. Why don't you come on over and let's talk about what you're looking for."

"Now?"

"Sure, I'm not busy. Do you have a half hour or hour to chat now?"

"That would be awesome. Me and Barb?"

"No, just you for now. Then I'd like to talk to Barbara for a few minutes alone before we get you two together."

"I can be there in ten minutes."

"I still have an office in the church, meet me there."

When Chris walked into the Pastor's reception area, the secretary Maureen told him to go on in—Pastor John would be in shortly. Chris looked around the office. It was filled with mementos of a long and fruitful ministry. Pictures of baptisms and weddings covered the walls. Bookshelves held as many handmade gifts as they did books. Birth announcements, greeting cards, and childish hand drawn pictures covered several cork boards. His desk was covered in books and papers and more pictures—the pictures on the desk were of his family. The room had two couches and two chairs in a conversation area. There were also two seats in front of the desk. Chris moved toward the conversation area and sat on one of the chairs.

Pastor Davidson walked in and shook Chris's hand. "Sorry to keep you waiting." He sat in the other chair. "Tell me about the rumors."

Chris told Pastor Davidson all about Irene and what she'd tried to do and what he did in return. He told him about what she'd said to Barbara and that Barbara had kicked him out. Then Chris related what had happened last night.

Pastor Davidson listened carefully. "You want to live apart for a few weeks and get some counseling to see if you can make your marriage stronger. Are you sure you're not punishing Barbara?"

"Yes sir. I believe we need to work through some issues."

"Okay then, tell me the last time Barbara made you angry."

Chris frowned. "When she kicked me out with no idea why, that made me pretty darn angry."

"Yes it would, but that was due to outside influence. When was the last time before that?"

"I don't get angry at her too often—disappointed, but not angry. Oh, except I did get angry when she went to Florida."

"Tell me about it."

"I came home from work on a Monday night and found her packing a bag. I had no warning whatsoever. Of course, I did realize later, my phone was turned off and I had missed her calls. If I hadn't come home when I did, she'd have been gone with no warning."

"Why did she go to Florida?"

"Oh, to do alterations on one of her wedding dresses. The bride had lost weight and it was falling off."

"She went for her business?"

"Yes."

"Then why were you angry?"

"Because she just left. For her business, yes. But why does her business come first before everything else?"

"What everything else are you talking about?"

"Me and the town."

"What about the town?"

"Oh, she promised to be at the meeting last week. The one where I told the town about the amusement park."

"That's a fine idea by the way, and your presentation was well done—other than Irene's late entrance. I suppose that was all part of her scheme to discredit you."

"Yeah, several people mentioned it. Frankly, I was too nervous to even notice."

"Barbara didn't let the town down by not being there with you."

"Well, not exactly, but it felt like she let everyone down."

"Everyone or you?"

"Me."

"Now, tell me about some other times Barbara disappointed you."

"Before that, I suppose it would have been when she

told me she was coming with me to talk to Mayor Carol about the amusement park idea. She told me she was coming, then when she didn't show up she said it was because she finally figured out something she was trying to do with a dress. I had to talk to Mayor Carol alone. Later that night, I kept waiting for her to finish something on the wedding dress before we went to dinner. We were going to tell Amber about using the land for an amusement park. I waited about two hours and finally went alone."

"If I'm hearing you right, she's been busy working on her business and hasn't supported you when meeting with other people to share your dream of an amusement park. Is that correct?"

"Yeah, I just need her support."

"I do believe you have some issues to work on, both together and separately. Each time we have a session I'll meet for about a half hour to an hour with each of you individually and then give you homework. A few days after the individual sessions you will both bring your completed homework back and we will talk about it—all three of us together. Thursdays work well for the individual meetings and we can have a group session on Mondays."

"Okay, um. We were wondering if you think the separation idea will be good for us or bad."

"I think it might be beneficial for a short time. But not too long."

"And, um, we were also wondering if you thought it would be right for us to abstain from relations," Chris said, his cheeks heating.

"Relations? Oh, sex. Yes, I think it might be a good idea to abstain for a while—again, not too long. We don't want to break your relationship, but make it better. Sex is often the glue that holds a relationship together during the rocky periods. But it can also be a distraction that causes you not to see issues that need work."

"Interesting."

"Now, please call Barbara and have her come in to see me—today, if possible. Then go set up regular appointments with my secretary for eight weeks to start. After that, we'll assess how it's going."

"Okay."

"Your homework for this session is to write down in detail how you felt when Barbara was busy working on her business and she wasn't emotionally or physically available to be with you at your presentations."

"Gotcha."

"I'm going to get a cup of coffee. Can you call Barbara now and let me know when she'll be by today?"

"I will," Chris said, as Pastor Davidson walked out the door.

Chris called Barbara. "Hi, Barb, Pastor Davidson is willing to work with us. I'm in his office now and he'd like to see you alone for a few minutes today sometime."

"Alone?"

"Yeah, he wants to see each of us individually each Thursday. He's giving us homework, and we'll all meet together on Mondays."

"I can come now, or pretty much any time."

"I think now would be best for him, since he's already here and I just talked to him."

"At the church?"

"Yes."

"Tell him I'm on my way."

"Will do, love you."

"Love you back."

When the pastor walked back in, Chris said, "She's on her way now."

"Perfect, go ahead and talk to my secretary and I'll see you on Monday. Unless you decide to come to church on Sunday."

"Um, yeah. Maybe…" Chris hurried out the door.

Chris saw Pastor Davidson smirk as he ran away.

Chris waited for Barbara in the parking lot. He opened her car door when she parked and helped her out and into his arms. He gave her a warm kiss and hugged her close.

When they came up for air, Barbara asked, "What did he say about sex?"

"He said it would be good for us to abstain for a short while, but not too long. That sex can be the glue that holds marriages together during hard times. However, it can also hide the issues."

She sighed. "Oh, well. Okay then. I think I'm going to want it more than normal only because I can't have it."

He laughed. "You might be right about that. I'm going to go work on the park now. Do you want to meet for dinner?"

"I could do that."

"Six at Amber's?"

"Sure, have a good day."

Barbara went into the pastor's office and glanced quickly around as she walked over to the desk and sat in one of the chairs facing it.

Pastor John came in the door. "Good morning, Barbara. Sorry to keep you waiting."

Barbara heard the fire alarm go off on the radio while the town fire siren started blaring. Because so many people in town were volunteer firefighters—most homes and businesses had a radio. Both Barbara and Pastor Davidson listened to the dispatcher say they had a car fire.

"Do you need to go?" Barbara asked.

Scott Davidson, the pastor's son and the new minister, looked in to say he was going to respond.

"Okay Scott." Turning to Barbara he said, "No, they should be able to handle it. If they call for backup I'll go, but otherwise we'll let the young guys handle it today. Now tell me your side of the story."

Barbara told him about how Irene had insinuated Chris had been unfaithful and how she'd reacted. She told him about her trip to Kristen's and how Kristen hadn't bought into Irene's lies. Barbara shared what Mary Ann had said, then the dinner she and Chris had talked through.

When she finished, Pastor Davidson asked her the same questions he had asked Chris. "So when did Chris last make you angry?"

"The lies Irene told made me angry at Chris, but I don't suppose it counts. I guess the time before was when he was angry with me about going to Florida. I told him I had to go. I had tried to talk the bride into another seamstress from her area, but she had insisted I come since I had created the dress. I did agree with her I should do it. But I don't like travelling or going to a new city—it wasn't like going made me happy. So him being angry wasn't fair and I got angry back."

"Now tell me the last few times Chris disappointed you."

"I was disappointed when he said he wanted to live apart for a while. I thought he was punishing me."

"I asked him the same question, but his answer seemed to negate that idea."

Barbara smiled. "Yes he was perfectly reasonable with me too, the rat. I guess before that was when he invited Irene to come help him with the park."

"Tell me why you didn't like that."

"You know Chris and I fell in love while we were working closely together in high school, even though he was dating Sandy at the time. I thought if he was with Irene for long periods of time he might fall in love with her."

"You were scared of history repeating itself?"

"Yes, and I probably added in what my father did to

us."

"Oh yes, leaving you all for a younger woman. Is Irene younger?"

"Yes, she's in her early to mid-twenties."

"You and Chris are what? Twenty-seven or twenty-eight? Only a few years younger. Not like your father who went for a woman fifteen years younger."

"Correct, but still…"

Pastor Davidson interrupted. "I know, anything else?"

"He doesn't seem to see my business as important. He's disappointed if I work on it when he wants to do something else. Like one night I had finally figured out how to fix a problem I was having with a dress and he wanted me to drop it and go to dinner."

"Oh. He couldn't eat dinner at home?"

"He wanted to talk to Amber about his amusement park idea and he wanted me to go with him."

"Oh, so he had a purpose for the dinner."

"Yes."

"And you told him you couldn't go."

Barbara shook her head. "No, not exactly. I told him we could go, but for him to give me an hour."

"Oh and he was unreasonable?"

"No, he waited. And then, he actually waited a second hour. But I was still working on it, so he went alone."

"I see, so you didn't set the correct expectations."

"Um, no. I guess not."

"Did Chris explain my plans for counseling you two?"

Barbara blinked at the abrupt change of subject. "Yes."

"Good. Set the times up with my secretary. Your homework for Monday is to write out all your feelings about the times we talked about when Chris made you angry or disappointed."

"Okay."

"I'll see you Monday."

"We're done?"

"Yes, thanks for coming in this morning. It did make it easier on me. Oh, and I hear the fire trucks signing back in—sounds like the fire wasn't a big issue."

As she walked to her car, she wondered why Pastor Davidson hadn't said much about her revelations. Even the one where she'd kept Chris waiting. She hadn't realized she was setting false expectations and she wanted to make sure she didn't do it again. Why hadn't he talked about it more? It was clearly an area she needed to work on.

Barbara spent the next few days working on costumes for the town and writing her heart out on her homework assignment. She and Chris got together nearly every evening for dinner and to share their day. Chris was being charming and he brought her small tokens of his love. A bag of her favorite hard candies, a cookie or tart from Samantha's bakery, a quick sketch he'd done of something he knew she'd find funny, a sappy greeting card—he seemed to bring whatever struck his fancy. She was charmed by his attention and she made sure she was prompt to spend the time with him. In fact, she'd been stopping work early to primp for her dates.

Not having him around all the time and thinking

consciously about their time together, she realized how much she'd taken their marriage for granted. She liked this and vowed to herself she'd not fall back into those old patterns once they were living under the same roof.

He was the love of her life and she'd been treating him like a roommate, maybe a roommate with benefits, but definitely not the most important person in her life. Her wedding dress business came first nearly every time. She needed to treat it as a job and work it that way. Not let herself get so burned out and she wondered if fatigue had played a part in her difficulty with some aspects of the Florida bride's dress. Maybe if she'd been more balanced in her life and work, she'd have been clearer minded. Probably…and that was something she could fix.

CHRIS SPENT HIS DAYS working on the amusement park. A couple of guys were clearing the land in the area they would need to start building. He had what he felt was a good design for the first phase and was looking forward to breaking ground in the next few weeks. The temperatures would be high enough to get started and they had little to no snow in late February and early March as a trend. He hoped the weather would cooperate this year; they had a short time to build the first few amusements if they wanted to open in late June when the most tourists started coming to Lake Chelan. There were a couple of engineers

Sandy's game company had recommended who would be in town next week to look over what needed to be done and to help him get started.

He wasn't solely focused on the park—he was also focused on his wife and marriage. The homework the pastor assigned helped him to see where he needed to change, the act of writing it down really caused him to think about what was needed and how to go about it. For instance, he liked having Barbara's support for the amusement park, but he really didn't need her to be at every meeting, that was asking too much. He was an adult and he could manage to give out information without her there to hold his hand.

Wooing his wife was giving him a lot of enjoyment. He loved her excitement when he brought her a treat. That didn't have to stop once they were back living together. Him trying to decide what to surprise her with was putting back into their relationship the missing spark. There was no reason he couldn't continue to focus on her for an hour each day to find some way to charm her. And he was charming her because he noticed she was taking the time to look pretty for him. He thought she was beautiful in her baggy sweats, no makeup, and hair jacked up in a messy bun. But she'd been looking especially pretty for their *dates* with nice clothes and even a bit of makeup.

Chapter Twenty-Five

CHRIS AND BARBARA DECIDED they would go together to the Monday morning counseling session. They had both expressed a nervousness about going, and decided it would be less scary to with a united front. Barbara carried a steno notebook she'd done her homework in and Chris had a folder with printouts from his computer. They held hands on the way into the church. Maureen was on the phone and waved them toward the office. The door was open, and they paused in the doorway.

Chris cleared his throat. "Pastor…"

"Come in, come in. Have a seat. Would you like some coffee or water?"

Chris and Barbara looked at each other and Chris croaked, "Maybe some water."

Pastor Davidson walked over to a mini-fridge and got

out three bottles of water. He handed one to each of them and took a seat on one of the chairs while Barbara and Chris sat on one of the sofas together.

"Did you come together?"

"Yes."

"Did you bring your homework?"

They both nodded.

"Now we can do this one of three ways. I can read them out loud, or you can each read your own out loud, or you can read each other's out loud. Which would you prefer?"

"We have to read them out loud?" Barbara squeaked. "I thought they were like a journal—our own private thoughts. I didn't know Chris would hear them, or you for that matter." She glanced at Chris and he was nodding.

"You thought wrong. I think for today I will read them out loud. It might be easier to hear that way." Pastor John held out his hand for their assignments. Both of them were reluctant to hand them over, but they did. Chris reached for Barbara's hand at the same time she reached for his. Pastor John noticed and smiled to himself. They had a strong marriage, it may need some work, but the foundation was solid.

Pastor John started by reading Chris's first. The more he read, the closer they got to each other. By the time he'd read aloud both sets of homework, Chris had his arm around her shoulder and she had hers around his waist. Their opposite hands were clinging together in front of them. Yes, they had a good foundation. When challenges came they clung together, closing ranks rather than getting angry with each other.

Before John could say a word, Chris said in a croaky voice, "Oh baby, I'm so sorry. I don't mean to diminish your business. It's a strong business and I'm proud of what you've done building it."

Barbara spoke at nearly the same moment saying with tears in her eyes, "Honey, I didn't know my support meant that much. I have so much confidence in you. I'm sorry."

Then they both laughed through their emotions. Embarrassed to be so upset for each other.

Pastor John smiled at them. "Maybe you should take turns. Go ahead and talk it out." Then he got up and went over to his desk to give them privacy.

When they appeared to be finished talking and were just holding each other, Pastor John moved back to the seating area. "Everything good?"

They nodded and he continued, "The purpose of these sessions is to get out in the open the issues. To hear and understand where each of you is coming from, and to talk them through together. Too often in a marriage we let the hurts and even the pleasures go by without talking and sharing how we feel. Usually not sharing is for a good reason. Like for instance the upset or disappointment is minor and you think there is no reason to talk it through— you'll get over it. Or on the positive side, you assume your spouse knows how you feel so you don't need to share it with them. But it's not true. We don't always know what the other is thinking and feeling. We can't understand why the other person is hurt or disappointed. We don't always know when we've made our spouse feel good either. I'm going to teach you how to share in a non-threatening way. And also in a way you don't have to talk it to death. You both have busy lives, you don't want—or need—to spend hours sharing. You could put each other in a coma that way."

They laughed and he continued, "But quickly sharing can be an awesome way to protect and strengthen your marriage. For example, if you'd been practicing it when Irene pulled her stunt, she probably wouldn't have gotten as far with it as she did. If you'd both been sharing your disappointments and joys, the insecurity wouldn't have been there for Irene to poke at."

Chris and Barbara both nodded.

Chris said, "I can see if Barbara knew how much I love and appreciate her she'd know I wouldn't stray. And if I had voiced my feelings of abandonment, she probably would have told me of her confidence in me. And saying it out loud to her might have helped me to see my fear more clearly. Her leaving wouldn't have been blown out of proportion and we would have built each other up while separated, rather than letting it fester."

"Good, now keep talking issues through until we meet again on Thursday."

"Thanks pastor," they both said in unison. Then holding hands and with a lightness in their step they walked out of his office.

John smiled as they left. Yes, those two were going to

be a joy to work with. He certainly had some information and techniques to teach them, but they were open and they were committed to learning and strengthening their marriage. He wished more couples would seek guidance early like they were doing—before decades of hurts had built a wall between them so strong it took months or years to break through.

As CHRIS AND BARBARA walked to his truck they were quiet. Chris opened her door and helped her up into the seat, but before he closed the door he looked her in the eye. "I love you. I love the way you have confidence in me. I love your dedication to your business. I love that you've been primping for me. I love that we're taking time to work on our marriage. I love you in so many ways I can't even come close to telling you all of them. God, Barbara, you're everything to me."

Barbara took his face in her hands and looked back into his eyes with tears in hers. "I love you, Chris. I love that you put up with my one-track mind when I'm working on a dress. I'm proud of you for working on your degree. I love the tokens of your love you're bringing me. I love taking the time to have dinner and an evening together away from my business and your education. I love that we're putting our marriage first. I love you so much it hurts sometimes. I'm sorry I got scared you were leaving me and pushed you away."

"No recriminations—that's in the past and we are going forward. We are going to show Irene and the whole town that her lies and manipulations didn't hurt us, but made us twice as strong and twice as committed and twice as in love."

"Only twice?"

Chris laughed. "You're right maybe ten times, maybe a hundred."

"There you go."

He kissed her softly and then with growing heat. Chris groaned and pulled back. "I better get you home or neither one of us is going to get any work done today. I think the town might be a bit shocked if we made love in the church parking lot."

"You think it would shock some people do you?"

He laughed. "Brat," he said before shutting her door and going to his side. He got the truck started and moving, then reached for her hand.

He dropped her off at their home and she said, "How about I cook dinner tonight? What would you like?"

"Enchiladas?"

"Great."

Chapter Twenty-Six

CHRIS DECIDED HE WANTED to commemorate their breakthrough with the pastor. He went to the jewelry store and bought Barbara a heart-shaped locket. They would need to get their picture taken together and put it inside. When Chris walked into the office, he wondered what he should do to get some more people to help him design the park. The first few rides were mostly planned and the bubble seats for the spinning ride had been ordered. He wasn't sure how long it would take to get them, but he hoped it wouldn't be too long. On his voice messages he heard one from a man asking about an interview for one of the engineer positions he'd posted on Craig's List and ran in a few newspapers around the country. This man was in the Seattle area and he was interested.

Chris had also put an ad in the local paper over the

weekend for an administrative professional and there were a couple of messages asking about the position. He spent the day making phone calls and emailing some of what he was looking for to the engineer in Seattle.

THE FABRIC SHE'D ordered last week should arrive anytime. She had ordered a lot, and she knew the supplier worked quickly on large orders and sent it express shipping. Barbara called the three women she'd recruited to help sew the costumes for the town and amusement park. She wanted to meet with them to solidify the way they would be working together so they were ready to start when they had material. She set up a meeting for later in the afternoon and gathered together the patterns and drawing she'd made for the various costumes. She wanted to let the women pick out the designs they wanted to work on.

Once that was done, she turned her mind to Chris coming over. She wanted to make it a festive affair to commemorate their first counseling session. She had a good feeling this was going to be an important step for their marriage. She had some brightly colored placemats, which had a Spanish look to them. She got those out with some bright yellow plates. She thought maybe margaritas would be fun to have with dinner. Oh, and she had a peasant blouse and festive skirt she could wear to look the part.

CHRIS WALKED INTO their house that evening, grabbed Barbara, and swung her around.

"I had a great day."

"I can tell, and I had a great day too."

"Yay for us both having a great day."

"The enchiladas are in the oven for about twenty minutes longer. Let's take our margaritas into the living room—there are some chips and salsa in there for an appetizer."

"Excellent." They took the margaritas and sat on the sofa next to the chips and salsa.

"You go first, Chris."

"When I got to the office I had a number of calls from people responding to the ads I ran over the weekend. Some people from town calling about the admin position. A couple of them came in today for interviews and a couple more are coming tomorrow. It's a bit odd having people you've known all your life treating you like an employer—it freaked me out. I mean Francine Scott came in to interview. She was my babysitter when I was little."

"I know what you mean. But we'll get to my day next."

He took her hand and kissed her knuckles. Then he grabbed a chip and some salsa and stuffed it in his mouth. "I had another call on voicemail. It was from an engineer in Seattle who wants to talk about helping me design the park."

"Oh no! Another one?"

"Paul is a male, married, mechanical engineer in his late forties with two kids."

"Oh, well, that's fine then." Barbara nibbled on a chip with some salsa and sour cream.

Chris laughed. "But you haven't heard the best part. He was an intern at Disneyland when he was getting his education in LA."

"Disneyland? Really? That's cool."

"Right? Anyway, he didn't stay because his high school sweetheart and now wife didn't want to live in California. He moved back to Issaquah and has worked in the Seattle area designing various amusements for the last twenty years. He wasn't looking for a new position, but he loves to read the want ads in the Seattle Times and was drawn to my ad." Chris grabbed a couple more chips with salsa and guacamole.

"Hmm, interesting."

"Yeah, he called me up and we talked for a while. He seemed knowledgeable and made some suggestions right away. Hints he learned while an intern. Do you know when you visit Disneyland you are never farther than thirty feet from a trash can?"

"No. Really?"

"Yep, it cuts down on trash being dropped because a trash can is always handy. And they have tunnels under the part of the park to move costumes and food and equipment, so the visitors never see the behind the scenes activities. Walt Disney wanted people in the park not to see anything that didn't fit with the theme of an area. He called it being *on stage* and nothing is allowed to detract from the feeling of, well, magic."

"It would make it more special, like you're immersed in the world."

"Exactly. Anyway, Paul and his wife have been kicking around the idea of getting out of the city. Their youngest is a senior in high school and is heading for the Colorado School of Mines to become a petroleum engineer and the oldest is at UCLA."

"The Colorado School of Minds? Never heard of it."

"No, mines—like gold mines. They are an excellent mineral engineering school. Students come from all over the world to attend."

"Oh." Barbara had another chip with beans and sour cream.

"Anyway, it leaves them free to relocate, if they want to. He is going to drive over on Wednesday to talk and look around at the town. And he's got another engineer friend—Brad, also male—who might be interested, too. He's an electrical engineer. Paul said he's got friends and coworkers in every discipline, which he thinks would be happy to help remotely or even drive over for a week or two if needed."

"You've had a busy and productive day."

"Tell me about yours," he said as he took another chip and loaded it up with beans, salsa, guacamole, and sour cream. He barely got it in his mouth before the chip cracked from the weight.

She laughed at him. "I will, but let's sit down to eat, then I can talk. The dinner should be done and I want to toss the salad. You, my dear husband, seem to be starving."

"Yeah, I'm a little hungry. You take the drinks and I'll bring the chips and salsa."

Chris poured them more margaritas from the pitcher she'd made and got them both large glasses of ice water. He also filled up the chip bowl. Barbara tossed the salad and got the enchiladas to the table.

WHILE THEY ATE, she told him, "I got together with the three ladies who are going to be sewing costumes with me. We decided who would do which costumes and decided we would each start with one costume and come back together to look them all over and offer suggestions on techniques and possible changes to the design. We could bring in the four people who would be wearing them and have them try them on and offer suggestions also. The fabric and notions I ordered should be in on the ferry later this week. Or it might need to come on the barge, if the ferry can't carry it all with whatever else they might be bringing to town."

"That does sound like a good plan."

"Yeah and that's why I understand your feelings about people you've known all your life treating you like an employer. One of the women is the one who actually taught me to sew back in high school. It was weird having her defer to me."

"She probably taught you the basics and you taught yourself how to design and create patterns and all that."

"Yes, that's true. But it was still weird."

"Yeah, I know how you feel."

"Also on top of that I got a wedding dress commission I'm excited about."

"Oh, can you do both the costumes and the dress?"

"Yes, it's not a rush. I've got a long time to design and create it."

"Good, and if the women work out well on the costumes you can pass on a lot of that work."

"Exactly."

"It sounds like we're both getting the help we need. This dinner was awesome, babe, thanks for cooking. And the table looks pretty. Of course, not as pretty as you look."

"I wanted something special to commemorate our first counseling session."

"Great minds." Chris muttered. "Stay right here for one second. I'll be right back."

Barbara took a long drink of her ice water while she waited for Chris.

Chris came back into the room with a small package wrapped in pretty paper. "I kind of felt like commemorating too."

Barbara took the box and opened it. "Oh Chris, it's lovely. Is it a locket? We need a picture to put inside of the two of us."

"Yes we should get someone to take a nice one for us instead of a selfie."

"Amber has a good eye for photos, let's ask her."

"We'll do it this week. Do you want me to help you put it on?"

"Yes please." She lifted her hair, he put the necklace on her and kissed the soft spot between her neck and shoulder, which made her shiver.

"Chris," she said on a sigh.

"Yeah, baby. I know we are abstaining, but I couldn't resist. It was there and needed a kiss. Let me help you clean this all up. It will give us something to do."

"Do you want some coffee?"

"Decaf. I want to sleep tonight and you on my mind is going to make it hard enough without adding caffeine."

"I'll put some on while we clean up."

∞

WHEN THE KITCHEN was clean, they sat in the breakfast nook and enjoyed their coffee. Chris tried not to get caught up in the heat sparking between them. He brought up every subject he could think of to keep things light and easy. She seemed to be doing the same thing, babbling about random stuff.

Finally, Chris couldn't take any more. "I think I better go now. Out into the cold. Right. Now."

"How much longer do we have to do this abstaining

and living apart?"

"At least a few weeks longer. We've had exactly one session."

"No, you had one and I had one and we had one together. That counts as three in my book."

Chris groaned and smiled at the same time. "You aren't making this easy."

"No, and I don't think I have it in me to do so. I want you back home where you belong."

"I know, sweetheart— and I will be. But let's learn a few more tips about communicating before it happens, okay?"

"You are making me very disappointed right now. How's that for communicating?" she said with her arms crossed and a sparkle in her eye.

"Stinker."

"Meany."

"God, I love you, Barb."

"I love you too, Chris. Now, get out of here before I pull out the big guns."

"And what are the big guns?"

"Strawberries. Chocolate sauce. Whipped cream."

"Oh. Now that's cruel." Then he leaned over and kissed her hard. "You save that idea for later." He got up and nearly ran out of the house.

As the door shut, he heard her laugh and say, "Gotcha."

Chapter Twenty-Seven

CHRIS ENDED UP HIRING Francine, Paul the engineer from Seattle, and his friend Brad. They started the following week. Francine moved right in and was efficiently handling everything by mid-morning. Paul and Brad came over to get started while they made arrangements to move into town. They looked over all the plans and Paul suggested they create a 3D model of the entire park as it was designed on paper and see how it worked.

Chris loved doing crafty things. It was one of the reasons he had picked civil engineering for his degree. They gathered all kinds of materials to build with. Lots of wood, wire, cardboard, Styrofoam, fishing floats, sand, toy trees, and toy people. The only figures of the right size they had in town was a bag of toy soldiers. Chris did his model building in wood and if he needed something cut he would head over to Terry's workshop. While Terry made the cuts for him, Chris would do some sanding on whatever carousel animal Terry was working on. Often Greg was there painting the finished ones. Chris realized the hands-on-work was a great source of stress relief.

Paul used the wire to design the Ferris wheel and Chris introduced him to Kyle for any other metal work he wanted to do. Brad worked with the cardboard, Styrofoam, and the landscaping. As they put in the designed pieces, they noticed bottle neck areas and corrected them both in the model and also the engineering plans.

They also modeled the underground layer—where the access tunnels would be—along with storage rooms, break rooms, plumbing, and electricity. The models helped them to see the park on both levels and even experiment with colors.

BARBARA SPENT HER days working on the wedding dress and also directing the seamstresses on the costumes. They were getting a lot done, which was satisfying. The women were eager to make money and it was fun to sew the costumes. They all especially enjoyed the fitting days, when they would bring their completed costumes over to Barbara's house and the person the costume was intended for would come and put it on. Putting on a costume brought out their playfulness as they hammed it up as the character they portrayed.

Chris and Barbara continued their dinners together—sometimes at the house and sometimes going out. They decided that Friday night was date night, so they always went out for dinner and then went to a movie or to Greg's bar.

Barbara teased him when he came into the house one night with sawdust on him. "So now you're becoming Terry, are you? Covered in sawdust."

"No, just sanding, while I wait for Terry to get the wood I bring him into the shape I need."

"I kinda like the sawdust. It's better than the grease and oil from the garage and easier to get out of your clothes, I'll bet."

"Yeah, that's for sure."

"So, for our jobs, you now play in sawdust and I play in satin."

Chris laughed. "Ha, sawdust and satin. Sounds like a cheesy romance novel."

"Both use our creative side."

"I never thought of it that way. I always saw engineering as using science, but it is creative too." Chris looked a little shy as he said, "Speaking of sawdust, I made you something."

He handed her a flat package about an inch thick. She tore off the paper and opened the box. Inside was a tree made of cherry wood. In the trunk of the tree was a heart with their initials carved inside and the word *forever*. "Oh, Chris. It's awesome," she said walking into his arms and holding on tight. He hugged her back and she sniffed.

"Now what's this, not tears?"

"Happy tears, it's beautiful. And means a lot to me. Where should we hang it?"

"Somewhere you will see it every day and be reminded, I am always going to love you."

BARBARA AND CHRIS kept up their counseling sessions. Barbara was surprised at all the different areas they talked about. Each week had a different theme. They started with anger and disappointment, then talked about their fears and failures. After that they talked about how their spouse brought them joy and happiness. Their hopes for the future was next and finally they talked about their past and how it affected the present.

At one session, Pastor Davidson had them try praying out loud for each other. He had started the prayer session off, showing them how verbal prayer worked. She felt terribly self-conscious but she gave it a try. They each took a turn and Chris seemed as awkward about it as she was, but as they kept at it, she found it became easier. This was a completely new idea, they'd both been to church where the pastor prayed out loud and she had prayed silently from time to time and guessed Chris had too, but this was a whole new experience.

Pastor Davidson suggested they try it each evening, if

only for a few moments. He suggested they ask each other what they were feeling troubled about or what they were trying to figure out and pray for those issues. He said we often don't want to bother God with trivial matters, but God is interested in our lives and by having the spouse pray, it didn't feel silly. They agreed to try it and when they talked about it later she had said it felt very intimate, and Chris had agreed with her.

ONE EVENING AFTER they had dinner and watched a movie, he had suggested they pray together. He was trying to get a particular area of the park designed and everything they tried didn't seem to work. He asked Barbara to pray for him, so she prayed for God to help Chris, Paul, and Brad to find a good solution. Barbara then told him about taking a new wedding dress commission that was concerning her. The bride had asked for a quick turnaround, one his lovely wife shouldn't have accepted, but the bride had offered such a large incentive payment, she had relented. Chris felt like lecturing her about taking on too much, but instead he prayed that God would help her get it ready in time.

After they were done praying she asked him, "How much longer before you move back in? I miss you and want you back here."

"I know, babe. Let's ask Pastor Davidson on Monday."

"But it's only Tuesday that's almost a whole week," she whined.

"Yeah, so you talk to him Thursday and I will too. Then, we'll see what he thinks on Monday, will that work?"

"I suppose." Barbara huffed. "Are you sure you can't come back now? We've gotten a long way in our counseling. I feel closer to you than ever. We've worked through a lot of issues."

"Yes, we have." Chris nodded. "But let's wait and see what he says. He hasn't steered us wrong yet."

"Fine," Barbara said pouting at him.

Chris laughed and kissed her long and slow. "I have missed you, baby. I think we can convince Pastor Davidson it's time."

"Yeah, well, he better agree or I might have to resort to violence."

Chapter Twenty-Eight

Barbara was working on the wedding dress she should have turned down. The bride hadn't planned far enough in advance, and she wanted an elaborate gown too quickly. But she hadn't rejected it—she was spending all her time working on it. The only thing she wasn't going back on was her commitment to the marriage counseling and some of her evenings with Chris. She had explained about the dress and he was being supportive about her meeting him every other day for dinner.

Barbara heard the fire radio go off and listened to see what the call was. A house fire at old man Peterson's house. Not a surprising call, a lot of people were using space heaters now that the weather was getting warmer. People often decided heating the whole house wasn't necessary and then used portable heat. Most modern space heaters had safety mechanisms in place, but the older ones were still dangerous. And old man Peterson was a packrat—he was probably using something ancient. The fire department had fined him a couple of times for having so much junk his house was unsafe—which could make this call worse if he had newspapers and other stuff everywhere—but if they caught it quick enough it would be okay.

When they toned it the second time, calling in all-hands, she knew it wasn't going to be a simple fire. Chris would be there of course, along with most of the town. She took her sewing into the living room where the scanner was. She was working on a smaller beaded piece she'd sew onto the dress later, so it was portable. The light wasn't as strong in this room, but she wanted to hear what was happening on the fire. Sometimes the families were called on to make sandwiches or chili if the fire took a long time to put out. With the all-hands, she knew Amber would already be putting together coffee, drinks, and healthy snacks. Only if it were going to last through the night would they need to bring in other food.

She heard Chris on the radio. He was taking a hose in through the front door. He was a good firefighter, always careful about safety, but not fearful of going in to do the job.

She heard Chris say, "Hold up. Floor feels mushy and unstab—"

"Chris? Chris!" Terry said, "Greg, he fell through the floor. I stopped at the door when he said to hold up and now he's just gone."

Greg commanded, "Do not go in, Terry. That's an order. Do. Not. Go. In. Let's get a stable platform to work from."

"Ten-four."

Barbara dropped her sewing on the floor and was out the door in less than a minute.

GREG SAID TO KYLE, "Go find old man Peterson, stat."

Kyle hollered at some of the other guys and they spread out looking for the owner. Kyle found him and hauled him up to Greg who was in command.

"What's wrong with your floor?"

"Nothin."

Greg snapped, "I had a man fall through it and we can't see him. Now what's under there?"

"I might have dug me a little crawl space under the house."

"How deep?"

Peterson shrugged. "Um, eight feet maybe."

"How big?"

"Most of it."

"Most of the living room?" Greg asked.

"Most of the house."

Greg shouted, "You dug eight feet under the entire house?"

"No I left the edges and left some support columns.

I had to have somewhere to store my stuff. You guys kept nagging at me to clean out the house, so I put it under there," Peterson whined.

"What kind of support columns?"

"I kinda dug it out in the shapes of the rooms leaving the dirt columns along where the walls would be. I put in some support beams where it didn't feel stable."

"Iron beams?"

"No, some four by fours."

"Oh dear god, are you telling me the floors have no support under them, across the whole house?" Greg asked in disbelief.

"Um, yeah, I guess I am."

"Where is the entrance?"

"In the kitchen pantry."

Greg grabbed Peterson's arm and radioed, "I need a cop at command, now."

When officer Ben came over, Greg quickly explained the situation. "Ben, lock this clown up, we'll need to talk about this later."

Old man Peterson sputtered, "You can't do that, it's my house, I can do whatever I want with it."

Ben said, "Come with me now, I've got a hot meal with your name on it."

"But my house…"

"The boys will save it if they can."

Greg shook his head. *Some people are too stupid to live, how he managed not getting eaten by a bear is beyond me.* Now he had a house fire and one of his best friends was trapped below the inferno and he wasn't sure how to get to him.

CHRIS LOOKED AROUND disoriented. *Where the hell am I?* He could see the fire above him. He seemed to be in a basement of some sort. He was pretty sure these houses didn't have basements, and there was crap everywhere. How he'd managed to fall into a fairly open space was the question. He tried to stand up and there was screaming pain. His right leg seemed to be broken and wouldn't hold his weight. He collapsed back onto the floor. His left leg was throbbing too. Damn, there would be no walking out of here. He could probably crawl along on his arms—if he knew where to go, but he didn't.

Chris tried to radio, but it seemed like his microphone or transmitter was out. He could barely hear them talking. He listened close for any clues. He turned on his emergency beacon to let them know he was still functioning and he heard both Terry and Greg mutter, "Thank god he turned it on."

Greg said, "Chris, I assume your radio is out. If you can hear me turn off your beacon."

Chris turned it off.

"Now listen close. The foundation of the entire house has been dug out. Peterson said he left dirt walls and some wood four by fours as support. The entrance is in the kitchen in the pantry."

Damn, the kitchen wasn't too close to where he was.

"Chris, if you heard all that turn your beacon on for five seconds then turn it off."

Chris did.

"Good, now can you walk? Turn it on for yes, leave it off for no."

After a few moments, Chris heard Greg say, "Damn it. Then we have two options. We lay a ladder down and extend it over the floor to where you crashed through, anchoring it outside on stable ground and send someone down to get you. Or we can come in through the kitchen access and try to find you. If you can head toward the kitchen I like that option better since the fire is centered over the front of the house. If you can head that way turn your beacon on for five seconds."

Chris figured he could do it. He turned his beacon on and off.

"We will probably have to break through the wall. You start that way and we'll meet you. Now turn your beacon back on and leave it."

Chris turned it on and started dragging his body through the hollowed-out room, which wasn't easy because the senseless old man had a bunch of crap stored down there. There were paths through it all, so he followed the paths toward the back of the house. It was hard work to drag himself along by his arms. He was a big guy and the breathing apparatus and turnout gear was heavy. He prayed he'd get out of there. He needed to see Barbara.

What had he been thinking, not living with her? What if he never got to see her again? Or hold her? Or make love to her? Goddamn it, he wasn't giving up. He was going to crawl to that pantry if it was the last thing he did.

Behind him, fire rained down through the hole in the floor and ignited the boxes stored there. Fuck, wasn't that just dandy. Now he had a fire above him and one nipping at his heels and they couldn't bring hoses in to put out the fire, because all the floors would fall through. All they could do was pump the water in through doors and windows and from above. He couldn't imagine a worse scenario.

ONE OF THE HIGH school kids volunteering with crowd control came up to Greg.

"What?"

"Sir, Chris's wife…"

"Bring her over." Greg sighed.

The kid signaled his friend who had hold of Barbara's arm. He let go and Barbara ran over to him breathing hard.

Greg asked her, "What do you know?"

"Only that Chris fell through the floor. As soon as I heard I ran over here."

"But it's a mile and a half."

"Yeah, but I wouldn't get any closer in my car."

"Probably true. We're working to get Chris out. Old

man Peterson dug under his foundation—the whole floor is unstable. He can't talk to us, but he can hear us and he's moving to the kitchen area where the access ladder is. We're breaking in through the outer wall into the pantry to go down and get him. You can see him moving on the monitor there," Greg said pointing to a blue dot moving slowly through the house.

"Why's he moving so slow and what's the red and yellow?"

"He's hurt, maybe broken legs. He's crawling or dragging himself along."

"And the red and yellow?"

"I don't think you want to know, Barb."

"Dammit, Greg."

"Fire, red is close to him, yellow farther away—maybe the next floor up and above."

"What? He's surrounded!"

"No, now look, the red is behind him and most of the yellow is too."

"But it's really close behind him."

"Yes, but he has his turn out gear to protect him and he's moving."

Greg's radio crackled and he stopped talking to listen. "Carry on. Be careful, Terry." Greg signaled to one of the wives on the perimeter. "Now, Barb, I want you to go over with the wives. We've broken through the outer wall. It should be only a few minutes 'til we have him, but I need to concentrate." He squeezed her shoulder and pushed her into the arms of an older woman.

Then the longest ten minutes of Barbara's life started as they all waited for Chris. One of the wives had a portable scanner, so they could listen in on the conversation as they got down into the hollowed out foundation. She heard Terry talking to Chris, but couldn't hear what Chris was saying. Terry called for two air splints, some rope, and a gurney to be brought to the back. She heard Terry grunt when he lifted Chris and she heard Chris swear from the pain. She heard and saw the living room collapse in on itself.

She heard Terry say he was putting the splints on to lift Chris out of the house. Then Terry told the men up top to pull on the rope while he guided from underneath. More house collapsed. Fire and sparks shot into the air.

Finally, she heard Terry say Chris was out of the house and he'd be right behind him. Six firefighters ran— carrying the gurney—around the side of the house with Terry running behind them just as the rest of the house collapsed into what should have been the foundation, but was now a big hole.

They rushed Chris over to where Dr. Sorenson had set up a triage center and Barbara ran after them. Chris was on his stomach because they hadn't taken the time to remove his breathing apparatus. His helmet was unfastened and laying over the back of his head.

Terry told Doc, "I think his legs are broken. You better transport him to the clinic to look. You're going to need x-rays."

"Let's get him in the ambulance," the doctor said and

looked at Barb. "You coming?"

"Yes," she and Chris said in unison.

"Right. Then get in and see if you and young Josh here can get some of the equipment off him while we drive. Gloves, breathing apparatus, bunker coat, whatever you can get off without hurting him. Leave the air splints, boots and pants—we'll cut them off."

She climbed in with the technician and leaned down to see Chris's face. "You okay?"

"Been better."

"You're out and alive and you are moving home, now. No more of this separation crap, do you understand? You scared ten years off my life."

"Yes, ma'am. God, honey, I was afraid I wouldn't see you again."

"Me too, now let's get some of this off you."

"Always trying to get me naked."

She laughed hysterically. "Yes, I am. Now give me your hand."

She wrestled his right glove off while the technician removed the left. Then Chris got his freed hands under his chest enough to get the latch for the SCBA open, and between her and the technician, they got that off his back.

Chris breathed a sigh of relief when the tank was off, "Finally, that thing is fricken heavy." Chris reached back under him to unfasten the coat and they got it off him, too.

They got him into the clinic and Doc Sorenson said to Barbara, "This is going to be highly unusual. I'm going to need your help to get him ready. Josh and I can't manage him alone and we had to leave the nurse at the fire to deal with other injuries. Can you handle it?"

"Yes. Whatever you need."

"I want to check his upper body quickly. We'll leave him face down do a fast check on his back, then turn him over and do the same to his chest. That's where I'll need your help, to get him turned over. Your husband isn't a little guy."

"I understand."

"Then I need to get the splints off to make sure he's not bleeding under his turnout pants and boots. Getting all that cut off while keeping his legs stabilized is another place you can help. If he's not bleeding anywhere, we'll get some X-rays done."

"Any questions?"

"No."

"Let's get started."

They did as Dr. Sorenson had said. Chris whined about them cutting off his favorite shirt and he grit his teeth when they couldn't keep him completely immobile. His upper body had some bruising, but nothing seemed broken. His legs, when they finally got through all the layers, were not bleeding, which was very good indeed. But his right leg wasn't aligned and it was clear he'd broken some bones on the sudden eight-foot drop, with the extra weight of the fire gear.

Barbara was calm as she helped the doctor, not letting anyone see her inner turmoil and fear. Once the doctor had the X-rays and had determined what was needed, he sat down with them.

Doc Sorenson said, "You've got a couple options. Chris, you need surgery on your right leg. We need to put a plate in to stabilize the broken bones. The break could have been more severe, you got lucky, but it will still need support. Your left leg has a break also, but it only needs a cast and then it should be fine, the bones are still aligned."

Chris nodded.

Doc continued. "We have the hardware and a surgical room and we can do the surgery here once Wendy, my nurse, gets back from the fire. So we can do the surgery right here in Chedwick. We have two recovery rooms and they can be used for overnight observation and I would want you to stay the night.

"The other option would be to call a helicopter from Chelan to come get you and take you to their hospital, they do have more resources than we do here. If you needed anything we don't have here during or after surgery they would be better equipped to handle it. The flight is about twenty thousand dollars, but I imagine the fire department's insurance would cover most if not all of that expense. I'm certain they have very fine doctors in Chelan and you would get good care, but I need to stay here."

Chris shook his head. "No, Doc, I know you and I have confidence in you. I would rather be here in town than at some hospital with doctors and nurses I don't know." Chris looked at Barbara. "What do you think, babe?"

"That's fine with me, if you're happy here, I'm happy here. We have our support system here, not in Chelan."

"Alright then, Josh and I will get things ready for surgery and as soon as Wendy gets back from the fire we'll get 'er done." They heard a door close. Doc said "I'll bet that's her now. We'll be back for you in a few minutes Chris. Barbara, you can sit in the waiting room once we come to get him."

She nodded and bent down to give Chris a kiss. "I love you and I know everything will be just fine."

"Yeah, it will, so don't worry."

Chapter Twenty-Nine

WHILE BARBARA WAITED, she put their new praying to work. When she finished praying, she knew she needed to make some phone calls. Just as she hung up from the last call, Terry and Greg came into the waiting room. They had taken off their turnout gear, but were still covered in sweat and smelled like smoke.

"Sorry we couldn't get here earlier. We came as soon as the fire was out and we could leave the scene. We left the rest of the crew cleaning up, but I imagine they'll all be here soon. What did Doc say?" Terry asked.

"Oh Terry," Barbara said as she rushed into his arms, her composure finally breaking. She sobbed on him. "He's in surgery now. The doctor has to put a plate in his right leg. The left is fractured too, but not as bad—he can set it."

Terry held her while Greg awkwardly patted her back,

both of them muttering soothing words. Greg muttered something about coming back and she heard him walk out. Terry continued to hold her until she was done crying, then they sat in chairs. Terry kept a firm hold on her hand and she was glad she could hold on to him for strength.

When Greg didn't come back right away Barbara asked, "Where did Greg go?

"He went back to see if they needed another hand. He's EMT trained, as are most of us. He might be able to help."

Some other people started showing up in the waiting room, including Amber. She rushed in. "I'm sorry, after I dropped off the food I went back to the restaurant and did the payroll. I never listen to the radio while a fire is raging—it makes me too anxious. I didn't even know Chris was hurt until I went into the kitchen and the cook gaped at me and asked me why I wasn't at the hospital. I didn't know."

"It never occurred to me to call you. I'm sorry too."

"What's the verdict?"

"Both legs have breaks, the right is worse than the left, he's in surgery for the right now. The other one can be set," Barbara said as tears filled both her eyes and Amber's.

"Oh, no. That sounds serious."

"Yeah. I'm so scared. It seems like he's been in there forever."

"No, it hasn't been long for surgery," Terry said. "He'll be fine. Although, I don't know when he'll be able to be up and around."

Just then, Dr. Sorenson came into the room. "Barbara, Chris is doing fine. We got the left leg set and the surgery went well on the right leg. He's in recovery now. You can go in and see him in fifteen minutes. He's going to have to stay on his back for a week at least, and recovery will be six to eight weeks. I want him to stay here overnight tonight, so we can keep an eye on him. You can take him home tomorrow, if you can get your house setup quickly. If not, he can stay another day or two here."

Greg walked in, still in scrubs. "Terry and I will help her get setup and also help her with him for the first week or so."

"I imagine some of the other townsfolks will want to help too." Terry said.

"Good, you can spend the night here if you want, Barbara. The room has two beds and you can use the other one."

"Yes please—but I don't have anything with me."

Amber said, "After I see he's okay, I'll go get you both some items. I don't imagine his clothes survived."

"No, we cut them off of him. Thanks, Amber. The door's unlocked—maybe not even closed. I can't remember if I closed it."

"Greg and I will see what we can do to get the house ready for him to come home."

"That would be awesome, thanks."

More people started streaming into the room and Terry was happy to talk to all of them and spread the news, while Greg gave everyone who asked a job to do to help out. Barbara finally escaped to see Chris after what seemed like a very long wait.

Chris was groggy and smiled up at her. "Hey, baby."

"Hey yourself."

"What's going on here? I feel kinda loopy."

"You had surgery on your leg, after you decided to fall through the floor in a burning building."

"Oh yeah, not my brightest idea. When are we getting out of here?"

"Not tonight. You have to stay tonight for observation, then the doc said I can take you home, if I can get the house setup to keep you flat on your back for a week."

"I don't have time to be flat on my back. Too much to do to get the amusement park going."

"You'll have to command the troops from your bed, darling."

He frowned. "I'll have to think about it later. Right now, I need a kiss and a nap."

She smiled and gave him a nice kiss then she stroked his hair back from his forehead. "Sleep, my love. I'll be right here with you."

"Good," he mumbled as his eyes closed.

Amber came in a few minutes later and whispered, "How is he?"

"Tired, but he was awake when I came in. He's more concerned about the amusement park than anything."

"That's a good sign. Of course, he's still on a lot of drugs, he may feel differently when the drugs wear off."

"Yeah, can you mention it to Greg and see if he has

any brilliant ideas about how we can keep him quiet while he heals. And still let him work on the amusement park—enough to keep him from doing something stupid."

"I will be happy to. I'm going to go to your house and get some clothes for both of you, and toothbrushes and stuff."

"Thanks. Oh and can you or someone who wants to help, go bring all his stuff back to the house from his rental and let Kyle know he won't be returning to it."

"Not letting him get away huh?"

"Nope he's coming home and that's final."

"Good for you."

Pastor Davidson came in a couple of hours later, when Chris was having a small snack.

Barbara looked at him and put her hands on her hips. "He's coming home with me and that's final. I've had enough of this living apart."

Pastor Davidson blinked. "You're still living apart? It's been nearly two months, hasn't it?"

"Yes," Barbara said, "and I want my husband back."

Pastor Davidson looked at Chris. "I told you a short time apart would be good to get some perspective, but two months? You are a stronger man than I'd be with such a pretty wife."

Chris looked confused. "You thought we were back living together?"

"Of course, I figured a week or two at the most—certainly not two months."

"Oh," Chris said.

At the same time, Barbara said, "Thank God."

"I do think we should continue meeting together for a while longer. I'll come to your house on the same schedule as before, if it's okay with you."

"Fine with me," Barbara agreed.

Chris still looked baffled. "Yes."

"I hear through the grape vine you have broken bones in both legs, although your right is worse than your left."

"Yeah and it's going to take six to eight weeks' recovery. It will be nearly summer. How am I going to get the amusement park built?"

"With a lot of help from other people."

"Yes, like your wife," Barbara said.

"But you have the dress you've been working on."

"Not anymore. I called the women who have been helping me with the costumes and they are going to finish the wedding dress. They are calling up some other women who sew to help with the costumes. I'm going to be spending all my time helping you get better and doing whatever you need me to do for the amusement park."

"Oh honey, you don't have to do that."

"Already done. You are more important to me than anything—including my wedding dress business."

"Let's pray for Chris's injury, the amusement park, and seamstresses. Then I'll get out of your way—but I'll see you Monday."

After they prayed, he left and Chris was tired from eating and talking. He fell back asleep.

After he'd been asleep about an hour, Gus came into the

room. He and Barbara talked quietly. She told him about the prognosis and the recovery time projected. Gus said he wanted to help by paying for a physical therapist to come stay in town while Chris was recovering. The insurance would pay for the treatments, but Gus was willing to foot the bill of living expenses and travel. Barbara was relieved to hear that idea. She knew Doc had some training in PT, but he was a busy guy, being the only doctor in town and it wasn't his specialty.

Chris woke up and Gus turned his attention to Chris.

"So ya decided to fall through a floor and have surgery to get a vacation did ya?"

Chris grimaced. "A vacation flat on my back is no vacation at all."

"Nope, not so much. I went up and looked at the model ya'll built of the whole park. It's looking real good. In fact, it's looking so good I thought about having a bigwig syndicated columnist come in and give us a review. Maybe generate some interest. I know Sandy's company is letting the gamers know, but another source of advertising might be even better."

"Okay."

"We would wait a few weeks 'til you're able to be a part of it, of course, but I wanted ya to be thinking 'bout it. Maybe planning what ya want to say."

"I can work on that even flat on my back."

"Yep, also need to think about staffing—maybe get some blurbs out to the colleges letting folks know we'll be staffing a theme park for the summer and could use some hard-working college kids. We'll need some for both the park and the hotel. Some of our own kids off at college will want in on it, but I don't think it'll cover all the workers we'll need to get it going."

"Yeah, it had crossed my mind."

"Maybe after this first week, ya could start by calling some of the local colleges and see how ya might advertise. Maybe cover all the colleges in the state."

"Maybe I could do some research online too."

"One other thing, I signed ya up in the International Association of Amusement Parks and Attractions, the IAAPA. It'd be good to look through their archives of information and start talking with other professionals in the business. Ya could also be doing that from home. Me, Paul, and Brad can keep an eye on the building and take deliveries of the things you've ordered for the park. Of course, we've got those other engineers Paul knows in Seattle to help with plumbing and electrical and such. We'll get some of them to come into town for a week or two and the others we can Skype with."

"Barbara has also cleared her schedule to take care of me and help if needed. Keep that in mind."

"Will do. She's going to be busy with ya the first few weeks, I imagine." He looked at Barbara and smiled. "If only keeping the stubborn man in bed."

"You understand perfectly." Barbara laughed.

Chris grumped, "Hey, I'm not that bad."

"I have my ways to keep him down." Barbara looked at him.

Chris looked like he about swallowed his tongue at the look she was giving him.

Gus cleared his throat. "I'm gonna get going. We'll keep in touch with ya, Chris. Now get well soon." He hurried out the door, before they could even respond.

They both laughed at his quick exit. Barbara said, "I guess we freaked him out."

"Any normal man would run away with you making such insinuations. You know I'm not going to be able to follow through with any of those hot ideas running through your brain."

"Oh you won't have to do a thing but lay still. I've already got an order into Safeway for some strawberries and chocolate sauce."

Chris groaned and said in a hoarse voice, "Babe, I just had surgery."

"Oh no worries. They'll keep a few days," she said with a smirk.

"You are an evil woman. But right now, I think my pain meds are wearing off. Can you see if the doctor has plans for that?"

She jumped up from her chair. "Oh honey, I'm sorry. Here I am teasing you and you're in pain. I'll go right—"

Chris grabbed her hand and pulled her close. "Don't panic, sweetheart. I love you teasing me and I'm not dying of pain, just a little uncomfortable. Now give me a kiss before you get the doctor. Kisses are the best medicine."

She gave him a nice long kiss and went to find the doctor.

Chapter Thirty

B Y THE TIME BARBARA, Terry, and Greg got Chris home it had been transformed. Her sewing supplies were gone—to be able to use the room as a recovery room for Chris. There was a hospital bed and rolling table. Their TV had been moved into that room. Several chairs were nearby for visitors to use. The couch was pushed against the wall and had pillows and blankets on it for her to sleep on for the first few days.

Terry and Greg helped ease Chris into the bed where he promptly passed out from the exertion. They covered him up and left him sleeping.

Her kitchen was a maze of food. The refrigerator and deep freeze were filled with home cooked meals labeled with reheating instructions. There were homemade muffins, cookies, and pies lining the counter. On the dining room table was assorted snacks and ideas to keep Chris occupied, but quiet at the same time. He could read magazines and books. He could tie fishing lures. He could play games. There were board games, card games, and computer games. His laptop had been brought from the office, along with the pieces of the model he'd been working on.

Barbara was amazed at the love and thoughtfulness she saw everywhere she looked. With tears in her eyes she said, "Oh you guys, the whole town must have brought stuff."

"Yes, of course. It's who we are," Terry said. "If you need anything there is a number of people willing to help. Several even volunteered to go to Chelan if you need something."

"But that takes two days. One day into Chelan on the afternoon down lake ferry then back the next morning."

"Yes, but if you need someone to go they will. Of course, you could probably just call whichever store you needed something from and it could be put on the next morning's ferry. But people are still willing to go if needed."

"I doubt we will need anything. But I'll keep it in mind." Barbara gave both Terry and Greg a hug. "Thanks for handling all this."

Greg said, "Sure. Now why don't you go take a shower and get into some clean clothes. We'll keep an eye on the big lug."

"Thanks, that would be amazing. You guys are the best."

"Nope, small town living," Terry said.

For the first few days Greg or Terry or one of the other firefighters were there around the clock. They all had medical training she didn't, and Barbara was grateful for their help and knowledge. The nurse and doctor both stopped by twice a day. Chris also had a number of visitors—no one stayed long, but they all stopped by the check on him.

By the time a week had passed, Barbara was worn out from company. She was introverted, so all those people at her house all day, every day, was wearing on her. Chris on the other hand thrived on the attention, although he did tire easily.

One afternoon Chris called her over to him and in a quiet voice said, "Honey, I think you should get out of the house for a few hours. Go somewhere quiet and peaceful and relax."

"Oh, I can't leave you."

"Of course you can. Greg is here hovering and Amber will be here during the afternoon lull. I know you're feeling overwhelmed—take a couple of hours and rejuvenate."

"You wouldn't mind?"

"No, you've been here with me every second of the day since I got hurt. I love you for it, but I know all these people are wearing on you. Go on now and I'll see you in a few hours."

Barbara left feeling like she'd escaped torture. She tried not to feel guilty. She knew all of them were trying to help and she loved them for it, but dear god, she was sick of people. A quiet location by the lake where she could sit in the silence for an hour sounded like heaven.

When she felt herself finally relax, she decided to drive by Chris's land, to see how the construction was coming. She drove down what would be the access road to the resort, which passed by the Tsilly Rock. She was surprised to see the resort looking so finished; she hadn't been by there since the ground-breaking ceremony, and she had no idea the first phase of the hotel had gone up so fast. There were people swarming around it. She knew there was still a lot of work going on, but the outside looked finished.

Barbara went back along the road which bordered Chris's property and drove toward the other end, past the school to where the amusement park would start. Eventually the park would spread all through the land to where the resort was. But to start with, there was a lot of land in between them.

Again, she was surprised to see so much accomplished. It was starting to look like a small town with buildings that would house the concessions, restrooms, and gift shops. She could see the attractions going up and it all looked rather enchanting to her. She had seen a lot of drawings and even the model, but seeing it actually coming together was a sight. She took some pictures of it all on her phone to show Chris. She didn't know how much of it he'd seen before his accident but she decided that it might help him to see the progress. So he wouldn't feel so out of the loop.

Then she drove by City Park and there in the middle of the park near the playground was a huge statue of Tsilly.

Of course, she knew it was a climbing structure for the kids, but she had no idea it had been installed. There were some mothers and babies in the park—since school was in session there were no older kids—but she imagined what it would look like when the older kids were out of school.

She looked wistfully at the mothers and babies and wondered if she and Chris would ever have children. She knew Chris was ready and she was the one holding back. Would she ever feel secure enough to bring a child into the world? Maybe—she was feeling more secure in her marriage. Nearly losing him in the fire had opened her eyes to the fact that nothing was certain in life and maybe it was time to stop hiding from it.

Barbara's last stop was the house she'd rented from Kyle the day Chris had gotten hurt. It was a three-story Victorian, one block off Main Street. She hadn't told anyone about renting it, except for her three seamstresses and she'd asked them and Kyle to keep it to themselves. She had rented it to give the ladies somewhere to bring all her sewing paraphernalia and to give them a place to work, if they wanted.

She parked in front and went up the stairs to the door. The house had a nice big porch, which in the summer looked pretty with hanging baskets of flowers. A few years ago some enterprising person had turned it into a boutique, but when the economy had the downturn, they had fled the area. Barbara didn't intend to keep the house into the summer, but she remembered how welcoming it had looked as a boutique.

Barbara went into the front room and stopped dead in her tracks, her mouth hanging open. In the middle of the long room was a raised floor, with three wide floor to ceiling mirrors, set at angles making a little alcove to see all sides of the dress. Fancy padded benches sat opposite the mirrors.

On her right was everything wedding. There were several mannequins with wedding dresses she'd designed for some of the townspeople. There was satin and silk draped artfully over tables and chairs. The dress she'd finished for the bride that had cancelled was hanging on a rack where other dresses could be added.

She looked to the left and that area was filled with costumes. Mannequins had on several of the costumes she'd created for the town. She wondered what the heck was going on here.

Just then Tina, Stephanie, and Christa appeared at the top of the stairs looking anxiously at her.

"Um, this isn't exactly what I had in mind when I asked you to move all my sewing stuff here."

Tina said, "We know, but this room needed something. We've set up the second floor as the work room—it has huge windows and lots of light. We couldn't just leave this area all deserted."

"Do you hate it?" Stephanie asked as they came down the stairs.

"No, it looks lovely and inviting, but I wasn't planning on making it a retail store and you certainly have it set up that way."

Christa said, "Yes we kind of hoped you would love it and let us run it as a small boutique. Maybe make up a few more wedding dresses. Come take a closer look."

The ladies guided her into the wedding area. She saw several of her wedding dress sketches framed and hanging on the wall in groupings by style. In another area were some of the photos grateful brides had sent her over the years.

"Where did you find those photos?"

"In the files from your filing cabinet. When we were moving everything, we saw them in there and thought it was a waste not to frame and display them. So when we started working on this area that's exactly what we did." Tina said.

"Of course, I forgot they were in there. They look nice all framed and grouped. I don't think much about the brides once the dress is shipped, but they all look happy."

Christa said, "Yes, Barbara. What you do makes people happy and beautiful. Some of the women in these photos wouldn't turn a person's head. But in the dresses you design? They all look amazing."

"Where did you get the mannequins? And the wedding dresses?"

"The dresses came from people in town. When they saw us moving stuff in here they asked what we were doing and volunteered them. Some mannequins were still in this house—from the boutique—and we found the others on Craig's List." Tina said.

"The satin and silks draped around are the remnants

from the bolts of fabric, aren't they?" Barbara asked.

"Yeah they were pretty. We thought they would be nice decoration. The pearls and beads looked like they were left overs too. Just a few of each kind, but sprinkled amid the fabric looks lovely," Stephanie said.

"Yes, they do."

Tina grabbed her hand. "Now, come see the costumes."

Again, her sketches had been framed and grouped into the different adventures the town had chosen to start off the tourist season with.

Tina said, "We put the costumes that are finished next to the sketches of them, so people can see how they look."

"Very clever, and it looks like you have some of the promotional items for the game."

"Yeah, Sandy sent us some," Stephanie said.

"And look, Kristen sent us some charms to fill a display case. The case was here from the boutique. We wanted to put something in it. Kristen gave us some of her sketches to keep the theme going. What do you think?" Christa asked.

"I like it. But do you think people will come in to look around? It's not like we have anything for them to buy. They could commission costumes or wedding dresses, but it's not exactly a *go on vacation and shop* kind of place."

Tina said, "No, but people might like to come in and look around—even if they don't buy anything. Although, we were thinking maybe we could get some veils and gloves and wedding accessories that could be sold."

"Hmm, maybe."

SHIRLEY PENICK

Stephanie said, "Come upstairs and see the workroom."

When they got to the second-floor Barbara said, "This room would be a delight to work in wouldn't it?"

Stephanie nodded and clapped her hands. "Oh, it is. The light is awesome, even in the winter. Since we have sunshine 300 days a year, we wouldn't need to use a lot of artificial light." They had set up their three sewing machines into areas where they had everything at their fingertips. In the fourth corner of the room was all the supplies. Her notions chest, bolts of fabric, and a nice large cutting table.

"The windows are huge and there is even sky lights in the section without the third story. You have to wonder what kind of workroom this was used for previously."

"We were thinking the boutique owner must have made something she sold. But come with me," Tina said.

Barbara followed them up to the third-floor room, clearly set up for her. There was a drafting table in one corner with strong light to draw her sketches. On the table were her sketchpads, pencils, colored pencils, and markers. Near that was a table to create the patterns. It was large and had the special paper with the markers she used to denote darts and sewing instructions on the patterns. Her sewing machine was also set up.

"Wow, you thought of everything."

"We have a nice desk tucked into the corner for you to use your laptop and communicate with the outside world. The internet people will be here on Monday to set it up," Tina said.

"Fine, then. We'll give it a try for the coming summer. But you three will need to do most of the work. Chris isn't going to be fully recovered for a few months and I want to help him as much as needed. I don't think I'd like doing the retail side anyway—I tried working retail in high school and it was awful."

"We know you are happiest in the background and we know Chris comes first," Christa said.

Barbara thought, he does come first right now, but in the past? Not so much.

Stephanie said, "There's a couple of other small rooms up here we didn't do much with. There's a kitchen and powder room downstairs behind the viewing platform. And a couple of small rooms that can be used for changing."

"All right then," Barbara said, "I have to get back to Chris now. But just carry on and we'll see how it goes."

"We're glad you stopped by. We've been anxious to show you, but didn't want to put any more burden on you with Chris to take care of," Christa said.

"I'm glad I stopped by, too. Call me if you need to."

They exchanged goodbyes and Barbara walked out to her car still in shock. It looked like she had a storefront.

Chapter Thirty-One

BARBARA DECIDED NOT TO mention her new enterprise to Chris, or anyone else for that matter, she needed to think through the whole idea. What role would she play? The ladies had clearly set her up as the designer and boss. She didn't have a problem with that and it was nice they had given her a private studio.

She couldn't be around people when she was designing. She focused all her energy on it and having people around wouldn't allow that. She knew she didn't want to be down in the retail part of the…shop? Boutique? Store? What was it, anyway? She supposed it would need a name. Her online presence was Wedding Dresses by Barbara. But this was more than just wedding dresses.

And what about payroll? Should she offer the ladies insurance? Did she need to change her business license, now that she had a real location? Would she need some kind of property insurance?

Stop. Too many questions. I am definitely not ready to talk about this. I don't even want to think about it.

When she got home there were several people in with Chris, all having a rousing discussion about the mayoral race. Steve had officially entered and so had an old man named Vernon Whitaker. Vernon was a good guy, but he was pretty set in his ways and didn't like change.

The consensus in the room seemed to be, they didn't like either candidate.

Amber said, "I heard a rumor our chief of police was going to run."

"James MacGregor?" Terry asked.

Amber raised an eyebrow. "Yes, do we have a different chief of police?"

Everyone greeted Barbara when she walked into the room and went over to give Chris a kiss.

Barbara smiled at them. "Hi, guys. It looks like we have a hot debate about the mayoral race going on in here. Do you think this motley group in here has all the answers?"

Terry said, "Maybe not all, but a good many." Turning to Amber he said, "Okay spill it."

Amber explained she'd heard bits of a discussion between Mayor Carol and Chief James. That he wanted to bring on another cop or two to free himself up.

As Amber talked, Chris whispered to Barbara, "You look better. Did you have a peaceful afternoon?"

"I did. I'll tell you all about it when we get rid of this

crowd."

"Perfect, now give me a good kiss." So she did.

Greg said, "I think Chief James would be a great mayor, but then we'll need a new chief of police. None of the officers we have now have enough experience to take over, except Ben and he's getting ready to retire, I think."

Everyone nodded agreeing with Greg.

"And that is what I think Chief James was talking about with Mayor Carol," Amber said. "He wants to hire a couple of experienced officers, from other places, to see if he can groom someone to take the position next year."

Barbara said, "We'll just have to see then, won't we. Now, I appreciate all of you keeping Chris occupied while I got out of the house for a while, but he's looking tired and needs to rest. I don't want to kick you out, but don't let the door hit you…"

They all laughed and Terry said, "Real subtle, Barb. Let's go folks and leave these two alone for a while. I'll come back in a few hours to help you get him settled for the night."

"Perfect, thanks everyone."

As they all made their way to the door Chris said, "I really am tired, can we talk after my nap?"

"Of course, you rest, sweetheart."

Barbara checked on Chris an hour and a half later and found him awake and looking rested.

"There you are, my lovely wife."

"Yes, here I am, you look well rested. I brought you a snack."

"Strawberries and chocolate sauce?"

"You think you're up to that already?"

"In reality, no I don't—but a man can hope."

"We'll get there, honey," she said as she set the sandwich, fruit, and glass of milk on his rolling tray and dragged it over so he could reach it. "While I was out I drove by the resort. I had no idea they were that far along. It looks great."

"Yeah, we had that stretch of nice weather, so they got the outside done as quickly as they could. Then they can work on the inside regardless of the weather. Same with the park. Did you go by there too?"

"I did and it's coming along faster than I guessed it would. You can see how it's going to be and it looks like fun. I took some pictures on my phone for you. I don't know how much of it was already up before you got hurt."

"Thanks honey, I would like to see them."

She climbed up on the bed, being careful not to jar him, and got her phone out of her pocket. As they scrolled through the pictures he told her about some of the thoughts behind different attractions.

"We want it to be appealing for everyone, not only kids and thrill seekers." Pointing to some benches, he said. "We want to have enjoyable places for tired moms and grandparents to sit while the kids play. And there are some picnic areas for people to enjoy the sunshine or shade and have lunch."

She flipped to the next photo. "I think this one is amazing, it's so beautiful, kind of like a fairy land or pretty little kingdom."

"Yeah, it's based on a castle and garden area in England. We thought the girls would have a fun time having lunch in the garden and then inside the 'castle' is a dress up room with mirrors, we ordered some different sized Halloween costumes of all the princesses. They can try them on and the parents can take pictures or we'll also have a photographer on hand for instant pictures. And for the boys in another room is pirate costumes and crowns like for a king and swords, stuff like that."

"That's so sweet, I know they'll love it. The whole thing is looking really great Chris and you did a fantastic job of designing it. It makes me so proud of you to see what you've accomplished." She put her head on his shoulder.

"Thanks babe." He cleared his throat. "I do feel bad about leaving all the work to the other guys to manage."

"It's what you're paying them for. But you'll be back out there helping them soon enough. I saw the Tsilly climbing structure in the park. I didn't know Kyle had finished it."

"Yeah they installed it two weeks ago, I told you about the ceremony they had when they put it in, but you said you were too busy to go."

"I did? I don't remember. I was probably distracted by that bride and her rush job."

"No doubt."

"I feel bad I missed it. God, I can be so absorbed and selfish."

"Now don't beat yourself up over it. You were trying to help a woman out with the most important day of her life."

Barbara wished it had been more about helping and less about money. But if she was honest, she had to admit to herself it was mostly about the money. She liked Chris's view of her much better than her own. He always thought the best of her.

"What else did you do while you were gone?"

"Oh, I sat out at Kissing Cove for a while."

"Without me?"

Barbara laughed at his pouty face. During high school, it had been one of the places they had spent a lot of time making out. "Alone, and that was the point, wasn't it?"

"I suppose, but still."

"I checked on the women helping me with the costumes and wedding dress."

"You were a busy girl going all those places. I'm surprised you could go to all their houses on top of everything else you did."

She could have told him about the shop right then, but she just wasn't ready to talk about it yet. Instead of starting that conversation she asked, "What do you want for dinner? We still have enough food to last a month."

Chris frowned at her change of subject. "Do we have any of Mary Ann's lasagna?"

"Yes, pasta boy, I believe there is a pan of it in the freezer. I'll go put it in the oven. It takes a while to heat up. Do you want me to get you anything?"

"If you could hand me my laptop, I think I'll check email and do some web surfing."

Barbara unplugged his laptop from the charger and

handed it to him before she went into the kitchen to get the lasagna in. She felt anxious as all the issues about the shop started swirling through her brain. No, she couldn't go there right now. She wasn't sure she'd ever want to go there, but she wasn't going to have a choice. *But not today. Right now my priority is Chris. Business is going to have to wait on me for a change. I've let it dictate my life for too long. How could I have not even heard Chris tell me about Kyle putting in the climbing structure? That is obsession at its best.*

Chapter Thirty-Two

THE PHYSICAL THERAPIST STARTED on Chris the next week. Chris thought she was trying to kill him. He'd never, in all his life, worked so hard. The woman was five feet tall at the most. He couldn't begin to guess her age, other than she was older than he was by at least ten years. And she was very opinionated. It was her way or the highway—only Chris couldn't run away. He knew he was getting excellent care from her, but she was just mean about it. And her bossiness didn't stop at the physical therapy.

The first words out of her mouth had been, "You aren't going to eat all that, are you?" She had arrived at the house right as Barbara had brought him in a nice large plate of Mary Ann's leftover lasagna. He had taken two bites and was raising the third to his mouth when she'd walked in.

He looked at her. "Yes I am. I always eat like this. I have a high metabolism."

"It might be true when you're up and moving, but with this injury and you being immobile you'll get as fat as a well fed rat if you keep it up."

He had deliberately taken another bite before asking, "And you are?"

"Your physical therapist and I'm going to own you."

Dear god, what had Gus gotten him into this time?

She asked, "What have you been doing to keep in shape?"

"Um, I'm not supposed to be doing anything."

"With your leg, yes, but what about your upper body. What have you been doing to maintain your strength?"

"Um…"

"Free weights? Resistance? Anything?"

"No."

"Nothing? Oh for god's sake, you're a firefighter, aren't you? You can't just sit here and let your upper body muscles atrophy. You could at least be doing some curls. How are you going to carry someone out of a burning building? Lifting that fork to your mouth, even loaded down with lasagna, isn't going to keep your upper body strong. I'll bet you've gained ten pounds eating like a pig and not exercising."

And so it had begun. Her tormenting him about food and working out. She wanted him to constantly push himself. He didn't like it—no, he didn't like it at all. He knew she was being paid to get him back on his feet and he was sure Gus had gotten him the best possible person to get him there, but a little bedside manner wouldn't kill her, would it?

Even his friends deserted him when she was in the house. Including Barbara, who had fled after the first ten words out of Attila's mouth. Her name was Abigail, but he felt Attila was more apropos. When Attila was there no one else came near. He wondered if she had a guard dog out front keeping them all at bay. But no, they were all probably scared she'd start in on them about eating too much and getting flabby.

He could take it; he worked hard when she told him to and grit his teeth. There was no way she was going to break him. Although she did break him. Every. Single. Session. Until he was a panting pool of sweat and quivering muscles.

Then she'd look him in the eye and say, "Not bad. Next time though, you're going to have to work harder."

He would smile, grit his teeth and not whimper like a little girl until she was out of the house.

Half an hour later, Greg or Terry would show up with Barbara and they would help him get cleaned up. He tried not to whine and moan. But he did accuse them of hiding from Attila. They would smile and say, "Yep I'm not stupid." Or something similar.

Barbara snuck away as soon as Abigail arrived and it gave her an hour at the shop. She was still trying to figure out a lot of pieces about how to run this. There were so many decisions to be made and she still had a lot of questions. She should probably tell Chris about it and get his input. He might have suggestions and answers to her many questions. But she was reluctant to tell him. Chris knowing would make it too real and she wasn't ready to go there.

She continued to drive by the construction sites to take more pictures for Chris with her phone, so he could see how they were progressing. The Ferris wheel was starting to look like a Ferris wheel. The carousel was up and Terry had taken some of the finished animals and installed them. He and Greg still had about a third of them to go, but the ones that were finished looked great. She'd gotten out of the car and taken lots of pictures that day.

Chris was excited to see all the pictures especially the ones from the carousel. He'd zoomed in on a lot of them to look closely. He'd seen many of the animals at Terry's shop when he'd been there. But now that they were installed he wanted to see how they looked. He figured Barbara was trying to keep his spirits up by taking the picture and he was happy she was taking them to show him, but it was frustrating to not be able to be a part of it.

His dream was going up without him. Not that he wanted the construction to wait for him, they had a deadline after all, but...

When he got too frustrated he went online and looked for trinkets to buy his wife. He wanted to continue to woo her, even though they were back living together. He wasn't about to take her for granted again. He also arranged for people, who got to get out in the real world, to bring by some of her favorite things. Like her favorite cookies from Samantha's bakery or a new book she might like to read while she was home with him.

She didn't seem to be doing any sewing, and he wondered about that. But she didn't seem to be stressed out about it—maybe she was doing some of it during his therapy sessions. He should try to remember to ask her.

Doc Sorenson finally declared his left leg was healed and he'd had enough physical therapy on it for him to use crutches and he could get out of the house—if he took it easy. Chris couldn't wait and Barbara said she'd take him, if he got Chris or Terry to come along and make sure he didn't get hurt. An hour later, he was dressed and waiting impatiently for Terry, who said he'd be happy to help.

When Terry walked into the room Chris said, "Finally. I thought I was going to have to call missing persons. What took you so long?"

"If you must know, I was putting the last few carousel animals in my truck. I thought you might like to be there when I installed them. But if you're going to be cranky..."

"No. No. I'm sorry. I'd love to see it. I just haven't been

out of this house in weeks and weeks and weeks."

"I know, let's get after it."

Chris was a bit shaky on the crutches, but Terry and Barbara flanked him so they could steady him as they went. It was a beautiful spring day—still on the chilly side, but the sunshine was bright and the sky blue. Chris took a deep breath of the clean air and felt like he'd been let out of jail. Some of Barbara's bulbs were blooming and the birds were singing. Life was good.

Then Chris looked to the right and there in his yard was a pair of crutches twenty feet high. He laughed out loud. "Oh you guys…" he said looking at Terry.

"What are you talking about?" Terry said innocently.

Chris shook his head, not believing the innocent act for a second. "The twenty foot wooden crutches in my yard. Since you're one of the few people with that much wood laying around, I know you had a hand in it, Terry Anderson. You and the firefighters."

Terry smirked. "I have no idea what you are insinuating, sir."

Then they both laughed, before getting in the vehicles to head to the amusement park. With Terry in the lead, he drove right up to the carousel, and Barbara followed him. She parked so Chris was right next to where Terry would be installing the animals. Greg drove up right then and it looked like he had some of the animals in his truck too. Terry and Greg started unloading the remaining animals. Chris marveled at them. There was a pair of lions, a pair of black bears, a pair of ostriches and a pair of camels. They weren't exactly to scale, but Terry had tried to get them as close as a children's ride would allow.

"We'll install them and then turn it on to see how it goes, sound good?" Terry asked.

"Sounds perfect. Too bad we don't have any kids to try it out," Chris said.

"Yeah, maybe you should open it up for an hour or so this weekend and let the local kids give it a try."

"That's not a bad idea Greg. I'll look into it, see if there are any restrictions we aren't aware of. There are probably some inspections needed at the very least, so maybe not this weekend but soon."

It took about an hour to get the last pairs installed and then they turned it on. It was a sight to behold. Terry had done a fine job with mixing the animals to be visually appealing for someone watching.

"Terry it's wonderful," Barbara said with a catch in her throat.

Chris was trying not to tear up himself. It was going to work. He looked around at the rest of the park. The Ferris wheel was up and they were installing the seats. He looked to where the twirling bubbles would be and noted the base looked finished, with Tsilly standing in the middle—the only thing missing were the bubble cars. He saw the big Noah's Ark, which would house the Old Testament bible stories. It was finished on the outside with work going on inside. The post-apocalyptic attraction was housed in a building, which looked like it had been bombed and was barely standing. The arcade was finished on the outside also. And the world geography play area had several structures standing—the Eiffel Tower and the Tower Bridge and the Coliseum. The US geography building looked like the Rocky Mountain range in Colorado—a left over design from Irene, but it was too impressive to change.

Since Sandy's company had sponsored several of the attractions, they were going to open with more than they had originally planned. Chris saw bathrooms and restaurants and lots of other pieces coming together. They would start the landscaping in a few weeks, when the heavy traffic of construction vehicles would slow down.

Now all they needed were people. He hoped the journalist who was coming in two weeks would give them a good review. He knew they already had some bookings from the publicity Sandy had started up.

Barbara said, "Babe, we need to get you home, Abigail will be there soon."

"First, I want to go by the resort."

"Okay. Terry or Greg—can one of you meet us at the house in half an hour? I'm going to drive Chris by the resort."

"Sure."

An hour later Chris sank down on the bed. Who knew crutching himself to the car and back was such work. He was glad Attila had been working his upper body along with the lower.

"You're late."

"Oh sorry. The doctor said I could finally get out of

this house, I've been gong stir-crazy so I didn't hesitate. Terry came by to help me get to the car and we went by the amusement park to watch Terry and Greg install the last few animals on the carousel. When they got all those installed we turned it on, it was amazing to see. Terry and Greg did all the animals by hand. It all took a little longer than we thought it would. Then Barbara drove me by the resort so I could see it too."

"Isn't she the most accommodating little thing. But I really d—"

"Now hold it right there! You can abuse me all you want, but you aren't going to dis my wife. I will not put up with that for one second."

Attila blinked twice and then a huge grin lit up her face. "There you are. Thank god, I was getting tired playing the bitch all the time. Who knew it would be your wife. Good for you. I'm always reluctant to hit on the wife. Too many men don't give a crap then I get depressed."

Chris shook his head. "What are you talking about?"

"You. Finally snapping back at me."

"What?"

"I work on the whole person—both the body and the spirit. Especially with cops and firefighters. They get into some scary shit and I have to make sure they haven't lost their nerve. I poke at my patients until they snap at me. Then I know they'll be fine."

"Are you kidding me? You really aren't mean and nasty to your patients?"

"No. Who do you take me for, Attila the Hun?" Chris

winced and she laughed out loud. "You do. That's the nickname you gave me, isn't it?"

"Well, um, yeah."

"I wish I'd known that earlier, I wouldn't have had to be so mean," Abigail said.

"You do a good mean."

"My father was a drill instructor. I learned from the best."

Chris laughed and shook his head. "Here I was, nearly biting my tongue in half and you were waiting for me to talk back. My mother taught me to respect women. Especially older women."

"Hey now. No need to get nasty."

They both laughed and started in on his therapy, but this time it was more fun. She still left him covered in sweat with quivering muscles, but he didn't feel like punching her and she didn't say anything mean when she was done.

In fact, she said, "Good workout. See you tomorrow. On time."

Chris laughed as she left.

BARBARA GOT HOME and Chris told her all about what Abigail had said. Barbara laughed at his bemused state. Who knew the woman could be nice?

Chris was getting cleaned up after his therapy session. Now that he could get around on crutches he didn't need as much care, so she left him in peace.

The doorbell rang and she went to answer it. The mailman handed her a large package. She was surprised by the delivery. She couldn't remember ordering anything and she was having the sewing items sent directly to the shop, since that's where they were needed. But her name was on the package. She took it into the kitchen to open it. Maybe it was something on back order and that's why it had been sent to the house. She didn't recognize the return address. Rather than take it to the shop, she decided to open it.

She set the box on the kitchen table and got some scissors to cut the tape. She looked inside and nearly fainted. The box was filled with sex toys. She laughed and looked through it. She guessed Chris was ready to resume their sex life with a little zing. One of the items in the box was a naughty nurse outfit. Barbara locked the doors and took the box to their room. The naughty nurse costume had a doctor's bag, which most the toys would easily fit in.

The hospital bed hadn't yet been removed, so she decided it would work perfectly. She put on the outfit, loaded the toys into the bag, and went into the makeshift hospital room.

CHRIS LOOKED UP when Barbara walked in and all the blood rushed south, leaving him light headed. His toys had arrived and the naughty nurse outfit was a perfect fit.

"Look what the mailman brought. You think you're up for this, do you?"

"As long as you do most of the work, yeah I think I can be up for it. In fact, I seem to be up already."

"Perfect, get on the bed, naked. Doctor's orders."

Chris had on sweats—it wasn't hard to do as she said. He sat on the bed and she went over to where he'd dropped his clothes. With her legs straight and her knees locked she bent down to pick up his things, giving him a fine view of her cleavage, which threatened to topple out of the top.

Chris groaned at the sight before him. "Oh my god, you're killing me."

"We nurses don't like to see things laying around—we have to make everything tidy." She folded the clothes and turned her back to him, walked over to the chair, slightly spread her legs and locked her knees, then bent at the waist—down low—to set the clothes in the chair.

"Babe, I'm not going to survive this."

She looked at him over her shoulder as she slowly straightened. "Sure you are." She sauntered toward him. "Now let's see what you ordered from the adult toy store," she said as she set the bag on his rolling table and opened it. "Lay down on your back so I can give you an exam."

Chris laid down grinning and as she came near he reached out to her, but she scooted out of his reach, took his hand and quickly attached it to the bed, with the velvet-lined hand cuffs. Then she walked around the bed to the other side and did the same to that hand. She also secured his legs—he couldn't move at all.

"There. Now you can just lie still while I do all the work."

She got the tickler out of the bag and started running it over his skin. Chris groaned. "This isn't exactly what I had in mind when I ordered that. I was planning to use it on you."

"We can do that another day—today is your turn." She ran it down his body and swirled it around his penis and balls. Then she ran it down his legs and back up, giving more attention to his male parts. Then up over his chest and arms.

His muscles jerked as she swept the feathers over him and he groaned at the sensations. "You know I'm not fully recovered yet—maybe you should go easy on me. At least this first time."

"Oh, you poor baby. Don't you want to try out the rest of your toys?"

"I certainly do want to try them. But maybe not all of them today. Please, babe. I need you."

"Good," Barbara said. She set down the tickler and leaned down to lick his nipple.

He nearly leaped out of his skin. "Whoa, works as advertised."

"Highly sensitive, are you?"

"You could say that."

"Good, maybe I'll have a taste of some other areas."

As she licked and nipped him all over. Chris thought he'd go out of his mind from the pleasure. "Babe please.

Ride me."

"I can do that," she said as she stripped out of her costume, climbed on board, and sank down on him. "Better?"

"Oh, sweetheart—I have missed your body united with mine."

"Me too, honey. Me too," she said as she moved on him slowly. He couldn't move, so she set the pace.

It didn't take either of them long before they were swept up into one of the most intense orgasms of their married lives. It had been so long, they both were overwhelmed by the pleasure and exploded together in a shower of lights. When she collapsed on top of him, she reached up and freed his hands so he could hold her close.

"Best purchase I ever made," Chris said sleepily. "Next time, it's your turn."

Chapter Thirty-Three

As Chris started to get around a bit better, Barbara had more free time. Greg or Terry were coming by in the late morning to take Chris out to the office or by the construction site or sometimes to Amber's for lunch, so he could chat with friends. After they got him back to the house, he had physical therapy.

With Chris occupied, Barbara spent more time at her shop. She didn't go into the retail and display areas on the first floor, but went in the back door and straight up to her office. She had a bride who wanted a full ensemble of dresses for herself, her bridesmaids, and flower girls. All in a similar style, but she hadn't decided on which style she wanted. Fortunately, the wedding was over a year away, so they had lots of time to decide. Barbara was drawing up many different ideas, with all the different types of dresses for each idea. She loved designing and had some pictures of the various people she was designing for, including the little girls who would grow in that year. She spent several hours each day drawing up the ideas. In about a month, she planned to ship the bride all the different ideas to look over.

She didn't know for sure what Tina, Stephanie, and Christa were working on, but they seemed busy and content, so she didn't ask. They had asked for a reasonable budget to *make up a few things*. Barbara agreed and was letting them run the show. She wasn't interested in the retail part—she was glad they were handling it and if it cost her a few thousand dollars in materials to make them happy she was all for it.

∞

CHRIS LOVED THE fact he was out of the house and able to contribute to the amusement park, even if it was only for a couple hours each day. Summer was quickly approaching; the crews were working overtime to get it ready. One morning several of them went down to meet the barge. The bubble cars were arriving that day and everyone was excited to see how they looked and worked.

The operator that called Chris said they would need several large vehicles to transport the delivery, so they had all driven down to the landing. Barbara was driving his pickup. Paul, Brad, Terry, Greg, and Kyle had brought their trucks also. When the barge pulled into the landing, they were all surprised to see the whole thing was filled with the bubbles. Each one was in two pieces and large enough for four people to sit inside. The bottom half had benches to sit on, but since they were the same color of clear light blue, you could barely see them. The tops looked like a solid half sphere, but when you got up close to them you could see there was a lot of ventilation built in.

They unloaded the pieces, but each pickup couldn't transport even one bubble.

"This wasn't very good planning. How are we going to get them to the park?" Chris asked.

Paul said, "It never occurred to me they would be this big. Although we did build a large platform for them."

Greg shook his head. "What we need is a flatbed truck. Or a flatbed semi-trailer would be even better, but I don't know any in town."

"Me neither," Terry said. "Maybe Gus or Carol would know someone who has something like that. Should we split up and go ask around?"

"We can't leave them here," Chris said.

Greg laughed. "Why not? They can't be stolen, or we would be able to transport them."

"Yeah, a thief would have to snap them together and roll them down the street," Barbara said.

Everyone turned and looked at Barbara.

"What? Why are you all looking at me?"

Chris looked at Terry. "It might work."

"It might."

"We could each roll one, with Chris and Barbara leading the pack with emergency flashers on and maybe even the fire department light."

"It would take two trips. Five at a time."

"Let's see if we can put one together and see if it rolls. We would have to leave the protective covering on the outside so they wouldn't get all scratched up and dirty. Which should be fine, because all the connections are on the inside, leaving the bubbles smooth on the outside."

And it's exactly what they did. The bubble actually went together easily, because it was designed to have the top lift up, allowing adults to walk out of the cars without stooping. They had a hinge on one side and some clamps to hold it shut on the other. Once the door was shut and the clamps were engaged, it was sturdy and rolled. It didn't move easily because it was so large and they had to keep the flat attachment side perpendicular to the road, and since that was the heavier side it made it challenging, but they could handle it. They put the first five together and with Chris and Barbara in the lead, the others started rolling the bubbles through town, on the way to the amusement park. People all along the street stopped to watch. Some people took pictures on their phones—no doubt to post on Facebook. Quickly it turned into a parade type atmosphere. When the people heard they would be bringing a second set through town in an hour or so, they all called friends and family. By the time the next bunch were ready, it was indeed a festive atmosphere.

They got the last set of bubbles through town and

over to the platform. As they started to secure them, a man stepped out of his car with a camera and microphone. He started asking questions. Chris was happy to explain the park and the rides and how they came to be rolling monster bubbles through the town.

When they were installed and they turned on the ride. The balls spun around on a platform designed to look like a lake. It was magical looking. The bubbles had a sheen and sparkle to them, and as they turned on the lake, it was beautiful. They stopped the ride and several people got in the spheres to see if they would turn fast and to see how comfortable it was inside the cars.

Greg and Terry got inside one and when they started it back up, they got their bubble spinning fast. Others were turning rapidly also, but Greg and Terry were flying.

"I hope when they get out they don't throw up all over your new ride," Barbara said.

"Yeah me too." Chris laughed. "But there *will* be people puking—it wouldn't hurt to give cleaning it up a test run."

When the ride stopped Greg and Terry emerged unscathed. Terry grinned. "Worked like a charm."

"Yep, you got yourself a winner there, Chris," Greg agreed.

"Sweet! Then we have two rides complete. The arcade has about half the games installed, with others on the way. The post-apocalyptic ride is ready except for the game footage. The boats are coming soon for the US geography river ride, and the world geography play area is coming along. I think it will all be ready to open in a few weeks.

We've decided to open it to the locals the weekend before the grand opening. That way we can give it a test run and also give our friends and neighbors a special day. The college students will be here then; we can do a staffing test at the same time. It's kinda scary—we're getting close to opening."

Terry slapped Chris on the back. "It's going to rock."

Just then Samantha arrived. She got a tray out of her car and brought it over to the assembled group. "I want you to see and taste the cookies I've designed."

"Oh man, Samantha. Twist my arm and make me eat cookies," Terry said as he and everyone else surrounded her, eager to try the cookies.

"Samantha, these are works of art. We shouldn't be eating them," Barbara said.

Samantha laughed. "Don't be silly, they're food."

"Yes, but they *are* works of art." Kyle nodded.

Samantha blushed at the compliment and held out the tray. She had made cookies that looked exactly like the animals on the carousel. There were also some that looked like Tsilly and Kalar. And more that looked like the Eiffel Tower, Tower Bridge, and Noah's Ark.

Terry happily bit off the head of a Kalar and moaned as he chewed it. "Not only a work of art to look at, but delicious. Great job Samantha. These are going to be a hit."

"Oh goody. I liked them, but I wanted some second opinions, so when I saw you rolling the bubbles down the street I knew where to find you. I'm a little surprised the rest of the town didn't follow to see what you were doing with the giant bubbles. They look awesome by the way. Did you try them out?"

"Yep, right before you got here. Greg and I had ours spinning like mad. People are going to love them."

Samantha said, "Yeah, providing they don't barf."

"Oh, there will be some of that, have no doubt," Chris said.

Chris saw out of the corner of his eye the man with the camera taking more pictures of the impromptu snack. He wondered for a moment who he was, but then his attention was drawn elsewhere and he forgot about him.

Chapter Thirty-Four

CHRIS WAS FINALLY RELEASED by both Doc Sorenson and Atilla to drive, he had a cane to give him more stability, but that's all he needed and he was able to get out alone. It had been a long process to get this far, Doc had taken the cast off and done more x-rays, when those looked fine he had a splint for when he got out on his crutches. Atilla had worked him over until she was happy with his ability to take weight and his stability.

So, the day they finally both cleared him, the first thing he did was he went to have lunch at Amber's counter with several friends. They were still talking about the mayoral race and whom they thought would or wouldn't do a good job. Several people had come forward to run, but the election was still a year out, so he guessed it would be a conversation subject for a long time.

Then the topic turned to the amusement park and the changes being seen around town to emphasize the game.

"You had a fine idea to focus the town on Sandy's game, Chris. I think the tourists are going to like it. I heard the resort is pretty booked up along with the hotel and a few B&Bs," Matt said.

Chris smiled. "I hope so. I like the climbing structure Kyle came up with and the signs along Main Street—he did a nice job on those too."

"I drove by the amusement park the other day. It's coming together nicely," Craig said around a mouthful of sandwich.

"Yeah I'm happy with it. Next year it will be a lot bigger. And the resort will be bigger too. I think it will be fun to open the amusement park for the town to try it out."

"My kids are looking forward to it," Matt said. "I am too, but that's a secret."

Chris laughed. "Amusement parks are for all ages—or at least they should be. I've geared mine toward that idea."

Matt sighed. "My kids are also bugging me to get them one of the costumes Barbara has in her shop."

Chris tried not to look confused and asked, "Barbara has costumes for kids?"

"Yeah, in her shop where the boutique was," Matt said.

"Oh, I thought she was focusing on costumes for adults."

"Well, yeah. She has those too, but she's got Kalar, Tsilly, and some other costumes made up for kids too," Matt elaborated.

"I take it you haven't been in her shop in a while," Craig said.

"Um, no. I haven't been allowed out too much and I've been focusing on the amusement park when I'm out."

Craig nodded. "Of course, it makes sense."

"Speaking of which, I need to get back to it. I still have physical therapy every afternoon."

"But you haven't gotten your pie yet," Matt said.

"Oh, I'll have Amber box it up for later. See you guys."

Chris went up to the counter and paid for his lunch. He left the restaurant in a hurry. He was going to go see Barbara's shop. He had worked hard to not look surprised when Matt had mentioned it. What the hell? A husband shouldn't be blindsided about his own wife's activities. Chris drove directly to the building the boutique had been in. There was no sign out front, but the building wasn't deserted and had an open sign in the front door.

Chris went in and a little bell tinkled as the door opened.

Someone said, "Go ahead and look around, I'll be right there."

Chris couldn't believe his eyes. Half the room was clearly Barbara's wedding dresses and the other half was the costumes she'd been working on, in all sizes. In the center was a raised platform with lots of mirrors—he assumed was for people to see what they were trying on. This wasn't some small operation. This was a full-blown store. There were mannequins displaying both the dresses and the costumes.

Christa came out of the back room. "Oh hi, Chris. We were wondering when you would come to see the shop, now that you're up and around more."

"Yeah, it looks great, Christa. Is Barbara here?"

"Oh yes, she's up in her office. She's still working on ideas for the bride who wants the women to have matching dresses, but has no idea what style she wants."

"Yeah a big job. Where is her office?"

"Up the stairs on the third floor."

Chris went slowly up the stairs and saw a large workroom taking up much of the second floor. But he kept moving upward. He knocked on the door and heard Barbara say come in, so he did.

Barbara had her back to him and was working at a drafting table. He just waited for her to turn. He knew it wouldn't do any good to say anything until she switched her focus off her drawing.

Barbara turned and startled. "Oh, Chris. What are you doing here?"

"I heard in town my wife, had a costume shop, so I came to see. It is clearly more than a costume shop. Were you going to tell me about it? I didn't like hearing about it from my old high school buddies."

"Of course, I was going to tell you. I just didn't want to." She looked guilty.

"What?"

"Oh, I don't mean it that way. I mean, well, I didn't want to think about it. And if I told you about it, I'd have to think about it."

"Barbara, you aren't making any sense. You have a full-blown wedding boutique downstairs with wedding gowns, veils, bridesmaid dresses, and all the accessories. And on the other side is a costume shop with all the costumes you've been working on, in all sizes from little kids to adults. And you don't want to think about it?" Chris said, getting louder with each word.

"What?"

"What do you mean, what?"

BARBARA GOT UP from her table and went out the door and down the stairs. She turned toward the wedding area and stopped dead, her mouth hanging open. She walked in and went over to the racks of readymade wedding dresses, recognizing the styles she'd designed over the years for various brides. And there were veils and bridesmaid dresses—including some she'd drawn recently. Who had made the patterns for those?

Then she turned and went into the costume area and by golly, Chris was right. There were costumes in all sizes. *What is going on here?*

Barbara turned to Chris. "I had no idea."

"What do you mean, you had no idea? You're here now."

"Yes, but I always come in the back door and go straight up to my office. I have been avoiding this area like the plague."

Christa came out of the back room. "Oh it's you guys. Isn't it great Chris?"

"Yeah, great."

"This is what you were doing with the supplies money? Making up ready-made dresses to sell?"

Christa nodded. "Yes, we ran out of the work you asked us to do, so we decided to make up some outfits to sell. When you said you weren't sure anyone would come in, it got us thinking. I did the wedding dresses. Stephanie did the bridesmaids dresses, and Tina did the costumes."

"You each made your own patterns?"

"No I used the ones I found in the notions chest. Tina cut the ones you had made for the townspeople down to kid sized. Stephanie did make her own patterns, but she only used your sketches to create the dresses—none of her own, since it's your shop."

Barbara laughed a little hysterically, at that. "Right, *my* shop."

Chris took Barbara firmly by the arm and said to Christa, "Barb and I are going to have a chat, we'll see you later. And yes, it is beautiful."

***

Chris slowly followed Barbara up the stairs and into her office, one hand on the cane and the other on the hand rail. Stairs were not that easy for him yet and two trips up would have made him tired, but he was running on adrenaline at that point. When he had the door firmly shut, he turned to her. "What in the hell is going on here?"

"Clearly, I have no idea."

"Tell me what you *do* know."

"I rented this place when you were in surgery. I wanted the sewing room cleared out so you could use it. I asked them to please move everything to this place and work on the wedding dress that was a rush job. I assumed they would do just that. But then the day you had me take some time off, I came by to check on the ladies and walked into a shop. Not nearly as elaborate as it is now, but still nice."

"That was weeks ago and you never told me about this?" Chris said, flabbergasted.

"Oh, Chris, it wasn't about you. All this freaked me out so bad I refused to think about it. But they had put so much effort into it—I didn't have the heart to have them take it apart. I never intended to keep the building after the few months you needed to recover. There are so many things I don't know. I've been avoiding it like the plague. And now it's even bigger. I don't know about insurance or employee benefits or even what to call it. I can't exactly call it Wedding Dresses by Barbara, now can I?"

"No. But Barbara, I could have helped you with some of those issues. I've had to research most of those same areas for the amusement park."

"I know, but I couldn't bear to even think about it. The whole idea of a shop freaks me out. I'm not a retail person. I design and sew up dresses. I don't want to run a shop, Chris."

"By the looks of it, you don't have to. Christa, Stephanie, and Tina seem to be doing a darn good job of it."

"I know and it's why I couldn't tell them no—they are excited and it is well done."

"Yes, but it does need a name, sweetheart."

"I know and I've thought of a thousand of them, but nothing clicked. I mean how does wedding dresses and costumes for 'Adventures with Tsilly' go together, for goodness sake?"

"Being married to you is an adventure. I happily go to lunch at Amber's and the next thing I know, the guys are talking about the shop my wife has opened—which I know nothing about. It hurt my feelings, Barb."

"I'm sorry, honey. I just wasn't ready to discuss it and I had no idea anyone would be talking about it."

"Apparently, Matt's kids have been in and want costumes."

"Really?"

"Hey, what about *Adventures*?"

"What?"

"For the name, just *Adventures*. Marriage is an adventure and the game has adventures too. You can call it *Adventures*."

"I like it. Yay, I have a name."

"We can talk more tonight. I'll see you later." Chris left the shop, still more than slightly irritated.

Barbara decided to stop by Samantha's bakery on the way home. She knew she'd hurt Chris's feelings and she thought a treat from Samantha's bakery might help smooth the way.

When she got to the bakery, she went up to the counter and got a few Tsilly cookies and a cherry pie. Turning to leave, Barbara noticed Abigail was there at a table having a cup of coffee and cinnamon streusel. She went over to say hi.

"Oh hi, Barbara, where's Chris?"

"Um, at home?"

"Oh, I must have misunderstood him. I thought when he cancelled his physical therapy today it was because he was doing something with you. It's not a good idea for him to cancel—he needs all the work he can get before summer starts and the tourists arrive."

"Chris cancelled his appointment?"

"Yes, I thought you knew."

"No, but I'm sure it was for a good reason. He is taking his PT seriously. He wants to fully recover and not have any lingering problems."

"I'm glad to hear that. I will plan on being there tomorrow then."

"Thanks for all your hard work with him, Abigail. We both appreciate it."

"Thanks, I do enjoy my job. It's satisfying to see Chris doing well."

Barbara called Chris's cell as soon as she was in her car, but he didn't answer and it went to voice mail. She decided not to leave a message. She wondered where he was. It wasn't like him to cancel his therapy appointment. She went home and looked in the freezer to see what food they still had left over from their neighbors. She found a casserole from Mayor Carol. Carol made yummy food, so Barbara put it in the oven to heat. When it was ready to be served, Barbara turned the heat down in the oven to keep it warm. Chris was still not home and he still wasn't answering his cell phone.

By nine o'clock she was getting worried and hungry. She took the casserole out and got a portion for herself, then covered the rest in foil and put it back in the oven.

She refused to panic and think the worst about where he was. She decided he was just busy with something and would be home when he could. She wasn't going to entertain foolish ideas he was leaving her or was out with someone else. She had finally learned to trust Chris and she wasn't going back to her previous negative thought patterns. With that firmly decided, she turned on a movie she loved and sat down to watch it. He finally got home about ten thirty. She stopped the movie and moved to the kitchen to greet him.

"Sorry I'm so late, babe, but I had a lot to do this afternoon. Here is what took the longest," Chris said as he lifted something wrapped in brown paper and handed it to her.

It was a large flat rectangle and it was heavy. She laid it down on the counter and tore the paper. When she got it open, her throat closed up. It was a wooden sign that said *Adventures* in large, slightly curved letters at the top. At the bottom in smaller letters, it said *Barbara Clarkson, proprietor.* There was a spool of thread carved into the top right corner with thread swirling around the words, down to a needle in the bottom left corner.

"Chris, it's beautiful."

"Yeah, Terry did a great job. He still needs to seal it, but I wanted to make sure you liked it first."

"I love it—it's wonderful."

"We weren't sure if we should stain it to make the words and thread and needle show up better or paint it in colors. Which would you prefer?"

"I think stain."

"Terry and I thought it would be best too, but we wanted to make sure."

"Oh, Chris, I can't believe you spent all afternoon and evening having Terry make this. You even cancelled your PT appointment."

"Oh, well—I didn't get to Terry's until about five. I spent the afternoon at City hall getting all your paperwork completed for your shop."

"What? Really? That's amazing. I thought you were mad at me."

"When I left, I still was pretty irritated you hadn't trusted me enough to tell me about your store. But then I decided to get over myself and help you with whatever I could. I went to City Hall and started in on the paperwork. That's when I thought of the sign. I called Terry to ask him if he had a nice piece of wood that size. He said he did, so after I had all the paperwork done the city requires, I went over and we worked out the design. Once we had the design it didn't take long for him to cut it. Not long in the way that it still took over five hours to create it."

"Oh, you are the best husband."

"I try."

"Well you do a good job. Are you hungry? I kept Mayor Carol's casserole warm for you."

"Oh good. Yes, I'm hungry. Terry and I snacked, but didn't have dinner."

While Chris ate, he told her the many things he'd accomplished. Barbara was amazed at all he'd done in one short afternoon.

When he was finished eating, Barbara took him by the hand and led him to their bedroom where she rewarded him for all his hard work. Afterward, when they had recovered, they had cherry pie in bed. Naked.

He said, "Gee, I need to help you out more often."

She laughed. "We should get to sleep."

He put their plates and forks on the nightstand. "We'll get to that." Then he pulled her in for a long, wet kiss and they did get to sleep. A long while later.

Chapter Thirty-Five

Gus walked into Chris's office with a newspaper in his hand. It was carefully folded to a column. At the top of the column was a picture of a man who looked vaguely familiar. The title of the article was "Amused at the Tsilly Amusement Park".

"What is this?" Chris asked.

"The article from the columnist who came to see the park."

"Oh, I didn't realize he was ever here. Although his picture looks familiar."

"Yes, he was here the day you got the bubble shipment. Look, here's a picture of the guys rolling them down the street."

The caption read: "The hillbilly way to take deliveries, and these people think they are running an amusement park. Beware!"

Chris quickly scanned the article. "I remember someone with a camera asking questions and taking pictures, but he never introduced himself. Gus, this article doesn't look complimentary."

"No, it's not."

"But…"

"It's giving us nationwide coverage in all the major newspapers. The columnist is famous and well read."

"But Gus, his article is doing nothing except making fun of our town, our idea, our park. How is this going to help? Other than turn people away?"

"Oh, you'll see. I'm off for lunch. Enjoy the article." With that, Gus walked out the door.

Chris sat back and read the article. Twice. When he was finished he hung his head in despair and said out loud, "This is going to kill us before we even start."

BARBARA RUSHED INTO Chris's office. She knew if he'd read the article in the paper he'd be devastated. How dare that man trash her husband's dream. Of course, he trashed the rest of the town right along with it—but the whole idea had been Chris's.

Chris was sitting at his desk staring into space. Oh no, he had read the article.

"Chris, honey, that guy is full of himself. Don't believe him for one minute longer."

"Gus said he was famous and well read."

"I don't care if he's the pope. He doesn't know what he's talking about."

"He called us hillbillies."

"Yes, I know. He said my wedding dresses were simple and plain. But brides love them and I have more work than I can handle, most of the time. Who cares what he thinks! And my costumes aren't silly, they are well-designed and people will love them."

"He said our attempt at an amusement park was pathetic and lame. That coming to it would be a waste of time and money. That the town was dying and good riddance."

"We'll show him. Our town isn't going to fade away. He's so full of shit, I'm sure his eyes are brown. Everyone who's tried out one of the rides loves them."

"Yes, but what do you expect from a bunch of hillbillies?"

"You stop that right now. Not everyone wants to be from a big city, Chris. There's nothing wrong with living in a remote area."

"He said our town was tiny and stranded in the boonies."

"Hey, baby. Now don't give up on this. That man's an asshole and this park and our town is going to thrive—regardless of what he says." She went over to him, pushed his chair back, and climbed on his lap. "Now give your wife a kiss."

He did and as they kissed, she could feel him relaxing. She held on tight while she relaxed him with kisses and murmurs.

Five minutes later Kyle marched into Chris's office waving a paper in his hand. "Did you read this bullshit? Who died and made him sheriff? My climbing structure is well-made and the kids love it. It is in no way flimsy and dangerous."

Samantha came into Chris's office, fighting tears. "Chris, are my cookies amateurish? I worked hard to make them special."

"Samantha, no they're not. They are wonderful," Kyle said going over to her, he wrapped her in his arms.

"But…"

"No buts, we all loved them and we don't give a hot damn what some jerk from New York thinks. Although, he did say they were tasty. I think you're the only one who got any compliment."

"He said I was unprofessional for bringing them to the park for you all to taste."

Barbara got off Chris's lap and went over to stroke Samantha's back. "Honey, we loved you bringing them to the park for us to taste. Where is the law which says all taste tests must be done in a closed environment with white table cloths, anyway?"

Chris said, "Samantha, the man attacked every corner

of our town and our plans. He even had the gall to say the Marquee resort wasn't up to their normal standards. And he came right out and said Sandy's game was on its last legs and we were unbelievably naïve to be pinning our town's future on a game which would be obsolete before we ever got the amusement park completed."

Mayor Carol walked in at that point. "I just got off the phone with Sandy and she's fit to be tied over his comments. They have no less than three more releases planned, all three years apart. She says that guy is a bunch of hot air. Her game company is furious too and plans to throw a lot more money into advertising—both the game and the park."

Marilyn came in laughing. "Oh my god, you should hear how furious the Marquee hotel people are over the article. They're on the east coast, so they've had hours to fume, and they've been taking cancellations from people afraid to come since seeing the article.

Chris groaned. "Oh, no. I'm sorry to have gotten us into this mess. It's all my fault—it was a horrible idea and now we've put all this money into it."

"Now, Chris, you can't give up, this might be a tiny set back, but we will thrive and people will love your park and the town's focus on the game," Mayor Carol said.

"Yeah, Chris," Terry said as he walked in. "This is the most excited people have been over an idea for the town since, well, forever. We aren't going to give up because some self-important twit decides he doesn't like it."

Greg followed Terry in the door. "It's gonna rock, Chris." Then he looked at Samantha. "Your cookies are works of art. There is nothing amateurish about them."

Everyone started talking at once to reaffirm their friends and neighbors.

Marilyn whistled loudly. "You didn't let me finish. The Marquee hotel people called to tell me they were going to throw a huge grand opening and fly in all their top people and many celebrities the whole week before the grand opening. They are giving everyone free tickets to the park."

"What?"

"They plan to fill the resort to capacity with celebrities and their head honchos. And they are going to give each person a week-long pass to the park."

Chris said, "But it's a hundred rooms, with a couple people in each room, will be a thousand tickets for five days."

"Seven days. Monday through Sunday. With a huge grand opening party for the resort on the Sunday prior. You'll probably want to move the soft opening for the town's people to the Friday and Saturday before that."

"But it's only two weeks from now."

"Yep, that's why I came straight here. So you can get after it."

Chris said, "Well, we know we'll have at least one decent week in sales."

Marilyn looked around the room. "There will be all those people in our town—you all need to be ready."

"We need to let everyone know."

"I'll call Sandy," Mayor Carol said.

Marilyn said, "I'm heading to Amber's next, to spread the word. That should take care of it."

Everyone laughed and said, "True." Or some equivalent phrase like, "Damn straight."

Chapter Thirty-Six

EVERYONE SPENT THE NEXT two weeks in a frenzy of activity to get ready for the soft opening of the amusement park and the resort grand opening. The college students who were coming to staff the park were offered a substantial bonus to come a week earlier. The town was cleaned from top to bottom.

Samantha baked like a fiend. The seamstresses all sewed like their life depended on it filling the shop to bursting with unique costumes and dresses. The barge and ferry were constantly filled with supplies for a weeklong party. Everyone pitched in to help wherever they were needed.

The high school moved graduation up a week and let all the middle and high school kids out early so they could pitch in and help get things ready. The older kids would be staffing the amusement park—having them there was not only helpful, but practical for learning where everything was. Using the underground tunnels they had built to move supplies when the park was open, was also a big plus. The college students started arriving by ferry and were taken to the various rentals available and some homes where people wanted to sponsor a student for the summer.

On Wednesday afternoon before the opening, Barbara called Chris. "You've got to come home right now."

"But I'm…"

"Now, Chris. Whatever you're doing can wait."

"Yeah, it can. I'll be right home. Do you need anything on my way?"

"No, just come straight home. Now."

When Chris got home he hollered, "Barb, where are you?"

"In our room."

Chris dropped all his work stuff on the kitchen table and hurried to their room."

"What's wrong? I…" Chris stopped dead in his tracks, his wife was standing by the window in a nightgown so sheer he was sure it must be made of cobwebs.

"Honey?"

"We're taking the rest of today and tonight to ourselves, before our life turns into madness. You are going to make love to me until you can't move."

"I am?"

"Yes you are, now strip."

Chris grinned and started unbuttoning his shirt.

When he got his phone out of his pocket she took it, turned it off, and put it in the drawer of the bedside table—next to her own turned off phone. Their landline phone was unplugged from the wall. He was guessing she'd even turned the sound off on the answering machine and maybe even locked the front door. She was serious about this.

Barbara walked over and started helping him remove his clothes, licking and nipping at him as skin was revealed. By the time he was naked he was fully aroused. She still had on the wispy nightgown. She pulled his head down for a hot, wet kiss while she molded her body to his. The material between them felt sexy. It was soft, but with a little edge of abrasion. He felt himself get harder as she moved against him. The nightgown caused some slight friction, which was the most erotic feeling ever.

Barbara walked Chris backward to the bed and pushed him down on his back, then she climbed up on top of him. "I'm gonna ride you, boy. Are you ready?"

"You go, girl."

And she did. She started slowly teasing him, rubbing her body over his and the friction of the nightgown strengthened the sensations. Then she sat up and arched her back to take him deeper. When he couldn't take it any longer, he flipped them both over and pounded into her. They never even managed to get the nightgown off.

Afterward as she lay cuddled in his arms, she sighed. "I'm thinking about bringing Christa, Stephanie, and Tina on as partners."

Chris looked at her. "Really? Why?"

"Stephanie is talented. She even has some of her own wedding dress designs, which are incredible. She is also willing to do the traveling to help hysterical brides."

"Oh. Well, that would be nice, I don't like you being gone."

"I don't either and I think she'd be better at it than I am. Christa, on the other hand, loves the retail side—she is a talented seamstress, but she loves the sales. She is also the one with the eye for decoration and she has a good grasp on which wedding accessory trend is currently in vogue. She does a lot of web browsing and seems to have a knack for selecting the hot new items to stock in the shop. Tina has been concentrating on the costumes and has been working up ideas for some of the other adventures in the game. She is a great organizer and has discovered other women in town who can sew. She isn't as talented with taking a vague idea and turning it into a pattern, but since that's my strong suit it's not an issue."

"You all complement each other."

"Yes, and I think they should have a stake in the shop since it was their idea and we are making money now."

"What are you thinking?"

"I was thinking I'd retain fifty-two per cent with which I'd continue to stock the store and buy all the materials needed. Then I could give them each sixteen percent. Do you think that's reasonable?"

"Sounds fair to me."

"Good." Barbara took a deep breath. "I was also

thinking maybe it's time to think about having a family."

She felt his breath hitch and he said in a soft voice, "Really? You're ready for kids?"

"Yes. Yes I am. I want to have babies with you, Chris. If you want to have babies with me."

"Yes my love, I would dearly love to have babies with you."

"Good."

"It's going to take a lot of work and practice," Chris said in a seductive voice.

"Oh yes, I'm sure it is."

"Let's get started then." He whipped off her nightgown and rolled her under him.

Chris was gentle with her, worshipping every inch of her body. He wrapped his arms around her and drew her close. His mouth met with hers, and she opened to him allowing his tongue to sweep inside.

She dug her fingers into his hips to hold on to him. She opened her legs and said, "Come make love to me and let's see if we can start a new life to love."

"Oh babe, I will be happy to do my part—I can't get enough of you." He lowered his head to her breast and licked then suckled her.

She moaned. "Inside, now."

"In a minute sweetheart—we don't want to rush now, do we?"

"Yes. Yes we do."

He just continued his assault on her other breast and she squirmed from the sensations he was eliciting. She pulled his head up, their mouths met, and she sucked on his tongue while she squeezed his ass and steered him into her. As he slid deep inside, she felt like she was coming home. She always felt complete when he was inside her and surrounding her. She wrapped her legs around his hips and drew him in farther.

He loved her with long slow strokes, both of them building higher. As they got closer to the summit, his movement became harder and faster, more frantic, and she loved it. She dug her nails into his ass to encourage him.

He moaned. "Oh Barb, you feel like heaven."

"Mmmm, faster Chris."

He sped up until he felt her start to tighten then he plunged into her and they both came together in sheer ecstasy.

When they woke up from their nap Barbara said, "I'm starving."

"Yeah me too."

"I got one of the last meals from your surgery out of the freezer and put it in the fridge to thaw. It's a fettuccini bake."

"Yum, want me to go put it in the oven?"

"Sure."

CHRIS WENT INTO the kitchen and opened the fridge. There was the baking dish with the glass lid on it, which he slid into the oven. But on the shelf below was a beautiful platter with strawberries, whipped cream, and chocolate sauce. The fettuccini instructions said to heat on a low heat for an hour. A perfect length of time to have an appetizer of strawberries and wife.

He grinned as he took it out of the fridge and into their bedroom. Barbara looked up as he entered the room and groaned. "Oh no, I forgot about the strawberries."

"Let me remind you. Besides I'm still moving and you commanded me to make love to you until I couldn't move."

"I've created a monster."

"No, just someone who loves you passionately," Chris said as he popped a small chocolate covered strawberry into her mouth.

"I think our baby is going to love strawberries."

"And chocolate and whipped cream."

They did eventually eat the Fettuccini bake and it was only a little dried out.

Chapter Thirty-Seven

THURSDAY NIGHT CHRIS didn't get much sleep. He was too worried about opening the park to relax. His mind kept whirling with all the details and thinking about whether he had them all covered. He knew his admin Francine—better known as the queen of the office—had taken care of many of those details and he totally trusted her. He hoped he'd told her all that was necessary. Of course, she probably knew more about it than he did. She was frightfully efficient and a super researcher. She had pointed out several issues they hadn't thought of, after doing some research online about amusement parks.

Paul and Brad had been running tests on all the equipment at the park. But what if they had forgotten something? Did they have enough food? Enough toilet paper and trash bags? Could the park handle a thousand people? Were there enough places to sit? Would people get bored or angry standing in lines? They had tried to anticipate those kinds of things; they had put entertaining signs and decorations to look at where people would be standing.

Chris tossed and turned all night, until shortly before dawn Barbara had woken up said, "Enough." And proceeded to wear him out with sex. That worked and he finally got a couple hours' sleep.

They opened the park at nine in the morning with nearly the whole town attending. As they opened the gates, everyone cheered and swarmed in. They didn't charge admission—all the rides would be free. But the food, souvenirs, and the arcade would cost.

Chris was near the front by the bubbles and watched as his friends filled them for the first official ride of the park. Everything went smoothly with some bubbles spinning like mad where the older kids were, and some spinning slowly when families of little kids filled the bubble. As the ride came to a halt, everyone got out of the ride smiling. Many of the people came by to tell him it was a fun ride and to thank him.

He wandered over to the carousel where people waiting in line commented on how unique the animals were. Terry and Greg stood there eavesdropping and grinning. One of the ladies pointed up to the top of the carousel and the three of them looked up. Perched on the very top of the carousel was the town peacock with his feathers out.

Greg said, "Well there is your official mark of approval,

Chris. If the town peacock likes it, everyone will."

Chris went into the arcade and it was packed—every machine was in use, the noise was deafening and it seemed like everyone was having a great time. The information booth was handing out souvenir maps of the current park detailed on one side and the planned expansion on the back. They also were giving all the kids Tsilly and Kalar stickers.

The Ferris wheel was going full speed with many people commenting on the huge pictures of Kalar and Tsilly on the side. The small petting area they had next to the Noah's Ark building seemed to be a huge hit with the little kids. Alyssa Jefferson, her ever-present best friend Rachel, and Alyssa's little sister Beth were standing by making sure everything was okay with the animals and showing the children how to pet them.

Chris continued on to the post-apocalyptic ride and saw lots of teenagers and adults waiting in line. As he walked around the park, he saw mothers or fathers with strollers and grandparents watching from the many benches spread throughout. His high school-aged employees were pointing out where to find different attractions or on hand to help with various tasks. Some had brooms and dustpans to cleanup snack crumbs or spills.

The two young women dressed as Kalar were having their picture taken over and over. The guy in the Tsilly costume was mugged by kids asking about adventures.

Barbara came out of the souvenir shop. "I just dropped off more kid costumes. I decided two each wasn't enough.

It was a good thing too—most of the first batch were already sold. The park's been open less than an hour. How's it going?"

"Great. So far, everything is going good. People seem to be enjoying themselves—lots of people have commented on how much fun they're having."

"Of course they are, this is going to be a hit."

"Want to walk over to the river ride with me? I haven't been there yet."

"Yes."

As they neared the ride, a family was coming out from the end of it and one of the kids was talking a mile a minute. "I've always wanted to see Mount Rushmore and the Grand Canyon and Yellowstone and we saw them all. Can we go again? I only had time to look at the things on my side of the boat. I want to go again to ride on the other side. Can we?" The parents just laughed and got back in line.

Barbara smiled at Chris. "Who knew US geography would be so fun?"

"Yeah, I wonder how he liked the first part of the ride with the alligators in Florida."

"Depends on which side of the boat it was on."

Chris laughed. "True."

"Are you going to take me on the Ferris wheel? It's kind of a romantic ride for a couple, isn't it?" Barbara asked.

"Of course. As it goes around we can smooch."

When they got to the top of the ride and it stopped to load and unload people, Barbara said, "I have something to show you." She pulled out her phone and after a couple of seconds turned a picture toward him.

"What is that? Some plastic thing with a plus on it? What does that mean?"

"It's a pregnancy test, my love."

He felt his mouth drop open and his throat closed up. He managed to croak out, "Are you…"

"Yes my darling I'm pregnant, are you ready to be a dad?"

"But… but we just talked about it, like two days ago."

"Yes and it's a good thing I wanted to start because this little guy or girl was already on its way. I've been feeling a little tired and achy and I can't remember when my last period was, way over four weeks anyway. I didn't think anything of it because we've been so busy. Kristen's the one that noticed the symptoms and suggested I take the test."

"I'm going to be a father? We're going to be parents? That's wonderful—what are we doing all the way up here on this thing. We have to get down, now, what if it's not safe? You can't be endangering our child in this manner."

She just laughed and kissed him.

BY THE END OF THE day everyone was exhausted, but thrilled with the success. They had few problems and could easily adjust things to fix them. The town had a fun day and the workers were happy with their part in helping people have fun. Mayor Carol had sought Chris out to tell him how pleased she was with the park. She had also complimented Barbara on the costumes and uniforms for the park staff. So many people had expressed their joy and enthusiasm for the park Chris was flying high. They planned to be open for more town people and the neighboring communities on Saturday. Chris had no trouble sleeping that night—in fact, he was probably asleep before his head hit the pillow, content with his wife snuggled in close.

The second day was as big a hit as the first and the park was also filled on Sunday—which had surprised them. With it no longer being a *free day* and since there was the big grand opening for the resort that day—with lots of activities planned—they hadn't expected many people. They weren't officially open, but they didn't turn away paying customers. Scattered among the locals was both celebrities who came over to check out the amusement park and some tourists.

The ticket sellers had asked the tourists how they knew the park was open and they had pointed out the Ferris wheel could be seen from the lake. They had been on the lake on Saturday when they saw it, they planned to come on Sunday. While they were back in Chelan for dinner, they had told some of the other tourists they ran into.

The grand opening for the resort was magnificent with amazing food, live music, giveaways, and at the end of the evening fireworks over the lake. There were celebrities from every genre—from sports to actors to rock stars to politicians. The townspeople had trouble not gawking. It was a fun and busy day, and all those people would be at the amusement park for the next week.

What would happen after that was anyone's guess.

The week was hectic, but profitable for the whole town. All the business owners were swamped with customers. Every time Chris saw anyone they mentioned it to him and each report thrilled him to hear of all the success the town people were having. Kyle said he was surprised to be kept busy showing houses for rent or sale. Apparently, many people seemed to like the town and several expressed an interest in a summer property.

Barbara had told him all about Kristen's challenges to keep up with demand. Kristen had originally sent a small amount of her jewelry to town to be placed in Barbara's shop *Adventures* and the resort gift shop. When there was nothing left by the fourth day, she had Mary Ann bring another larger batch to town. Kristen had been glad that she had many pieces set aside for shipment to other cities where her jewelry was sold in galleries, because she was selling so much in town she started sending those pieces down for sale. She said could make more for the galleries. And of course the Tsilly and Kalar charms were selling like hotcakes.

Terry told him that people loved the carousel ride, and when they heard a local wood worker designed it they had flooded his workshop to see his furniture. He said he'd taken a lot of orders for his exclusive furniture and some bought his extra pieces he had on hand, he had a large number of things to be shipped.

People even went into Greg's bar to seek out the man who had done the whimsical painting on the carousel animals, asking if he was available for custom murals or unique toys for their children. Greg said he turned down the murals; he didn't have time to fly around painting murals. But the toys were a different idea and he'd told the people he would talk to Terry about them.

The park and resort had stocked Jeremy's children's books and Sandy's games and those were selling quickly. Chris had called Sandy and asked her to bring more games with her when she came for the grand opening of the park. Jeremy reported he had called his publisher asking for more books to put in the resort gift shop and amusement park.

When the celebrities headed out of town, the business owners heaved a sigh of relief. They all came together in the school auditorium the Monday morning after the weeklong event, to discuss what was needed for the future.

Mayor Carol started the meeting. "Well, folks we made it through the first week now let's take stock of what happened, what we needed, what we didn't anticipate, and what we need to do better in the future. Don't forget to take into consideration this isn't even thirty percent of the plans that have been made for future construction on both the amusement park and the resort.

"But let's start out with good news. I want to hear any good news you want to share. I'll start. This last week in the town of Chedwick we had zero unemployment. Absolutely every person from fifteen to ninety was gainfully employed."

Kyle stood. "I sold three homes to people who want to make them their summer homes. I also sold three pieces of property."

"On two of those pieces I was asked to build homes," Marc Winthrop the contractor said.

Samantha smiled. "I sold more this last week in my bakery, the resort and the amusement park auxiliary shop than I have ever sold in a two-month period."

"I have commissions on three wedding dresses for celebrities, two of which will include bridesmaids' dresses. My team of seamstresses also sold a ton of premade clothing from the shop. Nearly every costume is gone— especially the children's costumes. I have maybe two of each one left. I could use a few more seamstresses this week to build back up the stock." Barbara sat down and jumped back up. "Oh and Kristen called me and said she had record sales too."

Chris cleared his throat. "And…"

Barbara blushed and said, "And Chris and I are expecting a new addition to our home in about nine months."

Everyone hooted and clapped and called out congratulations.

Chris said, "We'll all go celebrate after the meeting at Amber's for pie or something. Now let's get back to our regularly scheduled program. I don't think we got through all the good news since I just had to share the best news ever. Who else? Terry?"

Terry stood. "I have a shit ton of orders for my furniture. Greg and I will be working on some ideas for wooden toys for children, based on Sandy's game."

There were several other people who expressed their enthusiasm for new jobs and even some new business ideas. Mayor Carol then opened it up for areas that needed improvement. There were a number of suggestions which were discussed and promises were made to follow up on them. There were a few problem areas discussed, one of which was lack of accommodations for tourists when the resort was full.

When the discussion had run its course Mayor Carol said, "Chris please stand up." When he had risen, his hand tightly gripping Barbara's, Carol said, "Let's all give Chris a round of applause for his idea." The noise of clapping and hoots and hollers was deafening and Chris felt his cheeks heat, but he had a huge grin on his face.

"Thanks everyone," Chris said, "but it was all of us working together which made this a success. I hope we will build up to full capacity later this summer and next. I think we will all be happy for a small break and time to make plans for handling a larger crowd next summer."

Marilyn stood. "Begging your pardon Chris, but there isn't going to be a small break."

"But I thought we lost bookings for the summer when the article came out."

"Yes, we lost a dozen or so the first day, but we are booked to capacity for the whole summer—as is the hotel and the few B&Bs we have scattered around."

Chris said, "Filled to capacity?"

"Yes Chris, there is a whole ferry load of people coming into the landing in about an hour."

"But what about the article?"

"When the reservations started flooding in I did ask a few people about that and they said 'Anything that columnist dislikes we know we will love.' We have more bookings than we would have ever had, if he'd given us a good review."

Gus just laughed and said, "I love it when a plan comes together. Now let's go celebrate this young'un before the ferries start arriving."

The End

Coming soon, book two in the Lake Chelan Series

Designs on Her

Turn the page for a sneak peek.

Chapter One

NOLAN THOMPSON WHIPPED into the yard in his patrol car. *Damn people still here.*

"Dispatch I'm at the Mathews place, two vehicles fully loaded, but not evacuated. I'll get them out of here."

"Ten four Officer Thompson. Probably the tanks she needs help with."

The back door on the truck was open and there was a very fine rear end sticking out from the backseat. He'd like to paddle that read end. The fire was getting too close, he could smell the smoke even with the windows rolled up and a thick haze filled the yard. *Why hasn't this crazy woman evacuated?* He glanced around, there was an Airedale dog tied on the back porch. He also saw she'd done everything else right to prepare for a fire. She had a large fire break dug between her house and the forest. She had hoses pouring out water, although they weren't aimed at the house, but at a large shed. Her truck was parked close to the shed. He stepped out of the squad car and slammed the door. She turned out of the truck and Nolan had to change his question to *why hasn't this beautiful crazy woman evacuated yet?* He heard her say, thank God even over the roar of the fire. He didn't feel any heat from it, so it was still a safe distance away but that could change in an instant.

"Ma'am you need to get out of here right now, the fire is heading this way."

"Kristen, call me Kristen and yes—I know," she said and started dragging him by the arm towards the shed.

Nolan dug in his heels and said, "Did you get your household gas tanks loaded?"

"Yes, but—"

"Ma'am we really don't have time—"

Just then one of the hot shot fire jumpers ran into the yard. "We've got to get this place evacuated now."

"Oh two, hallelujah!" the crazy woman said and grabbed hold of the firefighter and started dragging them both towards the shed.

The firefighter said, "Ma'am just what is it in the shed that's so important to risk your life over."

"I'm Kristen. The tanks."

Nolan said, "But you told me they were loaded."

"The household tanks, yes—" she shoved both of them through the door to the shed "—but not those."

"Oh shit," the men said in unison. There, standing next to the door, was over a half dozen four-foot acetylene tanks.

"I can't carry them by myself or even with Mary Ann, they're too heavy," she said pointing to the other woman in the room. "We got them to the doors by rocking them, but…"

The firefighter touched his mic and said, "Chief this is Trey at the house on the ridge I need another couple of guys over here stat and have them bring at least two fire blankets."

"I was just sending them out. Is this an emergency?"

"The biggest one we've got right now. I'll explain later."

The men started carrying out the tanks and laying them in the cradles that neither had noticed in the truck bed. Two other fire jumpers ran into the yard and over to the shed. When they looked inside one of them said, "Oh fuck, over a half dozen A5's." While the other one said, "Thank you, Lord, for this woman refusing to leave these behind."

The four men made quick work of loading the tanks. Just as they got the last one in, and the firefighters were securing them, a truck roared into the yard and four men jumped out running over to help. Three of them ran into the shed and started hauling out everything they could, to fill their truck. The fire fighters joined them, helping to evacuate as much as possible.

Stoic, beautiful, Kristen burst into tears and ran into the arms of one of the men. She was babbling, "Oh, Chris, you came. I was so scared. You came, thank God. We couldn't lift them. They're too heavy. And the ground's too uneven. You came."

Chris stroked her hair saying, "It's okay, baby. I'm so sorry you were scared. Now, calm down and let's get the hell off this mountain pretending to be a volcano."

Kristen hickuped and nodded.

"I'll drive your truck," Chris said

Nolan, who felt a prick of disappointment that she had a boyfriend, said, "I'm going to ride with you, just in case we need two men for something. I need someone to drive the cruiser down."

Chris said, "Good. Terry can drive it, he's the mayor's son, so no worries."

"Perfect." While Nolan radioed into headquarters to notify them of the plan, Chris continued to bark out orders.

"Greg go with May Ann. Kyle drive my truck and take Farley with you, he's tied up on the back porch. Terry take the squad car and try not to act like a kid in it. Hotshots, we owe you for saving one of our own."

"Shit man," Trey said, "she saved our ass by not leaving these here."

Greg nodded. "Still, come into my bar, when you get a chance. On the house."

Kristen was finally calm enough to speak. "Trey, use the house if you can, there's food and beds and water, no electricity or gas but please feel free."

"Thanks, Kristen," the hotshots saluted and ran off towards the fire.

The rest of them piled into the vehicles with Terry

leading the way. Running lights and siren, they hauled ass down the mountain.

Once they were a safe distance from the fire Chris said, "Barbara is going to kick my ass for not getting up here sooner, I'm so sorry."

"Who's Barbara?" Nolan asked.

"My wife."

At the same time, Kristen said, "My sister."

"Oh," Nolan said, with an internal smile, maybe she wasn't taken after all. Not that he had time for a woman, he was trying to make his mark in a new town and a new job.

"What took you so long?"

"Being a dumbass! We were all busy, trying to get everything ready for evacuation. The barge radioed in and said they were on their way. I didn't know anyone had called them yet, so when Kyle pulled in I assumed it was him, but he said no. Then it hit all four of us at the same time, that it must have been you. We knew you had to have help with the big tanks, so we burned rubber and ran lights and siren getting out of town and up the mountain. Why didn't you call one of us?"

"As soon as I hung up from calling the barge I lost all communication and electricity. No cell, no landline, no radio. Apparently, I hadn't used the radio in such a long time the batteries had gone dead. So, I just started hauling out the household tanks and prayed like crazy that you guys would get up here in time. Then, I dug the fire break. Mary Ann showed up about the time I finished that, so we tried moving the big tanks and we did get them close to the door, but we couldn't lift them. I got the hoses started pouring water over the shed. Then we boxed up the metals and gems to take with me and loaded her car up with clothes and stuff. When you still weren't here, I tried to get Mary Ann to leave, but she wouldn't. So, we just kept boxing up more stuff."

"Damn, I'm sorry Kristen, you had to be scared."

"I was terrified. I just got that load of tanks last month. They are all full, if the fire got to them—"

Nolan interrupted, "You didn't show it."

"I felt like bawling when you drove up, because I figured the three of us could move those tanks. There wasn't time for hysterics."

Nolan said to Chris, "She was awesome. When I showed up trying to get her out, she just dragged me towards the shed. Then the first hot shot, Trey, showed up and she dragged us both towards the shed. She was cool as a cucumber, until they were loaded and you drove in."

"Yeah, that's our Kristen, totally in control until the danger has passed, then she freaks out."

"Hey," Kristen said.

"Am I lying?"

"No, but still, you don't have to tell everyone."

Nolan turned towards Kristen, her long straight brown hair was up in a crooked ponytail, she had dirt on her cheek, her big brown eyes were red and puffy from crying, her clothes were filthy, her hands were covered in grime, her fingernails torn and ragged. He laughed to himself, because he thought she was the most beautiful woman he had ever seen.

He said, "I'm Nolan Thompson, by the way. The new cop in town."

Kristen shook his outstretched hand. "Kristen Matthews, jewelry designer and currently a filthy hot mess, nice to meet you."

Nolan smiled and said, "A beautiful, hot mess, maybe. Jewelry designer, huh, I wondered what you had all those tanks for."

"Kyle, who does metal work, and I always split an order. The gas company requires orders of a dozen due to the fact we are so remote and they have to be put on the barge to get here. These will last me a year or two, providing they don't explode and kill everyone within a forty-mile radius."

"So, you plan to put them on the barge and then what?" Nolan asked.

"The barge will take them across Lake Chelan and put them on the other side in a large storage structure, that was built when I was a kid and we had a huge forest fire between us and Chelan. It's large enough to evacuate most of the town. I don't think we're quite there yet, but those of us who live on the mountain and people like Kyle and myself who have large amounts of flammable gas can put those over there for safety."

"Good, nice to know the town has plans in place for emergencies like this."

"Since, I had all that time to load up, I brought most

of my stuff down, Mary Ann's car is full and the truck and now your truck Chris. I don't know what to do with all of it, but I'm glad it won't burn up if the hot shots lose control up there."

"You can stay with us," Chris said.

"I know and I will for a day or two, but you know how long these things rage on, it could be a couple of months, even up to the first snow. I'll probably see if Kyle has anything I can rent. I have some orders I need to keep working on. So, if I can find a place to set up shop that would be better."

Chris's green eyes sparkled. "I think the guys got nearly everything out of your workroom, so you should have everything you need."

"Looks like we made it to town safe and sound," Nolan said with relief, as they turned the corner into town.

Kristen smiled at him. "Well, you've had quite an introduction to our town, Officer Thompson. Kind of a trial by fire."

Nolan laughed out loud. "Good one. I can hardly wait to see what's next."

19391802R00194

Printed in Poland
by Amazon Fulfillment
Poland Sp. z o.o., Wrocław